ALSO BY SHELDON RUSSELL

A Forgotten Evil

Winner of the 2020 Spur Award for
Best Western Historical Novel from the
Western Writers of America

A
Particular
Madness

A Particular Madness

SHELDON RUSSELL

cennan

PUBLISHED BY Cennan Books of Cynren Press
101 Lindenwood Drive, Suite 225
Malvern, PA 19355 USA
http://www.cynren.com/

Printed in the United States of America on acid-free paper

ISBN-13: 978-1-947976-26-9 (hbk)
ISBN-13: 978-1-947976-27-6 (ebk)

Library of Congress Control Number: 2021930543

COVER DESIGN BY Kevin Kane

For Keith and Judy

Whom the gods would destroy, they first make mad.

—*Sophocles*

CHAPTER 1

On my fifth birthday, I asked my mother where I came from. She said that a buzzard threw me up on a rock. From that day on, I knew that my family had somehow failed to tighten all the screws.

That same night, I stood at the window of the old farmhouse and watched a storm brewing on the horizon. It wasn't a house, really, not in the normal sense, but an old railroad shack that had been moved onto the land and set on a foundation of red sandstone that my father hauled in from the field. When the wind blew, which was nearly all the time on the Oklahoma prairie, the house moaned like someone in pain, or lost, or in mourning.

"Mom?" I said.

"What?"

"You making fudge?"

"No," she said.

"It's lightning out," I said.

"We could use the rain."

"I gathered black walnuts out of the shelterbelt this morning?"

"I saw."

"For making fudge, I mean."

I could hear her walking across the kitchen. The floorboards made a *bong, bong* sound that was peculiar to her.

"You *could* have shelled them," she said.

"Gea should shell them," I said. "She never does."

"Gea isn't here."

Gea is my sister, older sister. Her name means "earth," or "dirt," or something like that, and she is the one who said that if I gathered the walnuts, Mom would have to make fudge. But Gea never *picked* them or *shelled* them. She's a girl, and older than me, so she never has to do anything like that. Mom and Dad favor her.

And she's pretty, too, that much I know. Not to me, because she's my sister, but to the boys at West Liberty, the one-room school three miles away. Both Gea and me went there. I started at five, though I should have started at seven. My dad said, why not, he don't do nothing around here anyway.

When Gea was at school, the boys giggled and turned red and gave me rides on their shoulders. But when she was not around, they tied my shoelaces together and threw my Lone Ranger gloves down the outhouse hole.

I'd fallen under Gea's sway myself from time to time. I did her chores, opened the door at night so she could get in without waking the folks, said I liked her new dress, even when I didn't, or the way she'd changed her hair. I carried wadded notes to her from the boys, listened to her play the piano and sing what Dad said was perfect alto. I'd seen how my folks gathered about and centered on her smile. I knew why. It was her right.

"Jacob, there isn't any water in the water bucket," Mom said. "Didn't I tell you to draw water?"

Lightning cracked open the sky beyond the window and zigzagged through the blackness. My hair tingled, and I closed my eyes, the zigzag still burning on my eyelids.

"If you're not cooking fudge, what *are* you cooking?" I asked.

"Chicken gizzards," she said.

"Pencil erasers," I said.

"Don't talk about food that way, Jacob Roland, or you won't get anything."

My mother always says that about food, that it's not to be wasted and not to be talked about in a "dirigible" manner, whatever that means.

"Go draw the water," she said.

"It's dark, and it's storming."

"You should have thought of that earlier."

"Dad will do it when he gets home."

"Your dad's tired when he gets home, and it's your job to do."

My dad, Abbott Roland, works the seven to eleven shift at the Santa Fe roundhouse in town. We need the cash to make place payments. The cream check buys the flour, and sugar, and kerosene for the lantern, but little more. When Dad gets home, he goes straight to bed, rising again at daybreak to do the chores, fix fences, or chase cows all over the damn country. Sometimes he takes a short nap before leaving once again for the roundhouse.

"What if I get hit by lightning?" I said.

"I'll see that you're buried up on Casket Hill," Mom said.

Casket Hill is the cemetery that sits atop the mesa that rises between the Rolands' and the Franklins' places. Both families bury their dead there, the Rolands to the east, the Franklins to the west. The Cimarron runs at its base and marks the boundary between the Rolands' and Franklins' farms, but with each flood, the course of the river changes. Some years the mesa belongs to the Rolands. Some years it belongs to the Franklins. It's a constant source of irritation between the families, who don't much get along anyway. But when my dad, a Roland, married my mother, a Franklin, it brought the whole matter to a head.

On a July morning, my relatives from both sides gathered at the base of the mesa and decided that neither family would own it in the future, that it would be a cemetery to be used by both families instead. The deal was struck with a handshake, the first and only ever to pass between them. It became known as Casket Hill, and so it's been ever since.

What the mesa lacks in fertility, it gains in scenery. The gypsum cap rock is white as chalk, with red cliffs dropping away to the river. Even in the heat of summer, a blue haze shrouds the mesa, and sometimes ghosts sit in the shade of the cap rock. I've seen them.

Over eternity, the river has carved the mesa from earth red as blood, leaving behind a sheen of salt that kills all living things, save for the kangaroo rats and the green lizards that scuttle about in the rocks, and the diamondback rattlers that writhe in tangled balls deep in the gypsum caves. In the spring, the rattlers bask on the rocks in the sun's warmth but stay put on the mesa so long as the Cimarron runs water. They swallow whole the rats and lizards that wander in too close. They flick their tongues and level their beady eyes at each other.

But then there are years like this, when the rains stop, the river dries, and the salt gathers in white ripples across its bed. On years like this, the rattlers slither down the mesa on their bellies and into the valley like an invading army.

"You don't even *have* a casket," I said.

"I have a tow sack," Mom said. "Now, go draw the water."

CHAPTER 2

I lowered the bucket into the cistern and flipped the rope to upend it, thinking the while about that tow sack and those snakes. Drawing it up hand over hand, I could hear the water spilling and could smell its murkiness. Rainwater is slick as grease, and when Mom washes my hair in it, she says I look like Fuzzface, my dad's coon dog. He's half Black and Tan and half Airedale, and his whiskers sprout out his face like a wore-out toothbrush.

I worked at the screen door lock, which only opens if you hit it with the heel of your hand. The wind caught the door and whipped it against the house with a bang. Water sloshed into my shoe.

"Dammit," I said.

"Jacob, I'll not have cussing in this house," Mom said.

"I said 'darn it,'" I said, lifting the bucket onto the table next to the icebox.

I hooked the dipper handle over the side of the water bucket. Everyone in the family drank out of the dipper, which I didn't mind so much, except when my uncle, the one who always had tobacco stains on his chin, stayed overnight.

Mom lit the lantern and turned up the wick. A black curl floated out the chimney and rose to the ceiling. The lightning no longer zigzagged outside but pulsed instead, like on the newsreels about those German bombs that fell on London. The thunder growled, a low and constant rumble. Mom walked to the window and looked out.

"I wish your dad would get home," she said.

She always said that, because making decisions by herself was hard.

"I'll shell the walnuts, if you'll make the fudge," I said.

"Jacob, quit picking about that fudge. We might have to go to the cellar, and I don't want nothing on the stove."

The cellar was my dad's pride and joy. He'd built it by digging a trench in the shape of a rectangle with his posthole diggers and piling the dirt in the center. After that, he filled the trench with concrete and let it cure. Then he covered the pile of dirt in the center with concrete, and my sister and me put our handprints in it, "May 1948." When everything was cured again, he dug out all the dirt inside of it, and his storm cellar was made. The neighbor drove his John Deere tractor over the top of it to prove its worthiness.

It was a good cellar, except Dad had built it too far from the house. It didn't have steps or a floor, and the crickets in it were the size of prairie dogs.

A gust of wind rattled the windows, and a hailstone pinged off the side of the house.

"Maybe we should go now," Mom said.

"It's passing around," I said.

I said that because that's what Dad always said. He'd stand on the front porch and study the clouds and the lightning and say, "It's passing around, Vega." That was my mom's name, Vega.

But everyone knew that he didn't like to go to the cellar because of the big elm tree that grew just outside the door. When the wind blew hard, the limbs creaked through the vent pipe. Dad said there was no telling when that tree would fall over onto the door and trap everyone inside. I think he figured the best bet was not to go to the cellar at all, given that most storms pass around.

Another gust of wind blew in, harder this time, and the house shuddered. Sheets of rain swept the windows, and thunder rumbled under our feet. Mom sat next to the lamp with her elbows on the table. The flame flickered in her glasses, like the devil's eyes, but they weren't really the devil's eyes. Mom said I had an overactive imagination because I came from both the Rolands and the Franklins. She said it was putting cold water in hot grease and I'd be lucky if my head didn't explode someday.

"Mom?" I said.

"What, Jacob?"

"Do your eyes shoot out of your skull when your head explodes?"

She started to answer, but the rain stopped. The wind fell away, and the world took a deep breath, sucking up all the sound and air. My heart beat in my ears, and my skin tingled.

"Get your coat," Mom said.

I started to protest. "Mom—"

And the world exhaled. My ears popped, and the kitchen linoleum lifted a foot off the floor. The screen door broke loose from the lock and slammed against the side of the house.

She grabbed me by the arm. "Go, Jacob!" she said.

She hauled me out the door with my coat halfway on. The wind cut at my face and snuffed away my breath. Hail, no larger than match heads, screamed out of the sky like blasting sand and pelted my face and ears. Puddles of water gathered in the low spots, and balls of lightning danced along the old barbed wire fence. Mom covered her face with her arm and pushed through the storm, and by the time we reached the cellar, her hair hung in wet strands.

She struggled to lift the door, but it was heavy, too heavy against the wind, and the limbs of the elm were touching the ground. Dad had made the door from boxcar siding and said it would last forever. It didn't matter that no one but him could lift it.

"Help me," Mom said.

So I grabbed hold, and we lifted it six inches, no more, before another gust of wind slammed it closed again. Wind twisted through the yard, picking up dirt and grass and water.

Mom turned, rain dripping off the end of her nose. "What's that sound?" she said.

"What sound?"

And then I heard it, like the sound a mad bull makes when he's throwing dirt over his back, or the sound of a steam engine pulling grade up Curtis Hill.

"I don't know," I said.

"That's a tornado," she said. "Get in the cellar, now."

So we put our backs to it, along with a dose of fear, and it opened. The dank smell of old potatoes rose up from the blackness.

"Get down there," Mom said.

"It's dark," I said in my best whine.

"Get, Jacob, before we blow away."

I'd forgotten about the lack of steps, or, if I had not forgotten altogether, it didn't seem all that important under the circumstances. But what awaited me was a mud slide caused by rain water mixing with the red clay left behind from all the digging. My feet went out from under me, and I shot down the muddy chute and into the blackness of the cellar. Before I could say a word, Mom plunged down behind me, nearly knocking me over. I couldn't see her, but I could hear her groaning and breathing hard.

"Are you OK?" I asked, my voice reverberating inside the concrete walls.

"There're matches on the nail keg. Light the lantern," she said.

We kept a nail keg in the cellar for the kerosene lantern to sit on, and an old daybed for resting and storing potatoes on in the fall. It was black as night, so I swept my hand through the darkness slowly, so as not to knock anything over. I worked my way up to the base of the lantern and then the box of matches next to it. The elm tree creaked through the air vent overhead as it bent under the force of the storm.

"I found them," I said.

"Well, light it," she said.

I pushed my back against the coldness of the concrete wall and fished out a match from the box, striking it across the striking strip. Dampened from the humidity, it smoldered and went out, the cellar filling with the smell of phosphorous. I dug out another match and tried again. This time the match struggled to life. I lit the wick, put the chimney back on, and turned it up.

That's when it started—first a small scurrying sound in the rocks somewhere in the shadows, then a full-blown rattle that built to a crescendo and filled the cellar and my heart with dread.

CHAPTER 3

"It's a rattler," Mom said. "Get on the bed."

We both climbed up on the bed, balancing ourselves on the springs. The lamp light pushed our shadows up the wall and across the ceiling. My heart beat in my neck, and my ears rang. Rain streaked through the vent pipe overhead and onto our backs. We clung to each other as the rattling mounted, bouncing and echoing from every direction in the confines of the cellar.

"Where is it?" I asked, my voice pitched and thin.

"I'm not sure," Mom said.

"What are we going to do?"

"I think maybe it's by the door," she said. "I think we came right past it in the dark."

I peered through the dim lantern light but could see only darkness next to the door. Lightning shimmered through the vent pipe. The wind howled, and my ears popped against the pressure.

"I can't see anything," I said.

"I'm pretty certain that's where it is," she said.

The rattling stopped, only for a moment, but long enough for me to locate the sound when it commenced again.

"It's by the door," I said. "We can't get out."

Mom's arm trembled against mine, from the wet and cold, I think.

"Maybe we could hold the mattress between us and the snake and make it past the door," she said.

I had visions of our earlier plunge down the mud slide and what it would now take to climb out carrying a mattress, and with a rattlesnake waiting in the darkness.

"No," I said.

So we stood there, thinking, and listening to the storm rage above the relentless rattle of the snake.

Finally, Mom said, "I have an idea."

"What idea?" I said, hopeful that it was better than the mattress thing.

"There're rocks on the floor. We'll throw one at the snake to get it to move away from the door."

"I don't know," I said.

"It's hours before your dad gets home, Jacob. We can't stay up here all night."

"You want *me* to throw the rock?"

"You're better at throwing," she said.

"What if the snake is under the bed and bites me when I reach for a rock?" I said.

"It isn't under the bed, Jacob. You can hear it by the door, can't you?"

"Sort of."

"Jacob."

"All right," I said.

Working my way to the head of the bed, I got down on my knees, took a deep breath, and reached for a rock. Even though I could hear the snake by the door, its rattler beating like a snare drum, I could still feel its fangs sinking deep into my arm.

"I got a rock," I said.

"He's on the left," Mom said. "Throw it hard."

I put the three-fingered grip on the rock, the same way my cousin had showed me how to throw a baseball, reared back to pitch it with all I had, and knocked over the lantern with my hand. The lantern toppled to the floor; the cellar plunged into darkness, and the snake stopped rattling.

I could hear Mom breathing. "Dammit, Jacob," she said.

"Where is it now?" I asked.

"We don't know, do we?" she said.

"Can we light the lantern?" I asked.

"You know where it is?"

"No."

"Or the matches?"

"No."

"Or the snake?"

"No."

"So you want to put your hand down there and find them?"

"No."

"Well, neither do I."

So we stood there on the bed in the dark. The air had turned colder, and the storm sounded farther away.

"Mom?" I said.

"What?"

"Dad works a double shift sometimes."

"He won't," she said.

"Mom?"

"What *is* it, Jacob?"

"You think this is what it would be like to be buried up on Casket Hill, underground, I mean, and with rattlers everywhere?"

"It wouldn't be the same," she said.

"Why not?"

"They don't ask stupid questions on Casket Hill," she said.

What seemed like hours was only minutes, Dad said. But when he shined that flashlight down the vent pipe, both Mom and me let out a whoop. He came down the mud slide with shovel in hand and killed the snake. Holding it up by its tail, it was as tall as him, six feet, maybe more, and big around as a tree trunk.

"Come on up out of there," he said.

So we climbed out into the rain-cleaned air, and I was feeling good about surviving such an ordeal. Dad tossed the shovel in the back of the pickup and pitched the dead snake into the grass.

"I guess we managed that," I said. "I mean, what with you being at work and all."

"It was a bull snake," he said.

"It was rattling something awful," I said.

"Harmless as a puppy," he said. "You might want to think things over a little more before setting your hair on fire, Jacob. I swear, there's precious little connection between what goes in your head and what comes out of it."

I went to bed without eating, 'cause my stomach was shriveled up. Thunder rumbled somewhere a hundred miles away, and a few stars winked through my window. I lay there thinking for the longest time about that snake and about how scared I was and about how I should have thought things over.

Sometime later, I heard Mom and Dad laughing in the kitchen. I think Dad was right about me. There was something in my head that could spin a spark into a prairie fire.

CHAPTER 4

There were twenty of us in West Liberty School, grades one through eight, and four of us were in the first grade. It wasn't so hard, except for Mrs. Bransetter, the teacher, who walked up and down the aisles staring at us every second. She put me sitting at the same desk with Rudy Joe, who was in the eighth grade. Rudy couldn't read, and she said I could help him say the words.

I didn't mind that so much, except Rudy Joe stank, and he had a green band around his wrist from a copper bracelet he wore. I asked him what it was for, and he said it was to keep him from getting polio.

"It won't work," I said.

"I ain't never had it yet," he said.

Teaching Rudy Joe to read was probably one of the hardest things I ever did in my life. I'd teach him four or five new words out of our story every day, and the next day he wouldn't remember any of them. He wouldn't even remember the story. But *I* remembered them, and by the end of the year, I'd won a reading certificate award. It was a picture of a little boy holding up a lighted lantern on a dark night. That was me.

Rudy Joe had a mean streak and would push me to the side with his butt, until pretty soon I'd fall out of the seat into the aisle. He thought it was funny, but Mrs. Bransetter started watching us over the top of her glasses. One day while she was gone to the outhouse—she went to the outhouse a lot because she drank black tea all day long—he started pushing me again.

I figured it a good time to teach him a lesson, what with Bransetter gone, and so I bit his ear. I didn't just bite it, I hung on like a snapping turtle. Mrs. Bransetter returned about then, what with Rudy Joe screaming and pounding on his desk. She grabbed me up by the hair, slapped me in my mouth, and escorted me back to the first-grade desks.

Rudy Joe smirked from across the room, but he was holding his ear, and there was a trickle of blood running down his cheek.

When I got home, Mom asked me why my mouth was puffed up, and I told her a yellow jacket wasp stung me on the lip while I was in the outhouse. She said it could have been worse.

A West Liberty tradition was the annual field day at the end of each school year. Games of all kinds were held in the schoolyard, followed by a picnic, and the whole community showed up. This was of particular interest to my dad, him being a natural athlete. He loved games of all kinds and was especially good at playing pitch and throwing a baseball at bullet speeds. Everyone in the valley, and on the job, too, knew how strong he was.

While I, on the other hand, was the smallest boy in school. Not only were the other boys bigger than me but so were the girls. It was just an awkward stage, Mom said, but it made me last to be picked for games, save for marbles, which Mom said was just another form of gambling. I was dreading the field day like sin.

Field day arrived, and everyone showed up, along with my mom and dad, who had managed to find seats on the front row. I was put on the sprint team. I asked Rudy Joe what a sprint team did, and he said they sprint, idiot.

Rudy Joe won the mile, and my sister's team won their volleyball match. People clapped and cheered, and I could see the big smile on my dad's face over my sister's win. I figured she'd be singing perfect alto all week long now.

Time came to line up for the sprint. I looked at my feet and waited for the whistle to blow. Sweat ran into my eyes, and my stomach hurt. When the signal came, I took off running as hard as I could. At some point early in the race, I looked up to find that I was last—not a little last but a lot last. Everyone else was already making the turn, so I stopped and went back.

"Why didn't you finish the race?" Mom asked, plopping my hat on my head.

"I wasn't winning," I said.

"You're supposed to finish anyway."

"Why?"

"I swear, Jacob," she said.

"Where's Dad?" I asked.

"He caught a ride on home," she said.

Summer came as only it can in the country, and I spent long days alone
out in the shelterbelt or over at the pond. It was about June, I think,
when I finally figured out how the whole world works: all kids live
on top of the ground; adults live underground. There's a place in the
earth with a door on it and that's how adults get underground. Kids
don't know where it is and never get to go there.

Adults talk things over when they're underground and make all the
decisions about kids. They get to do things that kids can't. It's a big
secret, and nobody tells kids anything, not until they're adults. Only
then do they find out.

I also decided that summer that I was not going to die. It didn't
matter that everyone in all of history had died. My life was not going
to end that way. Something would come along to make dying a thing
of the past, a pill or something.

Dad bought me a BB gun at an auction, in hopes I'd become a hunter.
He said I could use his hunting rifle if I learned how to shoot. I made
the decision, after much thought, that I was going to kill something.
So I took my BB gun and went to where the shelterbelt trees grew
the biggest. Bullhead burs didn't grow much in the shade, so I went
barefooted. By that point in the summer, my feet were pretty tough
anyway, but they say that bullhead burs can puncture a tractor tire.

I sat down on a cedar log that had fallen across the path. It was
a hot day, one of those days when the locusts sing and the smell of
sunflowers is everywhere. I waited there for a long time for something
to shoot, maybe a bird or a cougar. There was talk that a cougar had
been taking pet dogs at night.

But no birds came close enough for me to shoot, and if there *was*
a cougar, he was probably sleeping somewhere in a cave. I started
thinking about stuff, too much stuff, Mom always said, the kind of
stuff that makes you go off into another world.

And at some point I spotted him, a fire ant climbing over twigs and
across cow tracks in the sand. I must have looked like just another tree
to him, and he was headed my way. I'd been stung plenty by fire ants,
and if anything needed a good killing, it was fire ants.

I aimed my BB gun, training in my sight like Dad had showed
me. I followed the ant closer and closer as it clambered toward me. It

worked its antennae and watched me with bulbous eyes. And when it was close, so close that I couldn't possibly miss, I held my breath and squeezed the trigger.

The pain in my big toe was pretty much like the time I jumped off the chicken house and ran a nail through my foot. I grabbed my toe and hopped around saying all the dirty words I could come up with, but it didn't help. I fell over and pulled my knee into my chest as the pain crawled up my leg like melted lead. I looked at my toe. The nail was turning purple. I tried to find the fire ant to stomp on it, but it was gone.

When I got home, Dad said, "What you limping for?"

"I shot a fire ant with that new gun," I said.

"What's that to do with you hopping around like a jackrabbit?" he asked.

"It was on my toe," I said.

Dad looked at Mom and then at me. "Bring me the gun," he said.

CHAPTER 5

I spent most of that summer alone. My nearest neighbor, a cousin, being three miles away, didn't get to come down often. So I walked the pasture in the cool of the day. I dug a fort out of the bank by the pond. I saw a spirit come out of the fish pond one evening at sunset. It smiled and then dove back into the pond. Spirits can do that. I buried milk buckets next to ant dens and waited for the ants to fall in. Then I dumped them in different dens, and wars commenced. Sometimes they lasted for days.

I sang songs, in something less than perfect alto. I made up stories in my head, even though Mom didn't like it. I made things the way they ought to be, and I couldn't see no harm in that. I changed the field day judges' decision about that sprint race, because they had made a big mistake. The other sprinters were not ahead of me but behind me by a full lap.

When it was announced that I had really won, everyone carried me around on their shoulders, and they named the field day the Jacob Roland Field Day. I pushed Rudy Joe out of his seat, and when he tried to get up, I cut his head off and put it on Mrs. Bransetter's desk. She died from fright, and I had to take over the school. I turned the school out for summer that same day, and everyone cheered, except Rudy Joe and Mrs. Bransetter.

Mom suggested that I should help Dad instead of spending all that time alone, that we had a place payment coming up, and there was lots of work to do. But Dad said some other time, that right now, he had to get the equipment up and running and shock the feed before it rained.

So I went back to walking the pasture and thinking. I decided I was probably just no more than thoughts myself. And if I *was* just thoughts, I probably would never die so long as my thoughts were around. But other people died all the time, probably because their thoughts were no longer around. If I was going to live forever, I had to find a way to keep the thoughts going, the problem being that I didn't know anyone who could do that forever, or even for a week.

One morning Mom sat me down after breakfast and said, "Jacob, you been acting peculiar all summer. Is there something you want to talk about?"

"No," I said.

"Jacob."

"I figured out how to live forever," I said.

She looked at me over the top of her coffee cup for the longest time. "I don't know if I want to hear this," she said, "but go on."

So I told her my idea about me being just a thought. She set her coffee cup down and studied me for a long time again. "Jacob," she said, "you got to learn to let your head cool off. It isn't healthy."

"It don't hurt nobody," I said.

"Sometimes there's a weakness passed down, you see, and you might have it."

"What do you mean?"

"Like when a family is all redheads or has crooked noses."

"We don't have redheads, Mom. Uncle Duny's nose is a little crooked, but that's because he got drunk and fell off the couch."

"Don't be cute, Jacob. I'm just using that as an example of how things can sometimes be passed down."

"Which family you talking about, Mom?"

"You might have noticed some things different with some of the Rolands from time to time."

"Uncle Berko don't talk that much," I said. "He just smokes cigarettes and drinks coffee all day."

"Yes, he does."

"Sometimes he talks to himself."

"I know, Jacob."

"And Uncle Ward sees Germans coming through the window at night."

"I'm not saying these are bad, Jacob. It's just you got to be careful not to let your mind spin off."

"But Uncle Duny isn't a Roland. He's a Franklin."

"What do you mean?"

"He's a Franklin, that's all."

"What's your point, Jacob?"

"Dad said Uncle Duny got drunk and left his car on the sidewalk in town and that he spent the night in jail."

"The Franklins are fun-loving people, that's all."

"Dad said they're poor managers. Does that come down through families too?"

"Go outside, Jacob, or you won't live long enough to find out."

Sometimes I took Fuzzface on my walks, because he always listened to what I had to say. When it got hot, we would take a nap under the big cottonwood that grew out of the creek bank. I'd put my head on his belly and listen to it growl. Sometimes I'd fall asleep. Dad fed him skimmed milk from the separator and mixed it with the wheat bran we used for hog feed. Dad said Fuzzface's number twos were long as a saddle rope.

I was well on my way to putting the final touches on my thought idea when I started losing weight. Mom upped my food, but it didn't help. She fed me pancakes topped with cream and homemade syrup and with sugar-cured bacon on the side. She fed me fried chicken and mashed potatoes and apple pie and plates of walnut fudge at night. Dad got a double chin, and Gea couldn't get in her dresses, but I lost more weight.

And then it started one night, a small scratchy noise somewhere in my head. If I moved, it would get louder, and my stomach would tip over. I lost more weight, and my britches hung slack. Gea called me spade butt. I quit going on walks, and I quit thinking about thinking and started thinking more about dying. I wondered when it would happen, and if they would bury me in a tow sack to save money for the place payment. I thought about that snake in the cellar because the noise in my head sounded just like that snake. Even if it was no more than a bull snake and harmless as a puppy, I didn't want it in my head.

I couldn't sleep but a few hours at a time, because when I'd move, the noise in my head would go off. It was like someone walking around breaking dishes. On top of that, it was August and hot as fire, even at night, so I moved out on the daybed we kept on the front porch. I liked sleeping outside and looking at the stars. Once in a while, I'd see a red blinking light far up in the blackness, an airplane, and I'd wonder what it would be like to be up there with the movie stars and gliding along through the night sky like that.

'Course, I worried some about sleeping outside, what with coyotes yipping just beyond the fence, but Dad said coyotes didn't have much taste for humans, especially ones skinny as me.

When I'd move the least bit, the noise in my head would start up again, and my stomach would shrivel. My ribs looked like piano keys, and my cheeks sunk into my face. Dad said I looked like ol' Pet, our milk cow that had bogged down in the pond last summer and starved to death.

When Mom thought I was asleep, she would come to look at me, and I could hear her and Dad talking. They were talking about me dying, I think, and where they were going to put me up on Casket Hill. Even Gea came in and gave me one of Mom's dill pickles. She said I should stop worrying the folks.

"You have to start gaining weight, Jacob," she said. "It's all Mom and Dad talk about anymore. They have a place payment, you know."

But it got worse every day. I couldn't move my head or touch my ear without it going off. I couldn't eat or sleep, and black splotches spread under my eyes. Mom came in one morning and said the decision had been made—they were taking me to the doctor. That's when I knew for sure that I was dying.

The whole family, even Gea, crammed into Dad's '49 Chevrolet coupe, to help carry the body home, I figured. Mom and Dad didn't say anything all the way to town. I think they were sad to spend the place payment.

The doctor's office was painted white. The doctor wore a white coat, and the nurse wore a white cap with wings on it. Everything was white, except my shoes, which were red with mud, and the soles were loose and flapped when I walked. I held my feet back under the chair.

The doctor checked my heart to see if it was still beating and looked in my mouth. He could see my heart, and he made humming sounds.

"Jacob," he said, "where does it hurt?"

I pointed to my ear. "Every time I move or touch it," I said.

He put his flashlight in my ear. He smelled like shaving soap, and his breath was warm on my neck.

"Oh my," he said. That's what doctors say when you're dying.

"My folks have some money," I said. "But it's the place payment."

"Do you have a pet, Jacob?"

"Just Fuzzface. He gets skunked all the time."

"Lie down on the table, Jacob. I need to have a closer look."

He stuck his tweezers into my ear, and the noise in my head exploded. My eyes watered, and my stomach rolled. I thought I was going to be sick all over his white coat.

"Would you look at this," he said, holding up the tweezers to show me a tick working its legs back and forth like rowing a boat. "This was on your eardrum, Jacob," he said.

"No it wasn't," I said.

"It's a wonder you didn't come down with encephalitis. I'll put it in a bottle so you can take it home."

I didn't want to take it home, but I took it. The nurse shook her head at me when I left.

No one said anything all the way home. When we turned at the mailbox, I threw the tick out the window.

Gea said, "What if my friends find out, Mom?"

"Who's to tell," Mom said.

"Jacob will be bragging all over," she said.

"We could have taken that damn tick out for nothing at home," Dad said.

CHAPTER 6

It was rare we ever went anywhere, what with Dad working a job and trying to raise cattle too. We milked eight cows morning and night and sold cream once a week at the creamery in town. Mom bought staples with the cream money. 'Course, we had chickens and kept a couple hogs for butchering in the fall. We rubbed the hams and shoulders down with Morton's Sugar Cure, wrapped them in brown paper bags, and hung them in the basement to cure out.

By the time they were cured and ready to eat, I'd pretty much forgotten the smell of hog guts and singed hair. Dad brought ice home from the ice plant at the roundhouse to keep the milk fresh. But keeping beef iced was out of the question. Dad always said the Rolands were ass deep in beef and couldn't buy a hamburger.

We planted a garden every spring with high hopes of fresh vegetables, but we had no water, save for what we hauled in from the county well and put in the cistern. Dad's old truck had a three-hundred-gallon tank on it, and once a week we drove up the hill to the county well. Sometimes we'd have to leave it sit until the windmill pumped it full. It could be an exciting ride back down the hill, what with a full load of water on, and bad brakes.

Between the Oklahoma heat and the grasshoppers that arrived on schedule every August, it was hard to grow much more than okra. Dad said he'd as soon eat tractor grease.

Sometimes Gea and me would beg Mom to go to the movies. Mostly, it was me did the begging. Gea said I did it better.

Mom would say we couldn't go to the movies, what with a place payment coming up, but that we could have a picnic instead. She'd fix an iron skillet full of potatoes with a gob of lard on top, and we'd go to the shelterbelt and fry potatoes over a camp fire. They were good, but not as good as the movies.

But then there was always the Roland reunion to look forward to every summer. The center of the clan was my Granddad and Grandma Roland. There were eleven offspring. Most had married up and produced more cousins than I could count. Granddad Roland was a preacher, an old-timey preacher, who had ridden the circuit back in territorial days. He lived by the Bible and expected all his children to do the same, no matter they were grown up on their own. They were

Rolands and would live their lives as he saw fit, if they expected to live at all.

He hated the government, education, and papists. The government stole a man's will, he said, not to mention his money. Papists worshiped idols, and education was a false god. He raised his family on cornbread and pork and refused to take his Social Security check. He sold watermelons and plums in the summer for cash, and if any man objected to the price, he gave them away free.

When Granddad said something, it was Jesus Himself talking. He'd memorized thousands of verses from the Bible and quoted them one after another, not in any particular order as far as I could make out. But the words were mysterious and drawn from the darkness, and didn't need understanding. He'd look at me, and his eyes would fill with tears, because he could see the evil inside me. He knew about the magazine I'd hidden in the hollow of that old cottonwood down on the creek, the one Rudy Joe had given to me with the naked girls in it, and he knew about the cigarette butt I'd smoked in the outhouse. He never said, but I knew that he knew.

The Rolands would arrive in the heat of the summer, seventy or eighty strong. A brush arbor would be waiting, built by Granddad Roland's own hand. A fatted calf would have been butchered and smoked by the darkies down the road, and the sermons to follow would be long. Hymns would be sung, followed by yet more verses. My stomach would growl at the aromas of smoked meat, corn on the cob, homegrown tomatoes. And when I was on the verge of collapse, a final prayer would be offered up, disguised as yet one more sermon.

My Grandma Roland, a small woman with braided white hair, would sit with folded hands and listen to sermons she'd heard a thousand times. She'd nod her head and cling to the words in her quiet way. Some said she was part Indian, coming out of the Cherokee country in northwest Arkansas, but if she was, she never said, not to anyone, not ever.

Odd things can sometimes be normal, you see. It was true that Uncle Berko rarely said anything, that he drank coffee all day long and smoked cigarettes through yellowed fingers, that he talked to himself. I knew it and expected it, because it had always been so. It was also true that Uncle Ward saw Germans coming through his windows, but it was no more than that. I'd seen glimpses of sadness in some of the Rolands' eyes, too. I'd seen them quiet with their heads down. But it was like being born with a missing finger—it's unusual only if it grows back. What was had always been. We were the Rolands and that was that, until now, because something in *me* had begun to change.

That summer, the steam engines were taken from railroad service and, one by one, parked on the siding north of town to await salvage. Dad's job changed from the machine shop to the ice plant and his hours to the midnight shift. Sleep came hard, and his temper shortened. There was never enough time to do what had to be done. Mom and me struggled to help, but there was so much we couldn't do. The milk cows stepped on my toes and swatted me with shit tails. The bucket calves sucked my elbows when I tried to feed them. The hogs knocked the slop bucket into the mud, and then me, too, when I tried to get it. They bit the head off my pet duck and ate it—the head, not the duck. A cow gutted herself on a tin culvert that had been ripped up by the road grader. Dad had to shoot her. We tied a ladder in the back of the old truck to paint the peak of the house, and Mom backed it through the wall.

I couldn't fix the fence or run the tractor. I put water in Dad's gas tank instead of the radiator. Fuzzface killed forty baby chicks and then took a nap under the car. Our boar hog escaped into the shelterbelt. Mom and me built a woven wire fence around him and left him there. The calves got screwworms in their heads where they'd been dehorned, and they had to be dug out with a stick. We pulled a calf at three in the morning, and I threw up when the afterbirth came out.

Dad worried and fretted about the work left undone. He developed boils on his neck that had to be lanced, and he grew thin from lack of sleep. He was angry to go to work and angry to get home. The more we tried to help, the worse things became. There was so little I could do, and even less I could do right.

What with the steam engines being salvaged, there'd soon be no work at all, Dad said, no cash money, and then what the hell was he supposed to do? He started going to work early and coming home late.

Mom said he was playing pitch at the pool hall, but sometimes I'd see her lying on the bed crying.

September came, and the shelterbelt lifted its bare limbs skyward. There was the smell of wood smoke trapped under morning fogs. Gea would be off to school in town this year, and I would be back to West Liberty. While I wasn't looking forward to it, I figured to survive. Perhaps I wasn't the smartest kid at West Liberty, but I would never be as dumb as Rudy Joe, and, with luck, the schoolhouse would burn before field day came around again.

But it was not to be. West Liberty School was closed at the last minute, and the lot of us were to be bussed into town to school. It struck me as a mistake to send a young kid like me to town alone.

"I think it's illegal, Mom," I said.

"You'll like it, Jacob. All those new friends."

"What if I get lost and die?"

"I'll send a note to your teacher," she said.

"Mom," I said, whining, "I'm serious."

"Gea will be there, if you have a problem."

"Gea hates me," I said.

"I can't figure why," she said.

"Do they have field day in town?"

"Get your coat and get out there before you miss the bus."

"If they have field day, I'm not going," I said.

"Go," she said, pointing to the door.

CHAPTER 7

The bus ride was an hour and a half of red dirt roads. The bus driver smoked a cigar and watched us in the mirror. We passed Rudy Joe working in the field next to his dad. He stopped and watched us go by. I guess he was through with school. Maybe he feared false gods, or maybe he was just fed up trying to learn words.

My new teacher's name was Mrs. Scarsdale. She had braided white hair stacked on the top of her head, and her eyes were black and beady, like the bull snake Dad killed in the cellar. She marched us into this big room and told us where to sit. She took a paddle out of her desk and had us count the holes aloud as she pointed to them. Six holes altogether. She said that holes in a paddle would take the skin right off your legs, so she hoped that she didn't have to use it. I hoped so too. She laid the paddle on her desk and then looked each one of us in the eyes, just daring us to say something. No one did.

I'd never seen so many kids my own age all gathered up in one place before. There were kids whose parents dropped them off at school in nice cars, and there were Mexican kids from Mexican town out by the roundhouse. They had black hair and black eyes and didn't talk much. One of them, a girl, sat in front of me. She looked back and smiled but said nothing.

There were other girls too. Some smelled like soap and wore dresses and giggled a lot. They passed notes when Mrs. Scarsdale left the room. Sometimes they would push the boys or pull them around by their collars. The boys had new shoes, new pencils, and new boxes of crayons. They stood around with their hands in their back pockets and acted like they knew something no one else did.

Recess came twice a day, with an electric bell that rang when it was time to go and time to come in. There was an indoor bathroom down the hall and a urinal where you could stand and go to the bathroom. The playground had slides and swings and a merry go round.

One day, the little Mexican girl who sat in front of me didn't come back from recess. Later, Mrs. Scarsdale came in with the principal. She was crying, and the principal told us that the little girl had hit her head on the schoolhouse wall while playing red rover and was killed.

Her coat hung on the back of the seat in front of me.

No one paid me any mind, except to look on my paper or to ask if I had gum. At recess the boys played games and chose up sides. The girls chased the boys and pushed them down. Mrs. Scarsdale had a million tortures she used to keep us quiet: Sit under the desk with your knees under your chin. Sit on the floor with your legs out in front of you and with your back straight. Put your nose in a circle on the blackboard while on your tiptoes. Stand in the corner with your arms straight out in front of you. Sometimes she'd just get out the paddle. Count the holes, she'd say. Six of them. Does everyone understand? Count them again where I can hear you. One, two, . . .

I had to sing choir after school one day and stand next to the prettiest girl in class. We held the songbook together. Her fingers touched mine. When choir was over, she looked back at the others and said, "I smell cow manure." I didn't look at my shoes. I didn't need to.

For three weeks the seat in front of me was empty, the one where the little Mexican girl had sat, and then one day there was a new kid sitting in it. He was larger than me, he wore thick glasses, and his hair was cut high on the sides.

He turned. "What's your name?" he asked.

"Jacob," I said. "What's yours?"

"Danny," he said. "Am I sitting in a dead person's seat?"

"Yes," I said.

"Did old lady Scarsdale kill her?"

"Yes," I said. "And there are six holes in her paddle."

"Want to hang out?" he asked.

"I don't play games."

"Only freaks play games," he said.

We met in the shade of the junior high building after lunch. He took out a pocketknife and sharpened the end of a stick.

"What's the matter?" he said, looking up.

"Nothing."

"I make science stuff all the time," he said.

"Like what?" I asked.

"Like, I made a magnet out of a battery and a spring coil. Do you make stuff?"

"No," I said. "But I think stuff."

He stopped whittling and looked up at me. "Like what?"

"I thought up a poem, and it was in the school paper."

"That dumb paper? All they got in it is the cafeteria menu and a picture of the principal."

"I think up other stuff too," I said.

"Yeah? Like what?"

I told him my idea about adults living underground and kids living on top. He thought about it for a little bit and said, "That's nuts."

"Why?"

"There'd have to be hundreds of tunnels, and how would the people breathe?"

"I hadn't thought of that," I said.

So I told him about how I figured out how to live forever. And he said, "To start with, you ain't a thought. You're made up of bones and guts. You have to keep your body from rotting if you want it to live forever."

"How?" I said.

"By freezing it," he said. "You could stay alive for a million years."

"In a million years, someone's going to thaw it out before that," I said.

He stuck his pocketknife blade in the ground and lay down on his side, his head propped up on his hand. "Why think up stuff in your head if you can't use it?" he asked.

"Because I can't help it," I said.

"If something can't be made out of it, it's just dumb."

"Maybe it's dumb to you," I said.

"Want to come home with me sometime?"

"Sure, I guess," I said. "If my folks let me. Where do you live?"

"The Railway Hotel," he said. "My grandparents own it. I have a room all to myself, and I have a stash too."

"A stash?"

"That's right."

"Where?"

"I'm not saying right off, because I don't trust you yet. For all I know you're in with Scarsdale, torturing kids and the like."

"I ain't," I said.

"Friday night," he said.

Mom said she guessed it would be all right if I stayed the night with Danny. Dad said I hadn't gathered the eggs like I ought, and the coons got 'em, but that I could stay over if I promised to keep up with my chores, so I promised.

Gea said she didn't want me showing up at school looking like some orphan.

"I wish I *was*," I said.

"Don't talk that way," Mom said.

"She talked that way first," I said.

"Jacob, you won't be going anywhere with a busted lip," Mom said.

"I saw Gea holding hands with Biff Housely on the school ground at noon the other day," I said.

"I was not," Gea said.

"All cow-eyed," I said.

"Mom," she said.

"I better not catch you holding hands. You ain't too big for a licking just yet. Now, there's the bus," Mom said. "Dad will pick you up Saturday, Jacob, and mind your manners."

Me and Danny walked to the Railway Hotel after school, which was right next to the tracks. His grandparents were really old and wore foggy glasses. We went to his room, which was on the top floor. I could see all the way to the roundhouse from his window.

We sat on the bed and looked at comic books. He had more comic books than I'd ever seen before.

"Why do you live with your grandparents?" I asked.

"My folks are dead," he said.

"What happened?" I asked.

"They were shot."

I looked at him, but he was busy reading his comic book. "Why?" I asked again.

"They were spies."

"Your parents were shot because they were spies?"

"They were spying on Hitler, and he shot them."

"Both on the same day?"

"Same second," he said.

I walked to the window and looked out at the roundhouse again. Smoke hung over it. I hoped I wouldn't have to work there when I grew up.

"Is that true?" I asked.

He tossed his comic book back on the pile. "If I want it to be true, it's true."

"Even if it's a lie?"

"It's not a lie if it's true for me," he said. "I can make it anything, and no one can stop me. You want to see my stash?"

"Sure."

"You have to take an oath first," he said.

"An oath?"

"Hold up your right hand."

"Like this?"

"That's not your right hand. The other one."

"It's the same hand as you."

"I'm facing you, dummy. Do you swear to God that you didn't help Scarsdale kill people or torture kids?"

"I do," I said.

"And that you will never tell anyone about my stash, even if they're cops or preachers?"

"I swear it," I said.

"OK, follow me."

We walked the tracks to the stockyards and then cut east to the cemetery. Danny talked about how he was going to build a rocket soon as he found a rain barrel big enough for the fuselage and enough gunpowder to get it into space.

We cut into the cemetery and stopped at a tombstone that had a huge granite ball on top. Danny said it was lit up twenty-four hours a day, first by the sun and then by the moon. A rose bush grew in a tangle next to it, and that's where Danny uncovered a wooden box.

"This is your stash?" I asked.

"This is it," he said, opening the box. In it was a can of Prince Albert smoking tobacco, a brand new pipe, and a girl's bracelet.

"The dead man's spirit in this grave will come for you if you ever tell," he said.

"I won't," I said. "Where did you get it?"

"I stole it from the drugstore in town," he said.

"Why?"

"They wouldn't let me read their comic books. Anyway, when I get enough stash saved up, I'll sell it and buy what I need to make a rocket. You want to smoke the pipe?"

"Sure," I said. "I smoke all the time."

We stayed until dark so that we could see the moon light up the sphere. We smoked the pipe until our tongues got sore and then put it back in the stash.

"Won't your grandparents be looking for you pretty soon?" I asked.

"They usually forget I'm staying there and go to bed," he said.

On the way back to the Railway Hotel, we passed the schoolhouse. I could hear music coming from the gym and people laughing. We cut through the parking lot, and there were lots of kids sitting in their cars. They were playing their radios and kissing.

CHAPTER 8

A few years after that, Danny moved away. I didn't know where he went. Maybe he built that rocket and flew it to the moon. That same year, Dad was laid off of the railroad, temporary, he said, until Bill McPhail retired.

We bought more bucket calves at the sale ring and tried to keep them alive on separated milk. But they scoured up and died and had to be hauled off to the shelterbelt. We planted a bigger garden, but it didn't rain. Mom canned what she could and sewed her dresses out of flour sacks. But sometimes the cream money didn't stretch.

Gea was chosen for cheerleader and needed pleated skirts and saddle shoes. She sang alto on the glee club and had to travel to school functions. She took piano lessons every Saturday in town and had to have gas for the car. Mom said maybe we couldn't afford it, but Dad said he thought it necessary, that we'd come up with the money somewhere.

I'd hear him getting up before dark to make coffee, even though he had no place to go. He'd sit by the woodstove. Sometimes he'd talk to himself or just sit in the dark.

On Sundays, he and Gea used to play the piano and sing hymns. But then Gea had glee club practice now and games to go to. He sang out in the barn while milking, but after a while, he quit that too.

Mom and him didn't talk so much as they used to. They didn't fight or nothing. It was just kind of quiet lots of times. Mom took to going to the church down the road. She said she especially liked the old pastor, who had been a missionary before he got old. He had white hair and wore suspenders. I asked her what missionaries did, and she said they saved folks over in Africa.

"Saved them from what?" I asked.

"From going to hell," she said.

"What did they do?"

"Nothing," she said.

"Then why they going to hell?" I asked.

"They're not Christians," she said. "You can't get into heaven if you aren't Christian."

"Rudy Joe ain't a Christian," I said. "Will he go to hell?"

"If he doesn't change his ways. And don't say *ain't*; it's ignorant."

"Will he burn up?"

"You don't burn *up,* Jacob. You burn *forever.*"

"Rudy Joe deserves it," I said.

Mom spiked her hands on her waist. "Go help your dad, while you're still able."

That summer, I spent my days walking and feeling lonely. I don't know why for sure, 'cept I had this feeling I had become invisible. I was the guy standing next to the tallest boy in the class photo, with my face behind his elbow. No one knew who I was, or cared. I was the one who sat at a table by myself in study hall, the one who hated recess. I wasn't dumb like Rudy Joe or cocky smart like Danny. I was invisible, an unimportant person in a world of important people.

Going to town school hadn't helped much with that, and then with Dad out of work, I wore last year's clothes to make do. Mom said it was only temporary until Dad's job came back. I didn't mind so much, until one of the girls asked me if I was expecting a flood. I guess I'd grown more than I thought. After that, I rolled my shirtsleeves up and pulled my britches low as I could.

Mom fixed boiled eggs, which we had lots of, and tomatoes out of the garden. We ate watermelon and corn on the cob. All of it was good. None of it was store bought. It's funny how hungry you can get for bologna, potato chips, and chocolate, though.

I came down with some kind of bug, plugged up and couldn't go. I didn't say anything for the longest time. It was just hard to talk about. Like, hey, everyone, I haven't gone to the bathroom in days. Just thought I'd let you know. Anyway, what was the point? We didn't go to the doctor for something so trivial as that.

Like I said, one time I jumped off the chicken house and ran a nail right out the top of my foot. It had an old rotten board still hooked to it. I screamed like a bobcat when Dad pulled the board off, so he soaked my foot in kerosene to take out the soreness and to keep me from getting lockjaw. He said if I got it, my jaw would lock up and I wouldn't be able to eat or talk. In fact, the more he thought about it, the more he liked the idea.

The notion of what might happen to me for not going to the bath-room was just too much to face. So I said nothing, my strategy of choice when it came to fear. Finally, Mom, a long-suffering victim of constipation herself, figured out what was going on. She fed me enormous quantities of mineral oil, glasses of sandhill plum juice, and canned blue plums. I ate an entire sack of prunes and bowls of boiled wheat, all to no effect, save for the peculiar noises emitting from my stomach.

That night, as I lay in bed, I could hear Mom and Dad talking in the kitchen. While I couldn't hear exactly what they were saying over the growls in my stomach, there was little doubt that it was about me, and that it wasn't good.

I awoke the next morning to Mom standing over my bed holding a red rubber bag with a hose attached. There was a black plastic tube at its end.

"Jacob," she said. "It's time."

I sat up in bed and rubbed my eyes. "Time for what?"

"Time for a soap enema," she said.

"A what?"

"An enema, Jacob. It goes into your body and cleans out your insides."

"I'm not drinking soap," I said.

"You don't drink it, Jacob," she said, holding up the tube. "This goes inside you."

"Inside me?"

"That's right, in your rear end."

"In my rear end?"

"Now, pull down your britches and lean over the bed."

I made a run for the door, just slipping under her arm. I could hear her coming after me as I dashed across the living room and outside. But here she came behind me like a crazed doctor, bag held over her head, her tube at the ready.

"Jacob Roland," she said, hollering, "you stop this minute, you hear?"

I wasn't much one to disobey her, particularly when she used that tone of voice, but the thought of having a tube stuck up my rear and soap water pumped inside me was simply more than I could face.

I hid behind a tree and waited as she circled the yard, her instrument of torture at the ready. Her voice grew louder, more impatient, and I knew I was in trouble no matter how it was cut. When I heard the front door of the house slam, I peeked around the corner. There it was, the dreaded instrument, on the front porch and even bigger than I thought. The tube on the end was two, maybe three feet long, all greased up and gleaming in the sun like a stiletto knife. I checked the house door. She was not to be seen, so I made a mad run for the enema bag, snatched it up, and headed for the pasture fast as I could go.

I threw that son of a bitch in the creek a quarter mile from the house and walked back, knowing the while there would be hell to pay, knowing also that I would never tell where that bag was no matter what.

I took my punishment, as was inevitable, hopping up and down like a jackrabbit to avoid the sting of that tamarack switch, but I never gave up my secret. Either the excitement or the exercise or a combination of the two soon enough worked, and I spent the remainder of that day sitting in the outhouse. It was nearly three years later, after a hard spring rain, that I spotted that bag floating down the creek on its way to the Gulf of Mexico.

My decision to go out for basketball was not well thought out, having been based solely on Dad's love of the game. Needless to say, I wasn't any good at it, me or Juan Lopez either one. He was taller than me, but fat, so the coach made us run the stairs, while the good players shot baskets. Some could make baskets from halfway down court. One day when we were running, I told Juan I'd had a poem published in the school paper.

"The one with the school menu in it?" he asked.

"Yeah," I said.

"I hate poems," he said.

By the end of the season, we still couldn't hit a basket, but I think Jaun lost fifty or sixty pounds, and I could run a full hour without breaking a sweat. Dad didn't go to a single game that year, for which I was most grateful.

It wasn't often that we went to visit the Franklin side of the family. Not because it wasn't fun but because they sometimes asked for money, a spare commodity at our house in any event. But now and then Mom would relent and take the long way to town to buy groceries, stopping in for that rare visit.

The Franklin house was an unpainted shack with cemetery roses growing up the trestle on the front porch. Grandma Franklin, a large woman with a large laugh, was the opposite of Grandma Roland. She smoked cigarettes, listened to soaps on the radio, and loved to go to the fiesta out at Mexican town, where she'd sit in the car and listen to the music.

The Franklin household lived off Social Security, government commodities, and springer rabbits they raised in the backyard. They had sixty acres of scrub, most of which grew little more than paddle cactus and mesquite, but no matter what was in the larder, Grandma could cook up the best meal I ever ate. If the little kids got whiney, she'd give them a chicken bone to suck on. If that failed to quiet them, she'd roll out one of the largest breasts known to the human species. "You need some titty, whiney boy?" she'd say, striking even the most ardent whiner stone silent.

Her first husband, my real grandpa, died from tetanus, after having an infected tooth pulled. Grandma raised the family, mostly on her own, a rowdy bunch quick to laugh, dance, and fight. She then married Roy, my step grandpa, a man as stoic and humorless as the rabbits he raised in the backyard. He chewed Days Work plug tobacco, cussed at will, and pinched all the kids until they hollered.

It made no mind to Grandma who you were or what you had done. She took everyone straight up. If you were a murderer, well, you were her murderer and probably the best one in the country. Grandma Franklin's house was the only place I was never invisible.

On this day, she invited us in, turned down her old radio, and said, "Had anything to eat?"

"Can't stay long," Mom said. "Just checking on you."

Grandma lit a cigarette and looked at me through the smoke. "Don't you feed this boy, Vega?"

"'Course I do. He eats more than me and Abbott put together."

"His arms look like spider legs."

"He's just naturally thin."

I said, "Gea eats in the school cafeteria, but I have to take a sack lunch."

"You don't treat this boy right, Vega."

"He's just a complainer."

"You a whiney baby, Jacob?"

"No."

"You need some titty, whiney baby?"

"No."

"Where's Jack and Duny?" Mom asked, Jack and Duny being her brothers.

"Jack's off to harvest. Haven't heard since he left. Duny's building fence for Old Man Tuttle. It's payday, so 'spect he'll be going to town."

"Drinking?" Mom said.

Grandma shrugged. "Duny's had a time since the war. Say, I got warm bread just out of the oven."

"We better get on home."

"Jacob here looks like he could use some homemade bread."

I looked at Mom.

"All right, but we can't stay long."

The bread was yeasty, warm, with puddles of butter melted on it.

"This kid's half-starved," Grandma said.

"You'd think so," Mom said.

"Mom and me pulled a calf," I said.

"Did?"

"I had to put my arm up the cow's butt," I said.

"Calves come out a cow's butt?" Grandma asked.

I nodded.

"I'll be. Here I had it wrong all this time."

"Let's go, Jacob," Mom said. "Before something else falls out of your mouth."

We went to the grocery store, which was across the street from the fire department and police station. Mom bought sugar, cornmeal, coffee, and twenty-five pounds of flour in a paisley sack. She asked the owner to put it on our bill. He looked at it and said, "Well, this time, Vega, but we need to get this taken care of soon."

We were loading up the groceries in the coupe when June Elliot, the city clerk, waved Mom over.

"You better come listen to this, Vega," she said.

"What?"

"It's Duny," she said. "The highway patrol is after him."

So we followed her into the clerk's office. Duny was Mom's youngest brother. "You sure it's Duny?" Mom asked.

June pointed to the two-way radio. "Just listen."

About then, a voice came over the radio. "He's headed across the field now," it said. "He's refusing to stop. The son of a bitch gave me the finger."

"Duny's drunk and on Tuttle's John Deere tractor," June said.

"Oh, no," Mom said.

"I'm going to crowd him," the voice said. Moments later, "Damn it, he drove through the fence, and he's headed across country. I'm going around the mile square. See if I can head him off." And then, "No, no, he's coming back toward the fence."

"Can't you stop him?" someone said.

"He's on a goddang tractor. I could use some help out here."

"We'll send out a unit, but it will take them a while to get there."

"Now he's back on the highway, and he's dragging a hundred feet of barbed wire and fence posts behind him. I've got to get him shut down before he kills someone."

"How?"

"I'm going to shoot the tires out."

"Oh, no," Mom said, taking my hand. "They might hit Duny."

There was the sound of a door opening, and then the crack of a rifle shot.

Several minutes passed with only the static of the radio, then, "This is unit twenty-four. He's in custody, and get Old Man Tuttle on the phone. He's got some fence to fix."

Mom didn't say anything as we drove home.

"Mom?" I said.

"What?"

"Didn't Uncle Duny drive a tank in the army?"

"Just shut up, Jacob," she said.

CHAPTER 9

A couple weeks later our phone rang, which it did with some frequency. There are fourteen people on our phone line, that's why it's called line fourteen, so when it rings in any one home, it rings in all fourteen. One could never know who might be listening, though most generally it was the same three or four neighbors. Eight short rings was the emergency signal, indicating a grass fire or some other calamity. One time a bolt of lightning hit the line and all fourteen phones jangled over and over as the electricity dissipated. Fifteen minutes later, a fire truck showed up from town.

Our phone rang again, two longs and two shorts. "Hello," I said.

"Jacob?"

"Yes."

"This is June, city clerk. Is your mother there?"

"Mom," I said. "It's June."

Mom came to the phone. "Hello," she said.

I stood up close so that I could hear.

"Vega?"

"Yes."

"This is June."

"Yes, June?"

"Thought you'd like to know, the highway patrol was just here. They said Duny was sentenced to thirty days in county."

"Oh?"

"He said Duny's taken up knitting."

"Knitting? "

"But the jailer would only give him one skein of wool."

"What can he do with only one skein, for heaven's sake?" Mom said.

"He's making a two-inch dick warmer for the jailer," she said, laughing.

Mom covered the phone with her hand and sent me out of the room.

August days blew in from the southwest, dry, torrid, and windy. Life crawled into whatever shade it could find and clamped its jaw against the blast. Gea spent fewer and fewer days at home, staying with friends in town. Sometimes she would call and say that she would catch a ride home later, but then she wouldn't show. Dad would slam the door, and Mom would grow quiet. I'd try to cheer her up by helping with the dishes or in the garden, but it seldom worked.

Dad took to going into town in the evenings to watch the softball games out at the park. If Mom objected, he would say she could come if she wanted. But she wouldn't, and he'd stomp out of the house and go anyway. Sometimes she'd lie on the bed and cry.

One night, he came home late. Gea was in town, and I was sleeping on the porch. I heard the car drive in. The lights came on in the house, and I could see them through the porch window. They were standing with their faces only inches apart, and their voices were loud and angry. Mom screamed something and pushed him. He took hold her of hands and bent them back until she went to her knees. Then he let her go and left.

The next morning, Mom fixed me toast and scrambled eggs. She turned the radio on and sipped at her coffee. Her little finger and the finger next to it were black and blue.

"Where's Dad?" I asked.

"He went to the field," she said.

"Where's Gea?" I asked.

"I don't know," she said.

I put sandhill plum butter on my toast and watched Fuzzface through the window. He was peeing on Mom's flowerpot.

"Mom?" I said.

"Yes?"

"What's a dick warmer?"

Mom poured herself another coffee and walked to the door. "Go do your chores," she said.

Labor Day was only three weeks away when I first noticed the twitch. It was there at the corner of my nose, like an itch, but not really an itch. For no reason, my nose started twitching, like I was making a face at something that tasted bad. The more I tried to stop it, the worse it got. I put a hot rag on it, but it didn't help.

Mom said, "You get those chores done?"

"Yes," I said.

Mom looked at me. "What?" she said.

"What, what?" I said, twitching.

"Don't you make a face at me," she said. "I'll slap you into next week."

I went to the bathroom and looked in the mirror. My nose twitched back. I put Vicks Salve on it, but it didn't help. I put a clothespin on it, and the clothespin bobbed up and down.

That night at the table, Dad set his fork down. "What the hell is the matter with this boy, Vega?"

"What do you mean?" she said.

"His nose is twitching."

"He's just being cute," she said.

"Go to your room," he said.

"I don't have a room," I said.

"Then go where you go and do it now."

So I went out on the front porch and lay down in the daybed. I could see a plane flying high in the blackness, its red lights blinking, blinking at exactly the same rate as my nose was twitching.

That night, one of Gea's girlfriends came home with her. They went straight to Gea's bedroom. The friend had stayed all night with Gea before. I liked her titties, which I could see through her nightgown when she came to breakfast in the morning.

I dozed, and when I woke up, I checked my nose. It was still twitching, and my stomach was growling. Twitching takes a lot of energy, so I decided to raid the icebox. Gea and her friend were already in the kitchen eating watermelon.

"What are you doing?" Gea asked.

"I'm hungry," I said.

"Well, we were in here first," she said.

I opened the icebox. There was nothing in it but tomatoes and half a watermelon. "I just want something to eat," I said.

"What's the matter with your brother's nose?" Gea's girlfriend asked.

Gea looked at my nose. "Just stop it, Jacob, or I'll tell Mom."

"Go ahead and tell her," I said. "Anyway, I'm going to bed." I stopped at the door. "You guys getting up for breakfast?" I asked.

By the time I started my first year in high school, my twitching nose had gone away, which I was really glad about. It was then that Mom decided to officially join the church down the road. She insisted that all of us start going regular too, including Gea and Dad. They both liked it because they could sing hymns in perfect alto, and all the people would say amen. Mom liked it because she was worried about the Africans going to hell. I didn't like it, because the sermons were as long as Grandad Roland's sermons, and there was no fatted calf waiting at the end.

About that same time, an older couple started coming to church from town. They drove a clean car and sat on the front row. The woman smelled like perfume, and the man wore a tie and freshly ironed shirt.

"Mom?" I asked on the way home.

"What, Jacob?"

"Why would those people drive all the way out here to go to church?"

"Maybe they're looking for a simpler way to serve God," she said.

"It's because we're goobers, isn't it?" I said.

"Who said that?"

"Danny."

"What does Danny know, nothing, that's what. Anyway, everyone's got a right to go to church where they want."

"I don't," I said.

Dad shook his head, and Mom looked at me over her elbow. "When you start buying your own groceries, then you can go to church anywhere you want," she said. "Until then, if you want to continue breathing, you'll go to church where I say. Understood?"

"Yes," I said.

It was the last weekend before school started when the townies brought their granddaughter to church with them. She was visiting for the weekend, the preacher said, and he had her stand up so all could see her. She was the most beautiful girl I had ever seen. She looked at me and smiled, and my ears turned hot.

The next Sunday, I took a bath and put on my best jeans and shirt. I

combed my hair and put on Hair Care wax to hold down my cowlick. I
used the last of Dad's shaving lotion and checked my teeth in the mirror.

When I got in the car, Mom said, "You look very nice today, Jacob."

"I could use a new pair of shoes," I said.

"I'm glad to see you taking an interest in church."

"I'm looking for a simpler way to God too," I said.

Dad turned up the radio. "Appears you found it," he said.

The townies were there like before, sitting on the front row, sharing
a songbook between them, except she was not with them. I heard them
tell the preacher that their granddaughter had gone home to start school.
I hardly heard a word after that. I'd only seen her for a brief moment,
but I knew that our lives were somehow linked.

CHAPTER 10

I stepped off the school bus to find that Uncle Duny, who had just gotten out of county jail, was waiting in our yard. He was driving an old Ford coupe with a cracked front window, and there was a mongrel dog sitting in the front seat with a rope around its neck. Duny was a giant, with a face red as blood and a voice that sounded like it was coming out of a rain barrel. Mom said he could dance smooth as glass, especially after he'd had a few, though I'd never seen it myself.

He'd done about everything there was to do in life: airplane mechanic, harvest hand, butcher, town cop, a guard at an asylum for the criminally insane. He even drove the bus for a country western band for a while. He'd do just fine long as he stayed out of town. There was no lengths to what he wouldn't go to stay out of town when he was drying out, because once he'd started drinking, there was no natural end to it.

"Jacob," he said, "your mom home?"

"I think so," I said.

"Go get her, will you?"

I nodded and went in, finding her running a tub of wet clothes through the wringer. She laid down her laundry stick. "Who?"

"Uncle Duny," I said. "He's outside."

"What does he want?"

I shrugged. "Don't know. He said he wanted to talk to you."

"Lord," she said. "He's wanting money. Drunk?"

"I don't think so."

Duny was sitting on the fender of his car smoking a cigarette when we got outside. He'd tied his dog to the bumper.

"See my new dog, Vega?" he said.

"I see it," Mom said. "When you get out?"

"Couple days," he said.

"Wonder you hadn't killed someone on that tractor, Duny."

"Oh, wasn't going *that* fast," he said.

"Whatever were you thinking?"

He squashed out his cigarette. "I just figured to discourage them some. All they had to do was wait, and I'd taken that tractor back."

"We got a place payment coming up, Duny."

"I didn't ask for money, Vega. I could use a place to stay for a while, though."

She wiped suds off her hands on her apron. "I don't know about that, Duny. Gea has the only bedroom. Jacob here is sleeping on the porch."

"I could put up in the separator house, help out with the chores."

"I don't know," she said. "We *could* use the help what with Abbott working night shift."

"For a few weeks," he said.

"I won't be putting up with drinking, Duny."

"No drinking," he said. "I could put that old daybed in the separator house, and I'd be milking the cows morning and night too."

"Why don't you just drink soda instead of that whiskey?" Mom said. "Sure would save a lot of trouble."

Duny looked up at her through the cigarette smoke. "Soda pop? Why, I hadn't thought of that, Vega," he said.

"Well, I guess you can stay for a few weeks. Don't go getting short with the kids, Duny. This is their home, you know."

"I'll be keeping to myself for the most part, Vega."

"You got clothes need washing? I'm right in the middle," she said.

"I only got the one change. Maybe Jacob here could help me move the bed?"

I nodded. "What's your dog's name?" I asked.

"Mortem," he said. "Named after the death dogs."

"Duny, don't start," Mom said, shaking her head.

We moved in the bed and carried in a cardboard box of old westerns he had in the trunk of his car. Duny's face lit red as fire and his hands shook some as we spread out the army blanket.

"Knock out your shoes before you put them on in the morning," I said. "I see scorpions out here all the time."

Duny sat down on his bed and lit a cigarette. "That's good to know. A scorpion in your shoe is no way to start the day."

I looked through some of his books. Most of them had the covers torn off.

"You like Zane Grey?" I asked.

He flipped the ash off his cigarette onto the floor. "Don't make a damn to me," he said. "As long as it's something to read."

"I think a person is kind of like a story," I said.

"Yeah, like I'm a goddang comic book," he said. "And you're a short story."

"What kind of dog is Mortem?" I asked.

"Rat terrier mostly," he said.

"Can he catch rats?"

"Only if they commit suicide first," he said.

I picked up his Prince Albert can and smelled it. "I like Bugler myself," I said.

"You smoke, do you?"

"Most all the time," I said. "Mom doesn't know."

"I 'spect not," he said.

"Were you really in jail?" I asked.

"Cops got the sense of humor of a stick," he said.

"Could you make me a dick warmer, Uncle Duny?"

He dabbed the sweat off his forehead. "Why, sure. Shouldn't take more than a minute or two," he said.

Danny came back for the school year to live with his grandparents again in the Railway Hotel. He hadn't grown a bit, but his face looked different, kind of old somehow, and a couple of black whiskers stuck out of his chin.

We gathered in the shade of the junior high building where we had spent so many recesses talking. He checked his pack of Kools and sat down on the steps.

"What you doing back, Danny?" I asked.

"I'm taking care of my grandparents," he said.

"Where have you been?"

"Alaska."

"Alaska? How you get up there?"

"With my folks."

"I thought they were shot by Hitler."

"That's what we thought at first, but they escaped."

"Did you really go to Alaska?"

"I got word my grandparents were dying, so I came back to help out with the hotel."

"What are they dying from?"

"Old age," he said.

I knew he was lying, but I liked his lies. They were more interesting by half than his real life.

"Uncle Duny is staying in our separator house," I said. "He's a drunk."

"I heard *all* the Franklins were," he said.

"Not all," I said.

"Are you?" he asked.

"No."

"A woman ever see you naked?"

"Why?"

"If you're a stud, you have to be careful. When they see a stud, they go crazy."

"We had a stud horse once," I said.

"Like that," he said. "I don't want to brag, but I'm sort of a stud myself."

"They go crazy when they see you naked?"

He nodded. "You have to be careful," he said. "This fella let his girlfriend see one time, right in broad daylight."

"Yeah?"

"She did it to herself until she died."

"Jesus."

"They could get you for murder," he said.

"Can guys do it to themselves until they die?"

"It would take a really lot. You don't know anything, do you?"

"Yes, I do."

And I did know to some degree. Not possible to live on a farm without knowing something about that and death. But I'd never seen anything die from doing it too much. 'Course, the guys talked about it, laughing and such. But they all seemed older than me, more experienced that way. Truth was, I could see that I was running behind in that respect. Some of the boys even had hair on their chests. Joe Bob Riley, the center on our football team, had to shave every day before he came to school.

But it was only in the last few months I'd noticed a change in my own body, my voice going high at unexpected times. And I thought about girls a lot, too, about their breasts, and their legs, and the way they smelled. I daydreamed, too, mostly about the girl I'd seen at church, and when I did, my stomach tightened up like on a roller coaster ride.

"I'd sure like to smoke a Kool right now," Danny said. "Listen, I get my driver's permit next month, and my grandpa said I could drive their Plymouth. He don't know you're supposed to have a licensed driver with you. Maybe you could stay in, and we could drive around town. Check out the girls."

"Sure," I said. "You're going to be fifteen already?"

"I didn't start school until I was nearly eight. They do it that way in Alaska."

"I got a while to go," I said.

"No problem. You buy the gas, and I'll drive the car."

By the time Danny got his driver's license, I was more or less out of the notion of driving around with him. I'd taken to being alone more and more, finding comfort in the isolation. If I'd see someone coming, someone I knew, I sometimes would change my direction, pretending I hadn't seen them. It was not that I didn't like them so much as I just wanted to be alone.

The more alone I was, the more I could live in my head, a place of my own making. My favorite place to be alone was on the porch roof. I would climb the trellis, sit back, and move into that private place where no one could enter except by permission. I often found life behind my eyes more interesting than life in front of them.

"What you doing on the goddang roof?" Uncle Duny said from below.

"Thinking," I said.

"You have to be on the roof to think?"

"No."

"Well, come on down. Me and Mortem are taking a ride in the water truck."

"Where you going?"

"Paris or the county well. Which do you figure?"

"Does Mom know?"

"You can't go to the well without telling your mom?"

"Sure, I can," I said, dropping down to the ground.

"Climb in and don't let the dog get out. He's a son of a bitch to catch."

Uncle Duny cranked up the truck, and we drove off. Mortem rode with his front feet on the dash, water dripping from his tongue. The old truck labored up the hill, and blue smoke boiled out the back. Uncle Duny shifted her into second and hooked his elbow out the window.

At the top, we pulled into the county well, dropped the hose in the tank, and opened the valve. Uncle Duny climbed the ladder and checked the water level. Climbing back down, he pulled the brake release on the windmill, and the tail whipped into the wind. She cranked over a couple times, but the wind was weak.

"Pump me some cold water up," he said.

I worked the handle and could hear the water climbing to the top of the pipe. When I looked up, Uncle Duny had a fifth of Hill & Hill whiskey tipped up, and bubbles were gurgling to the top of the bottle like an artesian well. He wiped his mouth with his arm, and his face turned the color of cranberries.

"Pump faster, boy," he said. "There ain't no better chaser than cold well water."

I pumped the handle faster, and he held out his cupped hands, drinking from them. "Oh, yes," he said. "That calls for another."

"Mom isn't going to like you drinking, Uncle Duny," I said.

"She'd have me drinking soda pop. Give me diabetes or who knows what." He took another swig. "Come on, let's find some shade while that tank fills."

We sat on the east side of the water tank in what was left of the morning shade. Uncle Duny drank from his bottle again and rolled a cigarette.

"You have a girlfriend?" he asked.

"Sure."

"What's her name?"

"I don't know," I said.

"You don't know her name?"

"Not yet."

"Sometimes it works out better that way," he said.

Mortem showed up with a sandbur in his hind foot. I pulled it out, and he chewed it up.

"Eating a sandbur is pretty dumb," I said.

Uncle Duny took another drink and set the bottle between his legs. "He's trying to tell you something," he said.

"What?"

"Something disturbs you, just eat it," he said. "It's the fastest way to solve a problem."

Seemed like the more Uncle Duny drank, the smarter he got.

Water spilled over the tank and onto the truck bed. Uncle Duny took a last swig and put the bottle under the truck seat. We took off with water sloshing and smoke bellowing, but it wasn't until we reached the crest of the hill that I remembered that the brakes didn't work so well with a load of water on back, the problem being that by that time we'd already picked up considerable speed. Uncle Duny pumped the brake pedal, but to no avail. The wind whipped his hair across his eyes, and he held on to the steering wheel with both hands.

He looked over at me. "What's the matter with the goddang brakes?" he shouted over the rattle and bang of the truck.

Before I could answer, we took the first curve, banking hard, and the water rushed to the right. The old truck careened into the grader ditch. Sunflowers gathered up in the bumper, and a cloud of dust rose up around the cab. Uncle Duny spun the wheel the other direction, and we shot back onto the road.

I could see the church at the bottom of the hill, and the sharp curve that would have to be negotiated when we got there. Uncle Duny had grown quiet, his eyes locked on the road ahead. The old truck bounced and rattled, and dust boiled up through the floorboard as we raced down the hill. I held on to the dash to keep from being thrown onto the floor. Mortem had fallen onto his back between the gearshift and the seat.

"We ain't going to make it," Uncle Duny said.

We shot across the road, through the church fence, and came to a dead stop at the front steps. The church mailbox rested on the hood of the truck. The Hill & Hill whiskey bottle rolled out from under the seat. Uncle Duny turned the key off, settled back, and took a deep breath. He looked at me and I looked at him. And we both looked at the mailbox.

"Are you a Christian, Jacob?" he asked.

"Yes, sir," I said. "Are you?"

"Am now," he said.

We walked the rest of the way home. Uncle Duny loaded Mortem into his car and rolled down the window.

"I'm going to run into town for a bit of business," he said.

"Aren't you going to tell Mom what happened?"

"Soon as I get back," he said. "And them damn brakes ought be fixed before someone gets killed."

Uncle Duny never came back. Dad pulled the truck out of the church yard and reset the mailbox. Mom never said anything, but the next day, I found Uncle Duny's clothes in the trash.

CHAPTER 11

Word came over line fourteen that they'd found Rudy Joe dead in the wheat field. He'd driven the tractor into a gully. It tipped over and crushed him. I can't say we were ever friends, but it was a pity him being dead, having never learned more than a half dozen reading words. Dad said that was six more than Rudy Joe's old man ever learned.

Danny drove his grandparents' Plymouth to school every day now. He'd sit in it at lunch hour and play the radio loud enough so that the girls could hear it. He kept at me about staying over so we could drive around. Finally, I asked Mom if I could. She said all right, though she wasn't at all certain about me staying with Danny after the talk around town. I ask what talk, but she didn't say.

After school, we got in his Plymouth, lit up a Kool, and drove around and around the town square. When we'd see a girl walking, Danny would slow down and blow smoke out the window. He said that girls liked nothing better than a guy smoking and driving a car with the radio on.

"Hey," he said, "want to go check the stash?"

"What stash?"

"The one out to the cemetery. Don't you remember?"

"That was a long time ago, Danny."

So we drove out to the big granite ball tombstone and dug around for a while. Pretty soon, we uncovered a pipe and a rusty Prince Albert can.

"It's still here," I said.

After we'd reburied the stash, Danny leaned back against the tombstone and crossed his legs at the ankles. "I admit I haven't been altogether truthful about some things," he said.

"Like what?"

"My folks weren't ever spies like I told you. They're divorced and don't want me around."

"That's all right," I said.

"It's just something I don't like talking about."

"Me too," I said. "I mean, there are things, you know."

"You got things?"

"I can't tell everyone," I said.

"You can tell me."

"You got an extra Kool?"

He dug one out of the pack and handed it to me. I lit up.

"What things exactly need saying?" he asked.

"Stuff happens in my head sometimes."

"Like what stuff?"

"Like sometimes I hear things. Least I think I do."

"Like someone talking to you?"

"Kind of. I can't always tell if it's real or something I make up in my head."

"That's weird," he said.

"I know."

"When did they start talking to you?"

"This summer. Sometimes things seem too real, bright, noisy, and it's all pulling me into a place I don't want to go. You think I'm crazy?"

He took a drag off his Kool. "Pretty much," he said. "Let's go see if we can find some women."

We didn't find any women, so we bought a magazine at the drugstore instead. Danny made me buy it. He said I looked older.

That night we lay in bed on the fourth floor of the Railway Hotel and looked at the naked pictures.

"Man," he said, "I wish I had a woman."

"Me too," I said.

"We could show old lady Mitchell in English class what we got in our pants. She'd probably give us an A," he said.

"Yeah," I said. "But I don't want to get charged with murder."

After a while, he said, "What do they say to you?"

"Who?"

"The voices that talk to you."

I shrugged. "That I'm different."

"How different?"

"That they only talk to me because I'm special. They tell me things that no one else knows. Sometimes they talk when I'm trying to talk to someone else or studying. It's hard then because I can't pay attention to everything. Sometimes I see pictures too. They come alive in my head."

"Are the voices talking to you now?"

"No."

"Can't you tell them to shut up and go away?"

"You aren't going to tell anyone, are you, Danny?"

"What do I care who you talk to? Maybe you need to figure a way to get rid of them."

"What do you mean?"

"I don't know. Maybe you could pay them off or something. Hey, I know, maybe they could give you the answers on tests."

"I don't think so," I said.

"Well, the way I figure it, if someone's going to talk to me, they better have something worth saying."

"Maybe it's just me talking to myself," I said.

"No wonder you don't know nothing. You can't even inhale."

"Yes, I can."

"And you have no girlfriend."

"I do," I said. "Sort of."

"What does that mean?"

"We haven't met."

"Is she in your head too?"

"No, I seen her at church."

Danny turned the page. "Hey, look at this one. Red hair."

"Whatever happened to that rocket you were going to build?" I asked.

"Gunpowder don't work," he said. "It's got to be liquid fuel. You can't buy liquid fuel."

"Like gas?"

"It has to be under pressure," he said. "Hey, look at the jugs on that one. I bet your church girlfriend don't have those."

"Don't talk about her that way, Danny."

"Come on, you don't even know her."

"I will," I said.

"All right, idiot. I stink. Want to shower?"

"Nah, I showered at home," I said.

"You don't even have running water at home," he said.

"I don't want to shower, Danny."

He took off his clothes and went to the bathroom to shower. Danny had pubic hair, and I didn't. I didn't want him to know. When he came out, he had a towel wrapped around himself.

"How can you be in love when you haven't even met her?" he asked.

"I didn't say I was in love."

"I heard the Rolands were weird," he said. "It's all that religion."

I threw the magazine onto the floor. "Knock it off, Danny."

"All right, take it easy," he said, picking up the magazine. "You can't take a joke?"

"At least I got folks who don't kick me out," I said.

Danny's face darkened, and he walked to the window. "I knew I shouldn't have told you," he said.

"I'm sorry," I said. "I got no business saying that."

"Forget it. Want to go window peeking?"

"Where?"

"Roof. You can see in all the windows from up there."

"Sure," I said.

We window peeked for a while. There was not much to see. An old guy in his shorts had fallen asleep in his chair. On the third floor, a couple lay on their bed watching television. They were eating something out of a box. We watched them a long time, thinking they might do it, but they never did.

We went back to the room and looked through the magazine again. Danny said, "Jacob, do you know I'm the only friend you have?"

"I don't need many friends, just one true one," I said.

"But how do you know if someone is your true friend?"

"They give you money," I said.

"I'm serious."

"A friend keeps your secrets," I said.

Danny turned onto his stomach with his legs up behind him and thought about it for a while.

"Anyone can keep a secret," he said. "Secret agents keep secrets, and they ain't your friend."

"What if they keep a secret for you that they shouldn't keep, then they'd be your true friend."

"What do you mean?"

"Like, if they didn't tell, it might get *them* into trouble as much as you, but they keep the secret anyway. That would be a true friend."

He turned over and stared at the ceiling for a while. "We need a friend test," he said.

"A friend test?"

"Come on. I got an idea."

We stopped at the hotel kitchen, and Danny got a squeeze bottle of ketchup. Outside, he opened the trunk of his Plymouth.

"Roll up your sleeve," he said.

"What?"

"Just do it."

I rolled up my sleeve, and he poured ketchup down my arm and over my hand.

"What's that for?" I asked, smelling my arm.

"Now, climb in the trunk and stick your arm out. Hold the trunk lid down with your other hand. If we see the cop, I'll tell you, and you can pull your arm in."

"What's the point of this, Danny?"

"Whoever doesn't turn us in is a true friend," he said.

"Turn us in for what?"

"Murder."

"But what if they do turn us in for murder?"

"There hasn't been a murder, Jacob."

"No, but—"

"Well, then, we haven't done anything illegal, have we?"

"I guess not."

"Get in then."

I climbed into the trunk and stuck my hand out. "Stick your *arm* out and let it dangle like it's dead," he said.

I stuck it all the way out. I could smell ketchup and rubber from the spare tire and Danny's old shoes he wore for seining minnows.

We drove off, slow like, and I could feel the cool wind on my arm. "I can talk to you through the back seat," he said. "Wait, here comes Old Man Stickle. I'm going to pull in front of him."

"It's hot in here, Danny."

"Ha ha," he said. "Yeah, yeah, we'll pull over in a minute. Oh, man, you should see his face. Hold it, there's the cop. Pull in your arm. Quick. OK, he's gone. Put it out again."

We made the square a second and third time. "Hey," he said. "Chester Finley just pulled in behind us. Ha ha, he's sees the arm. He's coming up close. I'm going out to the park and see what he says. Don't say anything."

Danny pulled over in the park and rolled down his window. "Hey, Chester," he said. "What's up?"

"Jeez," Chester said. "Is that a body?"

"What body?"

"There's a bloody arm hanging out your trunk, Danny. Did you kill someone?"

"Damn," Danny said. "I thought that trunk lid was down."

"What you doing with a body in your trunk?"

"It's a long story, Chester. I need to get rid of it. You ain't going to tell, are you?"

"You need some help?"

"Just keep it to yourself."

"Right," he said.

"Where do you figure would be a good place to bury a body?"

"No one would look for a body in the cemetery," he said.

"Great idea, Chester. See you at school."

"Yeah, see you at school."

Back at the hotel, I washed the ketchup off my arm. Danny and I laughed as the bloody water swirled down the drain.

"Well, you have a new true friend," I said.

"Yeah," Danny said. "And that's probably the only test Chester Finley will ever pass."

Mom stacked the clean dishes in the cabinet, while I looked through the icebox for something other than watermelon to eat.

"How was your stay over?" she asked.

"Good," I said. "Don't we have any bologna?"

"Did you meet Danny's grandparents?"

"They stay in their apartment pretty much," I said. "Watermelon and corn, that's all there is to eat?"

"Not everyone has watermelon and corn on the cob to eat fresh out of the garden, Jacob."

"Yeah, I know," I said, closing the door.

"Guess you heard the rumor?"

"What rumor?"

"Old Man Stickle reported to the police that he saw a dead body in the trunk of a green car. Its bloody arm was sticking out the back."

"Old Man Stickle? He was probably drunk again," I said.

CHAPTER 12

When I got my driver's license, I went to work driving a tractor for a nearby farmer. With the money I earned, I bought an old Mercury and set out to convert it to something other than an old lady's car. I put on moon hubcaps and fender skirts, and I painted the interior light with red fingernail polish. By midsummer, I'd paid it off, though my back was nearly ruined from the jerk and bounce of that damn tractor.

Mom had taken to going to church more and more, and with unusual gusto, which meant that the rest of the family was also required to get up Sunday mornings and go. My dad, having labored under this demand his whole life, was more or less resigned to it, and Gea enjoyed a certain celebrity with her singing and piano playing. I, on the other hand, suffered both mental and physical fatigue and wanted nothing more than to be left alone to sleep. On top of that, I had discovered that an old Mercury provided not only transportation but a certain amount of independence as well. But my objections were in vain, so every Sunday I climbed from bed, got dressed, and went to church.

On this particular Sunday, things were different. There she was, sitting in the front pew with her grandparents, just like I had imagined she might someday be. We took up the second pew, which put me directly behind her. I could see the sassy curls on her neck and the cup of her ear and could smell her perfume. When we stood to sing, she turned and smiled at me, and my knees buckled. She was everything I remembered and more.

After church, I hung around near my car. I had insisted on driving myself to church. It had rained the night before, and the sun shone bright. Pretty soon, she came out of the church to put her grandmother's purse in the car. On her way back in, she stopped and said, "Hi, what's your name?"

I tried to recall my name.

"I'm Rachael," she said. "Weren't you here last summer?"

"I'm Jacob," I said. "I saw you with your grandparents before."

"Do you live here?"

I pointed. "On a farm not far from here. Where do you live?"

"Denver, now," she said. "We've lived all over, even in Germany for a while."

"I've lived mainly here," I said. "I mean, it's the only place I've ever lived."

"What kind of farm is it?"

"Cattle mostly," I said.

She pushed back her hair with her fingers. "Are you going to college?"

I looked at my feet. "I haven't given it much thought," I said. "No one in my family has ever gone to college before."

"Well, it was nice meeting you." She climbed the steps and opened the door. Turning, she said, "Are you coming to church next Sunday?"

"Yes," I said. "I go nearly every Sunday."

"Good," she said. "Maybe I'll see you again."

After church, I ate dinner as fast as I could. Listening to Dad talking about the price of wheat and Mom talking about how June Booth's meatloaf tasted like dog food was more than I could bear. Gea had caught a ride into town with the preacher's wife and said she'd catch a ride back that same evening. Gea was gone more all the time, and she hardly ever talked to me now.

I sat in my Mercury and turned the radio to the one channel that came in clear enough to hear. The music had a clarity that it never had before, a beat that lifted me up, and I turned up the volume. I thought of Rachael, how different she was from the other girls in town, how her clothes were new and tailored, and how she sat erect with her hands in her lap. Her bosom was full and generous, though I'd never tell it to Danny. I hardly dared look upon them myself, and when she sang in church, her voice rose up singular and pure and distinct from the others.

I listened to the radio past dark, until Mom called me in to go to bed. I barely slept at all that night as I thought of all the ways I would change my life to impress Rachael and of all the things she must not find out about me or the way I lived. I wondered how her life must be different from mine, what with blue clean skies instead of heat and blowing dust, and how she and her friends must sit around and talk about movies and music, all the things I knew so little about, while Danny and I drove around with a dead body in the trunk. I thought most of all about how impossible it would be for this girl to see me for who I wanted to be. Anyway, she was probably looking for a stud like Danny.

That week at school, I hardly heard a word of what anyone said. I sat in the Mercury at noon, my radio on, the music surrounding my thoughts. Sometimes I could hear my mind speaking, hear it going over and over things, and sometimes the thoughts would get away from me, sort of fly off somewhere, and I couldn't get them back. But then the voices would talk to me, low like, telling me how lonely and sad I was and how disappointing to other people I was and how worthless and dirty I was.

I watched the groups of kids gather outside the school, four or five of them. They laughed and looked over their shoulders, and I knew they were saying things about me. How could someone like me ever matter? Not in a hundred years, not in a thousand.

Danny knocked on the window of my car. "Hey, goofball," he said. "Open up."

I unlocked the door, and he slid in. "What do you want, Danny?"

"Guess what?" he said.

"What?"

"Chester Finley asked me if I got the body buried."

"No he didn't."

"No shit. I mean, it was like asking me if I was going to lunch."

"You got a Kool?" I asked.

"Guess you can't buy your own."

"You want money for it, Danny?"

"What's with you, goofball? Can't take a joke?"

"Don't call me that."

"Hey, you heard the song 'The Purple People Eater'?"

"Yeah, so?"

"Well, old lady Mitchell was talking about it in her third hour, see. She called it 'The Purple *Peter* Eater.'" He looked at me. "Get it?"

"I get it, Danny."

"The class cracked up."

"Yeah, I'll bet."

"OK, goofball, what's the matter?"

"Nothing's the matter."

"You talking to ghosts again?"

"Just shut up, Danny."

"Mr. Sensitive," he said. "See if I give you any more Kools."

I squashed out my Kool in the ashtray. "You remember me talking to you about that girl?"

"The one you were in love with who you hadn't met yet?"

"Yeah, that one."

"I remember."

"She was at church last Sunday."

"The same girl?"

I nodded. "I talked to her."

"Is that what's wrong with you?"

"You think I should ask her for a date?"

"Why would she go out with someone who drives an old Mercury that looks like a hearse?"

"I don't know."

"Anyway, I always say you gotta ask. If they say no, to hell with 'em. Go to the next one."

"Maybe I will then."

Danny took out his Kools and counted them. "Does she have big knockers like in the magazine?"

"There's the bell," I said. "I have to go."

CHAPTER 13

Rachael was there at church, just like she said she'd be. Afterward, we had a pot luck dinner in the basement, and I watched her from across the room. Later, I went out to the Mercury to listen to the radio. Pretty soon, she came out, and I rolled down my window.

"Hi," she said.

"Hi," I said. "I wasn't sure you'd be here."

"This is my last Sunday," she said. "I'm going home this week. It's my junior year, you know?"

"Yeah," I said. "I know."

She leaned into the window, and I could smell her perfume. Her eyes were green, like spring grass, and she had a splash of freckles across her nose.

"You going into town?" she asked.

"Maybe," I said. "You want a ride in?"

"I'd have to ask my grandparents."

"Sure," I said.

She smiled, and my heart beat in the ends of my fingers. "Great. I'll be right back."

I watched her climb the steps, her skirt awhirl. She paused and gave a small wave back at me. I turned down my radio and checked out the inside of my car. There was a crescent wrench on the floorboard and an empty pack of Kools. I slid them under the seat.

Just then, Mom and Dad came out of the church and got into the old water truck. I could still see the dent in the bumper where Uncle Duny had run over the church mailbox. The cistern was nearly empty, and they were going to get water before going home. I hoped that Rachael wouldn't come out right then and see them with the water tank. She'd know right off that we didn't have running water, and I didn't want her to know that. They pulled away, smoke bellowing out the back of the truck.

Rachael slid in on the passenger side and put her purse between us. "They said OK but that I shouldn't stay out too long."

"Right," I said. "You want to go to town right now?"

"Let's drive around a bit," she said.

I cranked up the Mercury, which had an engine big enough to tow an iceberg. My dual straight pipes rumbled.

"Your car?" she asked.

I nodded. "I worked in the field all summer for it. It's not so much really."

"I think it's neat," she said.

I drove along the dirt roads, my elbow out the window. Her hair blew across her face, and she pushed it aside. "Is that your house there?" she asked.

"No," I said. "My house is the other direction."

"Oh," she said. "So, what are you going to do when you get out of school?"

"I hadn't decided just yet," I said. "I was thinking about going into the service."

"That would be nice," she said.

"And you're going to college?" I asked.

"I've applications out now. I'm hoping to get into the University of Colorado."

"That would be a good one, I guess?"

"It's ranked quite high, actually."

"What will you study?"

"I've been thinking literature. I've always loved it. My mother thinks I should go into something more practical, like medicine or business."

"I don't know much about any of them," I said.

"I met your sister," she said.

"Gea?"

"She's very pretty."

"Yes," I said.

"And your mom and dad seem nice."

"They're nice," I said. "And I like your grandparents, too, but I think they don't like me so much."

"Oh, you know how it is. They worry."

"What do your folks do?"

"Daddy's in business, owns a business actually. He doesn't talk much about it, and Mom stays at home. She has clubs and such. Oh, look, there's a view of the river. Let's stop."

I pulled over and shut off the car. The Cimarron roped through the countryside below, and buzzards circled a mile high in the summer sky. I turned the radio on and rocked the steering wheel back and forth. The wheel was ivory and the prettiest thing on the car.

"Do you think you'll be coming back here?" I asked.

"I think next summer."

"Maybe I'll see you?"

She nodded. "We could write in the meantime, if you want?"

"Yeah, I'd like that."

She looked through her purse, got a piece of paper, and we exchanged addresses.

"You write first," I said. "I'll know you want to that way."

"OK."

"I mean, I don't write so much."

"I can ask you some questions then," she said, smiling. "Maybe I'll send you a picture, and you can send me one?"

"Oh, sure. I'll have a school picture by then."

We sat for a while longer, listening to the radio and watching the river. She reached over and touched my hand. Electricity shot up my arm.

"I'll bet you have lots of friends?" I said.

"Don't you?"

"I guess you could call Danny a friend, but I'm not sure he could pass the friend test."

"Friend test? What's that?"

"Oh, it's nothing, really. A true friend keeps your secrets, even if it means he will get into trouble himself."

"I would do that for you," she said.

"Even if it was murder?"

"But you'd never do that," she said.

I tapped my fingers on the steering wheel to the beat of the music. "You have a boyfriend or anything?"

"Me?" she said, shaking her head.

"Me neither," I said.

"The boys there are, you know, just boys."

"You don't have to write if you don't want to," I said. "I'd understand."

"I want to. I'll write, but you have to write back."

I searched for something better on the radio. "We don't have so much, Rachael, I mean, not like town folks. And I don't know so much about literature and all that. We milk cows twice a day and sell cream. Dad works the railroad when he can and then the farming just to make place payments. I've never been anywhere or done anything that matters."

"Maybe you don't want to write me. Is that what you're saying?"

"No, I do."

"Then we will write, but we have to seal it first."

"Seal it?"

"With a kiss."

I looked at her, and my ears burned. "You mean right now?"

"We won't see each other for a year," she said.

We kissed. It was the first time I'd ever kissed a girl, and the world went awhirl.

"There, a seal that must not be broken," she said. "Now, you better get me home before Grandmother has a stroke."

I pulled in front of their house and turned down the radio. I looked at her, and she looked at me. "Rachael—"

She took my hand and held it for a moment. Her fingers were cool. "I know, Jacob," she said. "Me, too."

CHAPTER 14

School was a drag—worse, a nightmare. I hadn't the energy to engage in any of my classes. I didn't care about what the teachers had to say or the opinions of fellow students. I had no interest in my future, where I was going or not going. Being a junior for me was not the beginning of my life but its end.

Danny hung around, talking of rockets and outer space and women's jugs, telling me what a goofball I was to think that Rachael even remembered me. Sometimes when I was alone, Danny tuned in on my mind, like I tuned in the radio, skipping from station to station. Once he'd found the right spot, he'd turn up the volume, his voice blasting away in my head.

I cared only about Rachael, about the letter that was yet to come. Maybe she'd only said it by way of departing, like Mom always said: come back and visit sometime. Everywhere I looked, I could see Rachael, as clearly now as that day she'd touched my hand.

My grades dropped, and my teachers shook their heads in disappointment. I lived in my Mercury, spending as little time as possible with my family. When I ran out of gas and money, I sat in my car in the yard and listened to music until Dad called me in. I worked out a hundred different scenarios of how we would meet again or how we would never meet again, or how she'd meet someone else, someone smarter, better looking, someone who knew all about literature and movies.

Each day, I withdrew a little further from the people around me. Sometimes I would walk the pasture alone into the night. Under the stars, I would listen to the voices, those voices that knew more than me, more than anyone around me, and sometimes when the moon was bright, I could see their faces. They were the faces of strangers and dead people. They would talk among themselves and shake their heads in disappointment like my teachers.

I slept hardly at all, waking in the wee hours of the morning. Wailing voices would wake me from out of the darkness, and I would grow cold inside, like a giant piece of ice melting inside me. There was no one to talk to, to reach out to. Danny listened, so that he could comment on what a goofball I was, or why I didn't quit feeling sorry for myself, or just suck it up and be a man. But it wasn't like that. I didn't want comments, or sympathy, or explanations. I wanted someone to listen.

A week before Christmas, Dad learned that his job on the railroad was permanently gone. He stood at the window, talked to the window, though we were there in the room with him.

"They cut the job," he said. "I don't have the seniority to bump, not here. If we would move south—"

"I don't want to move," I said.

"We'd have to make it on cream money if I stay," he said. "Maybe we could raise a few bucket calves. But I don't know what about the place payment."

Mom poured water in the sink from the tea kettle to wash the dirty dishes. "Damn railroad," she said. "How are we to plan our lives with all this on and off?"

"If I could just make it on the farm," Dad said. "But then we have Gea and Jacob coming on too"

"I don't need anything," I said.

"I was your age, I was holding down a man's job," Dad said. "All this boy wants to do is sit in his car and mope or walk around talking to himself."

"There's lots I could do on my own."

"Like what?" Mom said, drying her hands. "Work the oil field? Hire out for some old farmer? Get yourself killed in the army?"

"Wind up drinking himself to death like his Uncle Duny," Dad said.

"Well, he'd be no worse off than some Rolands I know," Mom said.

"You don't have to worry about me," I said. "I'll find something."

"And then there's Gea," Mom said.

"She's apt to just up and get married," Dad said. "She hasn't lit on the ground since she discovered boys."

"We got the garden," Mom said. "And the cream check."

"I could work some fence building," Dad said. "Old Hinkle always looking for fence building."

"And the wood stove, and chickens. We could get by, Abbott, long as nothing goes wrong. Thing is, if someone turns up sick or the car breaks down, then what?"

"Some kids I know are going on to college," I said.

Dad poured himself a glass of buttermilk, peppered it up, and drank it down in one take. He wiped his mouth on his sleeve.

"College is fine for some, what can use it," he said. "But it's land makes the difference for the likes of us. A man without land is no more than the north wind. This boy hasn't given the slightest sign of having any book smarts. Sending him off to college would be a waste of his time and my money."

"Oh, Abbott, you sound ignorant when you talk that way," Mom said.

"Well, if he wants it bad enough, I figure he can get it," Dad said. "I'm going to go check the county well. I think we're getting low on water."

"Don't be going off to town to play pitch, Abbott," Mom said. "I got enough to do around here as it is."

Dad put on his hat and went out the door, rolling his shoulders. Pretty soon I heard the car pull off. I knew where he was going.

"Mom?" I said.

"What, Jacob?"

"You don't think I have any book smarts either?"

She put her hands on her waist and looked at me. "You learned to read earlier than most, Jacob, but it takes more than that. Why, your grades aren't any better than Rudy Joe's were, and he was dumber than a sledgehammer. Some folks are cut out for the intellectual life. Some not so much. There's no shame in working with your hands for a living."

I looked in the icebox. There was half a watermelon, cold corn on the cob, and what was left of the buttermilk. "Damn it," I said.

"What'd you say?"

"I said there's no sandwich meat."

"Sandwich meat has to be bought. You have money, go buy some."

"Are you saying I'm not cut out to be smart?"

"I see what I see, Jacob, and like your dad says, you've given no sign of being interested in anything but that car of yours. I swear it's like you live in a different world from the rest of us. And it appears to me to have gotten worse when that girl came to visit."

I took a cold roasting ear out of the icebox and buttered it up. It wasn't bologna, but it was better than buttermilk. "I sometimes think there is something wrong with my brain. I'll be thinking on one thing, and all of a sudden I'm thinking somewhere else, or dreaming up stuff that isn't there."

"Maybe you ought just grow up some, Jacob. Your dad and me work hard to keep our heads above water."

"It isn't that, Mom. I don't know what it is. There's stuff goes crazy in my head, and I can't tell what's real and what isn't."

"A man has to get on with his life, do with what he has. You understand? Real or not real, he has to make it his and go on with it. Now go get the cows in. Your dad's left the milking to us."

CHAPTER 15

Summer came, but I still didn't know what I was going to do. It was hard being so uncertain about who I was or what I was to be. I'd taken to sitting in my car a lot and was doing just that when I spotted an old yellow school bus coming down the road with a sign, "Eternity Is Forever," painted in red letters on its side. Tied on the front bumper was a wooden cross the size of a grown man and with a child's wagon wheels bolted through the bottom end. When the bus pulled into our yard, I snuffed out my Kool and got out. The driver shut the engine off, which continued to lope until finally falling silent in a cloud of blue smoke.

The door opened, and out climbed my Uncle Ward Roland. He had that look in his eye, the one I'd seen before when things weren't going well.

"Uncle Ward," I said. "Got you a bus, I see?"

"Yes, I do," he said. "It's got a bed across the back, a propane burner, and a kerosene light for reading through the night, if I've the notion."

"That's good," I said.

"I'll be looking for your dad. Is he home?"

"He's building fence. Laid off, you know?"

"Your dad never was one much for reporting family business. What about your mom?"

"It's her quilting day on Saturdays," I said. "I'm here by myself."

"You ain't never alone if you're God's child," he said.

"How's Granddad?" I asked.

"Me and him had a parting of the ways, so to speak."

"Oh?"

"He doesn't read the Bible same way as me, you know, and once he's taken an idea, there's no changing it."

"Some call it stubborn," I said.

"Want to see the inside of my bus?"

"Sure," I said.

There was a feather bed strung across the back, and the smell of kerosene and stale coffee hung in the air. His Bible lay open on the chair, and there was a half-empty pint of whiskey sitting on a makeshift shelf he'd built over the window.

"I could live in here through eternity, if need be," he said.

"Or 'til you ran out of food and kerosene," I said.

"Until the Rapture," he said. "When the end comes, and it will be soon enough, there will be a hill for all to gather on, and I'll be there in my bus."

"You think living in a bus has something to do with that, Uncle Ward?"

He sat down on the bed and rolled himself a cigarette. "Want one?"

"I only smoke Kools," I said.

He lit up and drew down on the cigarette. It turned red, shriveled up on the end, and dropped off as ash on his lap. He brushed it away and looked at the end of his cigarette.

"You're a Roland, if I ain't mistaken?" he said.

"Yes, sir."

"And the other half, Franklin."

"Far as I know," I said.

"Half archangel and half sprite," he said. "It's a mighty war inside you, isn't it, Jacob?"

"What do you mean, Uncle Ward?"

"Well, there are some folks closer to the hand of God than other folks. The Rolands have always been devout people. As for the Franklins, well, they've always had a powerful taste for liquor and dance. You must have seen that yourself, what with your Uncle Duny being around so much, living off your folks the way he does."

"How is it the Rolands get so close to the hand of God when others can't?" I asked.

"From study and passing down the word from one generation to the next. There isn't a Roland alive who hasn't been touched, knows it's in him. It's in the blood, and it's in you. The Rolands always step up when called."

"Step up to what, Uncle Ward?"

He snuffed out his cigarette in a jar lid that sat at the head of the bed. "To whatever their calling is," he said.

"Do you have a calling?" I asked.

"It's why I'm here, isn't it?"

"What would that be?"

"I'm building a town," he said. "A new town filled with folk as pure and clean as a mountain stream. And when the Rapture comes, as it surely will, those living in my town will be lifted up and carried off into the loving arms of God."

"Will there be any Franklins among them?"

He sat for some time, hands in his lap, and his eyes closed. "Strikes me as doubtful," he said.

"How do you know building this town is really your calling, Uncle Ward?"

"God told me," he said.

"He talked to you?"

"Yes, sir, He did. On a sunny day, it was."

"How do you know it was real?"

"It don't have to be real to be real," he said.

"Maybe it's just you talking to yourself, saying what you want to hear, seeing what you want to see. That happens sometimes. Maybe it's being scared, not knowing but what it's your own voice crying out."

"It's God making me do what I do, saying what I say. It's out of my hands altogether."

"Building a town strikes me as a mighty undertaking, Uncle Ward. What if it falls through?"

"Why, I'll just change it up, that's all."

"Changing up what God told you to do?"

"Whether I change it up or don't change it up, don't matter. Fail or don't fail, don't matter. It's all God's doings. Sometimes He makes it easy. Sometimes He makes it hard, mostly hard, but it's His command and that's that. It ain't man's place to understand everything, and it ain't his place to ask so dang many questions."

I got up and sat down in the driver's seat of the bus. The speedometer was missing, and there was a knob taped to the steering wheel. The cross that was fastened to the bumper stuck halfway across the windshield.

"What about this cross?" I said.

"It's what they hung Jesus on," he said.

"It's got wheels on it," I said.

"Morning and night, I put that cross on my shoulder and walk about wherever I am. It's damn heavy without wheels. You just try it and see."

"But why drag it around in the first place?"

"So folks will know about my new town, Valley View, and will know it to be a Christian town."

I turned in the seat and looked at him. "Valley View?"

"It's in a valley and it has a view," he said.

"You talking about that old railroad town site by the tracks? There's nothing been there for fifty years, Uncle Ward."

"I'm going to build a town of believers. I'm just the first of many to come, believers from across the world joining up to await the Rapture."

"How you going to eat?"

"God will provide, and I thought your mom might throw in a few canned goods for starts. She always could make the best plum butter in the county."

"You going to buy up the whole town yourself, Uncle Ward?"

He walked to the front of the bus and leaned on the hand rail. "That town site was divided into lots back when the railroad came through. I'm buying them up for the price of taxes with a little money I saved up.

"Is that your Mercury over there, boy?"

"Three hundred dollars and paid for," I said.

"Well, how about you follow me over to Valley View to park this bus and then take me back to town, so I can finalize those lots?"

"Maybe we ought to wait for Dad, Uncle Ward."

"I'll top off your gas tank and two dollars cash."

"Well," I said.

"Don't follow up too close on those hills. The compression isn't what it should be on this ol' bus."

While not particularly high, the Wild Cat Hills proved to be too much for Uncle Ward's bus. Halfway to the top, she crawled to a stop. Uncle Ward waved me back and commenced backing down the hill after me. At the bottom, he crawled out and came back to where I waited.

"I'll take her up in reverse," he said. "She's geared up for more climb than push."

I waited at the bottom while he made a run up the hill in reverse. The old bus roared and coughed and clawed her way to the summit, where she paused briefly before disappearing from sight down the other side.

By the time I caught up, Uncle Ward was under the bus cutting loose barbed wire from the back bumper where he'd plowed up the pasture fence. His wooden cross had broken away and now lay in the grader ditch. An hour later, we had disentangled the bus from the fence and pulled it back onto the road. We secured Uncle Ward's cross on top of my Mercury by means of a rope passed through the back windows, and by the time we reached the town site, the sun wobbled below the horizon.

The only thing left of Valley View was a storm cellar with the door missing, a few rocks left over from the track foreman's shack, and a single set of concrete steps that led nowhere. Nearby were the railroad tracks, which still served a doodlebug that ran a daily mail service to the Panhandle and back each day.

I carried Uncle Ward and his rolling cross back to town, while leaving his bus parked on-site next to the tracks. It turned out Uncle Ward had less money on hand then he'd estimated and couldn't fill my tank, leaving me to drive home with the gas gauge pegging on empty. The last I saw him was in my rearview mirror. He was rolling down Main with that cross leaning on his shoulder.

Since I was in town, I decided to drop over to see Danny, who was sitting at the reception desk of his grandparents' hotel. We smoked a Kool in the back, and he showed me some drawings he'd made for a wind generator. He said his folks' divorce was complete, and he didn't know if he was going to stay with his grandparents or travel around the world.

When I walked in the house, Mom and Dad were sitting in the kitchen. There was an empty coffee cup and a half glass of buttermilk on the table. Mom's eyes were red, and Dad's chin was parked in his hand.

"Where you been?" he asked.

"Nowhere," I said. "What's wrong?"

"Your Uncle Ward's in jail," Mom said. "They impounded his bus for sitting on railroad property. Assault and battery in town too."

Dad pushed his glass aside. "Assault and battery," he said after her. "And your Uncle Duny with him."

"Both in jail?"

Mom nodded her head. "Duny tried to sell that dog of his to your Uncle Ward for whiskey money. Uncle Ward tried to save him instead, and they ended up in a tussle down on Main. Uncle Duny took off with your Uncle Ward's cross and with Ward chasing after him down Main like some kind of maniac."

Dad got up and took his glass to the sink. "What I can't figure is how Ward got all the way to town without a car in the first place."

"I better get on with the chores," I said. "It's getting late."

CHAPTER 16

Mom handed me the letter without a word.

"What is it?" I asked.

"From Colorado," she said.

My heart pounded. "She said she'd write."

Mom turned for the kitchen. "Appears she has," she said.

I folded the letter into my pocket and headed for the shelterbelt. I had a place at the far end, a heavily wooded area that I'd go to sometimes when things got hectic or I just wanted to write stuff down.

I sat under an old elm tree that looked for the world like a woman with a broom. I held the letter to the light. I smelled it, and my hand trembled. The letter was from her sure enough, but maybe she'd written something bad. Maybe she'd say that she wouldn't be able to write letters to me anymore or would never be coming back this way.

I opened it and read it through. She was sorry that it had taken so long to write, that her dad had been sick and in the hospital and that from now on she would write me every week, if I would write her back. She'd been accepted into the University of Colorado and was going to major in English literature. She said she'd not forgotten her promise to write or the kiss that sealed that promise.

I sat for some time in the shade of the tree, her letter in my hand. Things were going to be better now. I had someone to talk to, someone to tell my feelings, but I wouldn't tell everything right off, not until I was absolutely sure.

I passed through my junior year with the same uncertainty as most do, I suppose. The closer I came to graduation, the less I understood about what lay ahead. The one thing that kept me going was the weekly letter from Rachael.

I liked writing the letters as well as getting them, because they helped make sense of things. Sometimes my thoughts scattered like leaves in the wind, even my dreams, which could leave me shaken with their starkness. But the letters were permanent, reassuring, and they stabilized my unstable world.

I bought tablets of lined writing paper and boxes of pencils that I sharpened a dozen at a time. I built a wooden box to put them in and one fall morning took them all to the end of the shelterbelt and buried them under the tree.

Rachael's letters were filled with plans and dreams. She longed to go to college, to be on her own and away from the control of her father, whom she loved but resented at the same time. Once she signed her letter "Love, Rachael," and each time thereafter she signed them the same, and so did I.

She talked about the books she was reading, and how she was going to live in the dorm with her friend from high school, and how she was going to major in literature. She said that one day maybe I could come to visit, and she would introduce me to her friends.

Her world was sound and planned, and I had only to read her letters to know that she knew where she was going and how she was going to get there. She told me how she loved me, and I told her the same. We were in love, though we'd shared but a single kiss in all that time.

But at other times I read her letters and felt her slipping away, her hand reaching out but never quite touching me. Those were the darkest moments, because I knew how far the distance was between us and how unlikely it was this thing could survive. I recorded my feelings faithfully in my tablets and wrapped them in bundles with binder twine that I took from Dad's shop. The letters grew, both in number and in length.

Mom called me into the living room and asked me to sit down. Her face was drawn and tired, and I knew that something was wrong.

"Jacob," she said, "I have something to tell you."

"It's Uncle Duny," I said.

"No, not that."

"Uncle Ward?"

"Jacob, it's about your sister."

I sat on the edge of the couch. "Gea?"

"I don't know how to say it, except to say it. Gea is pregnant."

My ears grew hot. "A baby?"

"The school has asked her to leave."

I knew of only one other girl who had gotten pregnant. She'd left town, and no one had heard from her again.

"Who's the—"

"John Bowker."

"They own the biggest store in town," I said.

"They don't want him to marry because he's too young, and it would ruin—"

"What does Gea want?"

Mom shrugged. "It's too late for what she wants, Jacob. She's going to have a baby, and that's that."

I walked to the window. I could see Dad working in the field. "He doesn't have a job," I said.

"I know."

"Won't they help out? I mean it's their baby, too."

"Your dad says no, that he doesn't need the help. The school has agreed that she can finish her studies here at home. The thing is, someone will have to pick up and return her assignments."

I turned. "You want me to do that?"

She nodded. "It's the only way I see it getting done."

"Gea is going to have a baby," I said. "They'll say things."

"Yes."

"There's something else," she said. Mom rubbed her face and then looked over at me. "I'm pregnant too."

I stood up. "What?"

"At forty-two, I didn't think it possible, but there you have it. The doctor says I'm healthy and it shouldn't be a problem."

"You and Gea both?"

"Two weeks apart. I know all this comes at a difficult time for you."

"I've a year of school left," I said.

"We'll get by," she said. "We aren't the first people who's had things . . . difficult things to deal with."

"I'll find work," I said.

"No, you should be thinking about your own future."

I got up and went to the door. "We will be OK," I said.

Tears welled in her eyes. "Yes," she said. "We'll get through."

I walked to the end of the shelterbelt and sat in the shade of the old elm. People would talk. They always did, and with two babies coming, things would be hard, and Dad without work. I had to think it through. Figure out what to do.

I took out my tablet and wrote Rachael. I told her about this family in town, about how the daughter and mother were both pregnant and how the father was out of work. While it looked for a while that things were going to be bad, someone secretly left five thousand dollars in an unmarked envelope on their front porch. I told her that no one knew who this was or why they did it but that I was happy there were still good people in this world. It was a lie, of course, but one I needed to believe.

Each week, I went to Gea's teachers to deliver Gea's work that she had completed at home in her bedroom. I would knock on the classroom doors, and the students would fall silent as the teachers explained to me Gea's next assignments. The teachers mostly smiled and said nothing beyond that.

At home, Gea cried a lot, and so did Mom. Dad worked at whatever he could find, work that no one else would do. He grew silent and sullen and sometimes would disappear on long walks into the pasture.

My own life was suspended. It failed to exist much beyond what the day demanded. School was idle hours passed. Eventually, I found part-time work plowing wheat fields, but it paid little more than what it cost me to drive there. My time at home was mostly chores and then off to my private place to write letters. The letters grew longer and more detailed as I censored them less. My mind roamed at will and went places that I couldn't predict. Rachael continued to write, but less frequently. She expressed concern that sometimes she didn't understand what I was saying.

The babies were born. Gea had a girl, Abbey, Mom a boy, Silas. Our lives were turned upside down with babies, diapers, and exhaustion. Money was short, so nothing beyond essentials was bought. My car sat idle for want of gas, and I rode the bus to school. And when Danny moved away once again, I refused to see him off. He could go to hell. Everyone could go to hell.

CHAPTER 17

The babies grew. They laughed and played as brother and sister, and the family closed about them. Gea went to work in a nearby town and came home on the weekends. I graduated with less than stellar grades and a future equally as bleak. I found a job in the oil field, working morning tower, a job of paydays, booze, and men with lost fingers. I couldn't sleep at home, a place teeming with children and noise. I retreated to my camp in the shelterbelt when possible, sleeping there on an old cot among the trees.

And then a letter came. She was out of school now and free for the summer. Why didn't I come? I put the letter away and told no one. The thought of packing up and going so far away was frightening to me. It would be her place, her friends, and I knew that I would probably not fit in. And then there were her parents, people who I knew instinctively would not approve of me.

There were moments I wished I had not received the letter at all. In some ways, it had been easier as a dream than as a reality. But I also suspected that my time at home had run its course. There were Gea and the babies, Dad's lack of work.

I retrieved the letter and read it again. Perhaps the time had come for me to find my own way. Perhaps this was where it lay. I told Mom and Dad of my plans, that I'd thought it out and made my decision.

In the end, it was the lack of objection that confirmed what I already knew. I collected my check and left without ceremony. I'd never been to a large city before, and as I approached that day, doubts flooded in.

The skyline reached to the heavens, as ominous and frightening as the Rockies behind it. My palms sweat as I negotiated the loops and mazes of city streets. I found the house at three in the afternoon and stood on the front porch at five.

The house was made of glass and brick and stretched to the corner, with grass like velvet and flowers heady with scent. I checked my shoes for manure and looked back at the Mercury, a black and ancient behemoth. I knocked on the door. My heart beat in my ears, and my mouth went dry.

She answered the door. "Jacob," she said. "You made it."

I nodded. She was as I remembered, taller perhaps, with a smile bright as morning and a voice like a bell.

"Come in," she said. "Mother and Father are in the living room."

I could see Rachael in her mother's eyes. Her father wore a tie and rimless glasses. He peered at me from across the room.

Rachael took my hand. "Father, Mother, this is Jacob," she said.

"Hello, Jacob," her mother said.

"Hello," I said.

Her father stood and shook my hand. It was a soft hand, with manicured nails and all fingers intact.

"How was your trip?" he asked.

"Fine," I said.

"Dinner is nearly ready," her mother said. "Won't you eat with us?"

I looked at Rachael, and she nodded. "OK," I said.

"Good," she said, directing us into the dining area. "Jacob, you sit here where you can visit while I get things on. Rachael, get Jacob something to drink."

Rachael's father bobbed his foot and studied me. "So, Jacob," he said, "I understand you've graduated high school?"

"Yes," I said.

"And you're working somewhere?"

"Oil field," I said.

"How interesting," he said. "I don't believe I've met anyone who works in the oil field. Do you like it?"

"It pays," I said.

"Yes, pay is important. Is it something you plan to do in the future, or is it temporary?"

"Temporary," I said, checking the bottom of my shoe.

"You're going to college then?"

"Well," I said, "I've thought about it."

"It's difficult to make a living, take care of a family, without a degree," he said. "Rachael has been accepted to the University of Colorado. She's quite bright, you know, and set on literature, though I'd like to see her go into something more lucrative, business or medicine perhaps."

"I figure she can do anything she sets out to do," I said.

"And what does your father do?"

"Farm," I said.

"He's a farmer?" he asked.

"He owns land," I said.

Rachael came in with a glass of ice tea. "Come with me. I want you to see my book collection," she said.

That evening, Rachael and I parked. We sat in the Mercury and talked and listened to the radio.

We kissed and held each other and then kissed some more. I told her about the letters and my writing and the wooden box in the trees. I told her how the words shaped my life and made things the way I wanted them to be.

"You mean the words aren't true?" she asked.

"They're true," I said. "But they're not real."

I started to touch her breasts, and then didn't. She reached for my hand and put it on her breast. It was warm and wonderful, and she smelled of perfume. I explored her carefully, reverentially, aware of the privilege, and that the experience had boundaries. I was, in the end, a curiosity to her, and one who would not be going to the University of Colorado.

We stood at her door. Moon shadows danced under the trees, and the smell of flowers filled the night.

"Where are you staying?" she asked.

"In a hotel," I said.

"How long can you stay?"

"I'm leaving in the morning," I said. "I have to get back to my job. Will you be coming to see your grandparents soon?"

"I hope to get away, but I've a tour scheduled of the campus this summer, and the family is taking a vacation. But you'll write?"

"Yes," I said.

We kissed again, and I took a long look at her in the moonlight so that I wouldn't forget.

That night I slept in the Mercury, somewhere on the outskirts of the city. I woke at three in the morning and headed back. I didn't know what I was going to do, but I did know with certainty that my life had changed. My family, my friends, and my future had been tipped upside down. I could see clearly now, not what I was, but what I wasn't.

Gea died an hour before I got home. She'd topped a hill a foot over the center line and was thrown into the windshield of Dad's car.

"You're back," Dad said, pulling me into him, something he'd never done. The embrace was quick, and he walked away to the barn. Mom was crying, while Abbey and Silas stood at her side, watching with sad faces.

"They tried to revive her," Mom said, shaking her head. "It was too late. The doctor said it was probably better that way."

I could see Dad through the kitchen window. He was headed for the pasture, his shoulders slumped.

"What happens now?" I asked.

Mom shrugged. "I don't know, Jacob. We have the children. Your dad was so crazy about Gea."

"Yes," I said.

"She played the piano. She sang."

"Alto," I said.

Mom walked into the kitchen and stood at the sink. Turning, she said, "You'll stay tonight? We need you here."

"I'll stay," I said.

"Are you hungry?"

"No," I said.

"You sleep in Gea's room," she said. "I can't stand to think of it empty."

That night I stayed in Gea's room as Mom asked, but I couldn't sleep. I shouldn't have been there. It was Gea's room, not mine. I got up and sat on the edge of the bed. Her closet door was open. I turned on the light and looked through her clothes. There was a plastic bag, with the name of the hospital on it, hanging on a hook behind the door. I slipped the bag off to find Gea's blouse inside. There was a blood spot on the collar. I went back to bed but awakened to someone singing in the night. The screen door closed, and the singing stopped. As soon as daylight broke, I rose to put Gea's blouse in the trunk of the Mercury.

We buried her on Casket Hill. Abbey stood next to me, her hand in mine. Uncle Ward, Uncle Berko, and an array of cousins stood at the grave. The Franklins gathered, too, but were few in number. Neither Uncle Duny nor Uncle Jack came. The Franklin clan was not big on death.

The Cimarron twisted through the valley below, dividing the disparate families. Locusts chanted in the heat, and mesquite clung to life in the harshness of the Wildcat Hills. We sang "Amazing Grace," with Dad taking the lead. I could hear Gea's alto from the valley below. If only I could have kept her thoughts alive. When I turned to leave, I saw Danny at the back of the circle, hat in hand. He nodded and turned away.

That night I took Gea's blouse and put it in the wooden box at the end of the shelterbelt. Afterward, I wrote of the day, of how Gea had sung in the valley and how I would remember her. I wrote of her spell on others and how her thoughts would remain in these words.

CHAPTER 18

The letters stopped coming from Rachael, and the days grew longer. Dad was gone most of the time now, and Mom, awash in children and hard work, seldom talked. The young family at home thrived in the freedom of country life, but it was a family set apart from me and of another time. We shared little beyond blood, separated as we were by the years.

I heard Danny was back and was wearing a beard. I found him sitting behind the reception desk at the hotel.

"Hey, Danny," I said.

He looked through his brows at me. "Hey, goofball. What's up?"

"Not much," I said. "What you doing back, Danny?"

He closed the reception book. "My granddad died," he said. "I'm helping out here."

"I hadn't heard. I would have come, you know."

"No big deal."

"I mean, I appreciated seeing you there at Gea's."

"Forget it, goofball. I'm finished up here. Want to take a spin? I got my own car now."

"Sure," I said.

We drove around the square, then out to the stash, where we smoked cigarettes and talked about what we were going to do now that we were graduated.

"I tried the oil field," I said. "Seven dollars an hour."

"Yeah," he said. "Why did you quit?"

"Morning tower is a killer, " I said. "Rough neck stories and whiskey at dawn. I was dying."

"It's 'cause you're so sensitive, goofball," he said.

We lit up another cigarette and turned the radio on. "And what about you?" I asked.

"Checking in train crews, cleaning rooms, taking Grandma to the doctor. What about that girl?" he asked.

"Rachael?" I said.

"At least you know her name now."

"I just got back from a trip to see her," I said.

"And?"

"Come on, Danny. Anyway, I've been thinking about going to college."

Danny studied me through the smoke. "Now isn't that rich," he said. "The local college, I mean."

"Don't you know people like us don't belong at no college? Anyway, how would you make a living?"

"My job is part time, and it's night work."

"There's tuition, books, all kinds of stuff. Maybe you should get on the railroad or something and forget the college shit."

"I got something to say, Danny."

He looked at me. "Well, say it."

"I don't mean like that. I mean, there's something in me I need to get out."

"That girl is going to college. That's it, isn't it? That's what this is all about. You want to go 'cause she's going. Look, I like you, but you're a goofball; no college is going to change that. Just saying."

"There's got to be more to living than a paycheck," I said.

He started the car and revved the engine. "When Grandma dies, I get the hotel, see. That's enough. You do what you want to do, but don't say I didn't warn you."

I wrote Rachael and told her I was thinking about college, that I was thinking about a lit major, like her. She wrote back and said that was very nice, but I shouldn't think that everyone had to go to college, because it wasn't for everyone.

I asked Mom what she thought, and she said that maybe I should think about it as something for the future, when money wasn't so tight.

That night I went to my place in the shelterbelt, and I wrote long pages about my thoughts. Once, I thought I heard Rachael laughing behind me. I built a fire and slept on the ground next to it. Something woke me in the night. There were voices beyond in the hills and a light in the night sky. My nose twitched a little like it used to, and then it went away.

CHAPTER 19

When I spotted Uncle Ward's bus in the gas station, I pulled in to see what was going on. Ward was cleaning the windshield, and Uncle Duny was sitting on the bus steps smoking a cigarette. Mortem was asleep in the front seat.

"Hi, Uncle Duny," I said. "When did you get out?"

"You have a dime, boy? I'm in sore need of an RC." I dug a dime out and handed it to him. "And a nickel? A man can't drink an RC without a package of peanuts in it."

Uncle Ward hung the hose in the pump and came around to pop the hood. "Hey, Jacob," he said.

"Hey, Uncle Ward. I thought you two were tied up with the government?"

"You ain't got a dime, have you? Taken my last for gas."

I looked in my other pocket and coughed up another dime.

Uncle Ward said, "Get me an RC, too, Duny. I'm going to check the oil."

Uncle Duny took my other dime and went inside, while Uncle Ward climbed up on the bumper.

"I thought you two been fighting?" I said.

Uncle Ward checked the oil. "Ain't you ever heard of forgiveness? Duny and me patched up our differences over a game of dominoes. Fact is, we're going into business together."

"Business?"

"Out to the town site."

"That's railroad property, Uncle Ward. That's why they impounded your bus in the first place."

"I was just parked up in the right of way. Railroad's not forgiving like your Uncle Duny. We sold his car and my cross. Along with my savings, we paid off our fines and have a sizable down payment on our new town, Dunyville."

"Dunyville?"

"Duny drives a hard bargain about some things," he said.

Uncle Duny came out of the station carrying two RCs and a package of peanuts, which he poured into the neck of each bottle, handing one to Uncle Ward. Mortem jumped out of the bus seat to come around and beg for some.

I said to Uncle Ward, "That town site sits out in the middle of nowhere. Isn't nobody going to move out there."

"You hear that, Duny? Jacob here gives up before he even starts."

"It's the Roland in him," Duny said.

Uncle Ward tipped his RC up and took a line of peanuts with it. "Anyways, we talked all that over," he said. "Wouldn't make no sense to build a new town inside an old town. A new town has to be out of town, or it isn't a new town at all, is it?"

"I guess not," I said.

"I'll be building a church for awaiting the Rapture, while your Uncle Duny here is undecided as to the type of business he'll be opening."

I looked over at Uncle Duny. "Possibilities have to be thought over," he said. "Sleep on it first, I always say, 'cause that's when the real thinking commences."

"I sure hope you two know what you're doing," I said.

"Listen to the businessman here," Uncle Ward said.

"There's not even electricity or water," I said. "It will be the smelliest and the smallest town in the state."

"There's that old windmill for water," Uncle Ward said. "And electricity isn't all it's cracked up to be. Damn stuff can kill you dead, if you ain't careful."

I turned to Uncle Duny. "Did you talk to Mom about this?"

He set his RC on top of the gas pump and lit a cigarette. "She's the woman what suggested I drink soda pop instead of whiskey, as I recall."

"She may not be much of an expert on drinking, Uncle Duny, but you aren't much on town building either, I'm thinking."

Uncle Ward gathered up the air hose to pump up the front tire. He looked at me over his shoulder. "We could use some young blood out to Dunyville. Why don't you join us up?"

"I've been thinking to go to college," I said.

"What for?" Uncle Duny said.

"College is a fine thing for educating a man," I said.

"Sure it is, if you figure on being governor or a schoolteacher," he said. "I'm thinking that isn't likely, is it."

"There are things I want to say, to get out of me," I said.

"Well, just stand up and say 'em," Uncle Duny said.

"That's just it, I don't know how."

Uncle Ward coiled up the air hose and hung it back on the hook. "Everything that needs saying has already been said in the Bible. Too much education will turn your mind to shit. First thing up, you'll be thinking you know more than the holy book."

"The future is with us in Dunyville," Uncle Duny said.

Mortem marked the back bus tire and then came around to the front.

"I don't think Mom would go for it," I said.

"Some men I know make their own life decisions," Uncle Duny said. "Ain't that so, Ward?"

Uncle Ward hooked his foot up on the bumper and leaned in on his knee. "Getting in on the ground floor of Dunyville is the chance of a lifetime. Most women wouldn't notice such an opportunity. Buy yourself a couple of them lots, and I guarantee you'll sell 'em for ten times that in six months."

"I'll sleep on it," I said.

Uncle Ward said, "The Rolands have always stood up when it came time to move ahead. Take your Grandpa Roland. Why, he never backed off nothing once his mind was set." He climbed into the bus, followed by Uncle Duny and Mortem. "When the graves open at the end of time and all are gathered into the sky, that college degree you're wanting isn't going to be worth a damn. That's all I got to say."

Once home, I poured myself a glass of buttermilk and sat down at the table, while Mom put the last of the dishes in the cabinet. She pushed the hair back from her face. Her hands were red from the dishwater, and her hair lay in curls against her neck. The kids were playing in an old cardboard box they'd dragged in from the garage. Mom threw her dish towel over her shoulder and went back to settle them down.

After the noise abated, she sat across from me and said, "Where's your dad gone?"

"I haven't seen him today," I said.

"These kids are driving me crazy," she said. "I could use a little help around here."

"Want some buttermilk?" I asked. "It's really good with black pepper."

"No one in the world puts black pepper in buttermilk, 'cept you and your dad. I suppose if he put rabbit pellets in it, so would you."

"It's the kids get on his nerves," I said. "He needs to get loose now and then."

"I can't imagine why," she said.

"And I think he misses Gea."

Her eyes filled. "Well, there's nothing I can do about that, is there."

"Guess who I saw today?"

"Who?"

"Uncle Duny. Guess who he was with?"

"This isn't charades, Jacob."

"Uncle Ward," I said.

"They were together?"

I nodded. "In Uncle Ward's bus. They bought up some lots over to that old Valley View town site. They're starting up a new town. They're calling it 'Dunyville.' "

Mom rolled her eyes. "They couldn't build an outhouse between them on a clear day."

"They asked me to come over to help out."

Mom dropped her chin in her hand. "A lunatic and a drunk sitting on a hill does not a town make. You got no business over there."

"Well, anyway," I said.

"Jacob, don't you think it's time you put things together for yourself?"

"What do you mean?"

"Stop moping around about that girl for one thing?"

I shrugged. "Just writing once in a while, that's all. Anyway, I'm thinking maybe I could get a railroad job."

"With your dad just being laid off?"

"Something else might come along."

"Nothing just comes along, Jacob, it's got to be wrestled to the ground."

"I'm getting things figured out," I said.

Mom rubbed at her arms. "It's just that with this new family and what with your dad out of work, I can't see an end to things."

I went to my place in the shelterbelt and wrote down what Mom said, so as to look at it, spell it out in words so I could kick its tires and walk around it. Afterward, I sorted through my wooden box, which was nearly half full of notes and letters and ramblings. Gea's blouse, the one with the bloodstain on the collar, was folded in the bottom. I took it out and looked at it. I thought maybe I should throw it away, but I didn't want to. I covered the box over and walked home in the dark. Above me, the sky spilled with stars, and tree shadows danced about my feet.

When I got back to the house, Dad's pickup was parked in the yard. The bedroom light was on. They'd be talking about Uncle Duny and Uncle Ward and about me needing to get out on my own. I sat on the back porch and wished Rachael would come for a visit like she said and that Dad would find work soon. I wished that I could get it together. But wishing didn't pay the bills, Mom always said. I'd sleep on it, like Uncle Duny. That's when the real thinking would commence.

CHAPTER 20

I made up my mind to leave. It was time, and just like my Granddad Roland, once I'd decided something, I'd decided. There comes a time to jump no matter what, and it was clear to me that time had come.

"But where are you going? How you going to make a living?" Mom asked.

"Old Man Hinkle is putting up bales. I'm thinking to check him out for work."

"You going over there to stay with Duny and Ward, aren't you?"

"Old Man Hinkle has a room over his garage. Maybe I'll stay there."

"Jacob," she said.

"Yeah?"

"I wish there was more we could do, but what with the job situation—"

"I know," I said.

"You stop by," she said. "I'll cut your hair. Save you that."

"That will help out," I said.

I drove off in my Mercury, watching Mom through the rearview mirror. She was standing on the porch waving as if she'd never see me again. I drove straight to the post office to set up a box with the postmaster. He pulled down his glasses and gave me the once-over.

"Where the hell is Dunyville?" he asked. I explained to him where it was, and he shook his head. "That's the goddangest thing I ever heard. You put up a box, and your mail will get delivered, but don't be putting no Dunyville on it, just your name and Route 3."

"Thanks," I said.

"And let us know if you move out of there. It's a hell of a long ways off-route."

"All right," I said.

I found Uncle Ward and Uncle Duny sitting around a campfire they'd built next to the bus. Parking my Mercury in the shade, I made my way over.

Uncle Ward flipped his cigarette butt into the fire and stood. "Will you look at who has come to Dunyville?" he said.

"I just came by for a visit," I said.

Uncle Duny poked the fire with a stick and said, "It's a good job someone showed up before I put this preacher fanatic out of his misery."

"All I did was bring up baptizing," Uncle Ward said. "Your Uncle Duny here don't give a damn if he burns in hell or not."

"You figuring on moving to Dunyville?" Duny asked.

"I was thinking on it," I said.

"Well, that's fine. As you can see, there's no place for living under a roof yet. I'm sleeping under the bus, while your Uncle Ward here sleeps inside where it's dry."

"I offered you to sleep on the front seat," Uncle Ward said.

"I'd as soon sleep in my grave," Uncle Duny said. "If I hear any more about the Rapture, I'm going to give someone a head start to hell."

Uncle Ward stoked the fire and set an enamel coffeepot in the coals. "You'll be investing in one or two of the town lots, I'm thinking?" he said to me.

"Maybe when I get a little ahead," I said.

"According to the town charter, anyone posting an address in Dunyville must be a property owner. Isn't that right, Duny?"

"It's our way of making sure we have the proper commitment of every citizen who takes up habitation, not to mention an up-to-date tax role," Duny said.

"Maybe I'll just have a cup of coffee and move on," I said. "I don't have funds for buying up a town lot just yet."

"Well, I suppose we could make arrangements, you being an upstanding citizen and close relative," Duny said.

"What kind of arrangements would that be?" I asked.

"Ten percent of your paydays until such time as your lots are paid off full and clear."

"How much would that come to per lot?"

"Five hundred dollars per, with a minimum requirement of two lots."

"A thousand dollars?"

"More or less," Ward said. "It's a small price to pay for being a property owner and lawful citizen of Dunyville."

I poured myself a cup of coffee and studied the fire. "I don't know," I said. "Where would I sleep?"

Duny said, "Park that Mercury on the lots of your choice and sleep in it. That's a hell of a lot better than sleeping under the bus."

"Maybe it could be a start," I said.

"Getting in on the ground floor is an opportunity most don't come to," Ward said. "You get pick of the choicest lots, and land appreciation is a guarantee."

"I plan on bucking bales this summer, but I don't have a job just yet."

Ward walked to the back of the bus and took a leak. When he came back, he said, "Seeing as how you're a favored nephew, I'm thinking we could postpone the first payment until such time as you've landed yourself a job. What to do you think, Duny?"

"Wouldn't do it for no one, but you being the son of my sister."

I sipped my coffee. "As you know, I was thinking I might go to college sooner or later," I said.

Uncle Ward looked over at Uncle Duny. "While that's commendable, I suppose, but it strikes me as a tad unrealistic. First of all, if you go to college, there ain't no paydays, which would jeopardize our arrangement. Second, harsh as it may sound, college isn't for the likes of everyone."

"I made it to the eighth and figured it lucky," Duny said.

"My girlfriend's going to the University of Colorado," I said.

Ward said, "Well, then maybe she's going to pay your way too?"

"She'll be coming to visit here to see her grandparents."

Duny rolled himself a cigarette and stuck it in the corner of his mouth. "Thing about city girls is they like to flirt with country boys, makes 'em feel superior, but when it comes to living day in and day out on a scrub farm, they'll be wanting their own kind. You'll learn that soon enough."

"Maybe she ain't that way," I said.

Ward said, "There's only one love you can depend on, and it's spelled out in the scripture."

"I'm thinking that's not the kind of love Jacob has in mind," Duny said.

I finished my coffee and set the cup aside. "I could sleep in the Mercury until I have enough to build a place?" I said.

"I don't see why not," Ward said.

"Why don't you put me down for it then. I'll be checking in with Old Man Hinkle tomorrow."

"Well, that's fine," Ward said. "In the meantime, you be thinking about getting baptized. My intention is to make Dunyville a Christian town. If the Rapture comes tomorrow, I want to be ready, want things as pure and clean as I can make them."

Uncle Duny said, "Baptizing isn't in the charter, Ward. That was our agreement. We believe in the separation of church and state here in Dunyville. You don't want baptized, then so be it."

Ward shook his head. "It's a sad start living without God's protection, but until we have the votes, I guess it's to be the case. Go ahead and pick out your lots. Any groceries or such used up will be kept on a running tab until such time as your paycheck comes through."

CHAPTER 21

I chose the two lots closest to the track crossing. Uncle Duny said once Dunyville took off, folks would be looking for property convenient for loading and unloading goods off the trains. I dug a hole, planted a post, and nailed a coffee can on top, painting on my name, *Jacob Roland, Rt. 3*. That evening, I parked my Mercury on the far west lot, rolled down all four windows, and went to bed in the backseat.

Deep in the night, I could hear Uncle Duny coughing, and I could smell tobacco smoke from his cigarette. I slept curled against the night cool, dreaming of sprint races. I heard Danny's voice, clear as spring-water, say, "Who do you think you are?"

Unable to stretch out, I woke early and half bent. Duny's campfire had gone out during the night, and no one was up yet. I could see Uncle Duny's toes sticking out from under his blanket.

I thought once to get an early start on some coffee, but I wasn't keen to be running up more grocery bills. Bucking bales started early, 'cause a single shower could turn the green-cut alfalfa into a brown mess, so I decided to get on my way.

I found Old Man Hinkle greasing up a race bearing underneath the baler. His straw hat was tossed over a lever, and his chewing tobacco was on the seat of the tractor. He peeked through the gears and belts, looking up at me. Climbing out, he said, "Ain't you a Roland?"

"Jacob Roland," I said. "My dad is Abbott Roland."

"What is it you want?"

"I heard you might be hiring," I said.

He ran his finger around his collar, which was buttoned tight about his neck. "I hired your Uncle Ward one time," he said. "He damn near preached me into the grave. And then he wanted an electric fan run all dang night on top of it. I told him to sleep with the window open like God intended."

"I wouldn't be needing board," I said. "I'm living at Dunyville, so it wouldn't take me long to get here in the mornings."

He put his foot up on the baler step and dug a sandbur out of his shoelace with his knife. "Dunyville? Where the hell is Dunyville?" he asked, dropping his knife back into his pocket.

"Used to be the old Valley View town site," I said. "Now it's Dunyville."

He took his straw hat off the clutch lever and screwed it onto his head. He lifted a three-finger cud out of his tobacco and loaded his jaw. There was a smear of grease across his glasses.

"Ain't you related to old Duny Franklin too?"

"He's my uncle."

"I thought so. You drink, boy?"

"No, sir. Duny and Ward are setting up a town. I'm buying in too. Soon as I get a job and all, I mean."

"That's going to be some kind of town, ain't it?" he said. "Duny drinking and Ward preaching. Neither one got the common sense of a jack mule."

"They ain't so bad when you get to know them," I said.

"I pay fifty cents an hour, twelve hour days until the hay is in the barn. Settle up every two weeks, no more than that. You can have Sundays off. The wife cooks dinner. Comes with the job. It ain't fancy, but it's filling. You don't do the work, you're gone back to Dunyville broke. Understood?"

"Yes, sir."

"I'm running this here sled behind the baler. We stack bales cross-wise, two, four, six deep, then stick that pole in the ground and slide 'em off. I won't be stopping 'til twelve-up dinner. When the field is stacked out, we'll haul 'em to the barn. I got three more fields just like this one. Them's ninety-pound bales, and they spit out pretty damn fast. You think you can handle it?"

"Yes, sir," I said.

"You got gloves?"

"No, sir."

"Well, there's some in the toolbox over there. I'll fire up the Johnny popper, and we'll get her on the road."

He poured gas into the primer cup and turned over the flywheel. She fired once and rolled to a stop. He repeated the prime, and the old popper fired off with confidence, gaining up speed. I could feel its power coming up through my shoes. He switched her over to kerosene, and she settled in for the ride.

The bales gathered up green and heavy, tied off with baling wire, and pushed out the back like a defecating giant. The wire cut through my gloves, and the heat sent my head to spinning. Hour after hour, we crawled around the field. Dust clogged my eyes and my nose, and grasshoppers crawled down my shirt. My arms burned and my legs trembled as I stabbed the pole in the earth and leaned into it as the Johnny popper dragged the stack off the sled.

Grubby with dust and alfalfa leaves, we washed our faces and arms in a galvanized tub on the porch. Old Lady Hinkle served up mashed potatoes, liver and onions, and a loaf of homemade bread. Leaning over the table, she scooped potatoes onto my plate. I could see her breasts through her sleeve, big as lard cans they were, and the hair curled with sweat in her armpits. She smelled of sour and wood smoke, and her fingernails were black from the garden.

We went back to the field as soon as dinner was finished. The sun bore down hot as fire, and salt rings grew in the brim of my hat and under my arms. Blisters gathered on my hands, filled with blood and water, and then broke into running sores.

By sunset, the field bristled with stacks of bales. Old Man Hinkle climbed from the Johnny popper and shut off the fuel. The tractor cycled out, coughing and choking as she starved down. My ears rang in the silence, and my back throbbed. Hinkle slapped the dust from his hat across his leg.

"Six o'clock," he said, turning for the house.

I crawled into my Mercury, my arms dead as fence posts, and drove back to Dunyville. Uncle Duny was playing solitaire on a stump he'd dragged in for such purposes. He said that Uncle Ward had gone to town in hopes of recruiting baptized Christians for buying up lots, for which he was glad, because he was damn tired of listening to him preach.

I took a shower under the fifty-gallon drum Duny and Ward had set up on creosote ties next to the windmill. They'd poked holes in a gallon bucket and hung it under the spout for showering. The water was warm from the sun and did an adequate job of washing away the day's toil. Too tired to talk or eat, I checked my mailbox to find only a black widow spider that had spun out her trap in the corner.

I slept hard and in dread of the dawn. Danny visited me in the dark of night, as he did from time to time while I slept, telling me that this was a goofball life, void of hope. He said there're things I didn't know, but things I was damn sure going to find out.

Two weeks passed as if a year, and in that time, my body hardened to rock. Calluses thickened like leather on my hands, and the sun tanned me to brown. Payday, I counted out my down payment to Uncle Ward. He gathered up his cash from a coffee can he kept under the bus seat and counted it out.

"I got enough at last," he said, looking up.

"Enough for what?" Uncle Duny said.

"For buying back my cross."

"We was to use that money for a Dunyville town sign," Duny said. "It's the sign what makes it a town."

"A gathering of unbaptized sinners is not a town," Ward said.

"Half that money is mine, Ward, and I'll have it now."

Uncle Ward looked at me and then back at Duny. "I can't be answerable for your soul, Duny."

"Give me," he said, holding out his hand.

Ward counted out the money into his palm. "The devil's share," he said. "Take me into town, Jacob. The Lord's work awaits."

Duny handed me a five spot. "Jack Daniels," he said.

"I'm not twenty-one, Duny."

"No one cares your age where there's five dollars to be had," he said.

When Ward and I drove off for town, Duny was standing stark naked under the shower barrel. He was singing "Amazing Grace."

Uncle Ward looked out his window most the way to town without saying a word. Now and then he'd lower his head, and I could hear him mumbling to himself.

"Where you want to go?" I asked, as we came into town.

"Salvage yard," he said, pointing. "I'll get back to Dunyville on my own."

"What you doing there?"

"Buying back my rolling cross."

"You sold your cross to the salvage yard?"

"I sold the wheels. The cross just happened to be hooked to them."

"Why?"

Climbing out, he slammed the door and said, "Damn good price, what you think?"

CHAPTER 22

I stopped at the package store like Duny had asked. The owner barely looked at me as he tucked the money into his cash register. By the time I got back, the sun was nearly set.

"You get it?" Duny asked, poking at his fire.

"Yes," I said, handing him the sack.

"Where did you leave off Ward?"

I took up a seat out of the smoke. "Salvage yard," I said.

"Crazy as a barn owl," he said. "He'll be paying double to get it back."

"He says it's penance for starting up a town full of heathens."

Duny twisted the bag around the neck of the bottle, screwed off the lid, and smelled it. Taking a slug, he wiped his mouth on his sleeve.

"Always saying as to how my soul is lost, saying as to how I'm to burn in hell for not being baptized. Well, he ain't getting his hands on me. I ain't no sheep to be herded around by the likes of your Uncle Ward or anyone else."

"Uncle Ward says he talks to God and knows stuff no one else does."

Duny took another slug and shook his head. "I talk to Mortem here my own damn self. Know what he says back?"

"What?"

"Nothing. Know why?"

"Why?"

"'Cause he's a dog, and dogs can't talk. I'd think a highly educated fellow like yourself would know that."

He tipped up his bottle again before settling it between his legs. "Mortem here never talks either, but then hellhounds are especially known for their silence."

"What is a hellhound exactly?" I asked.

"Everyone knows that," he said.

"Not me," I said.

He leaned back and rolled a cigarette. Taking a stick from the fire, he touched off the end of it, and embers floated up into the blackness. "It's a name given death dogs, and it's commonly known that their main purpose in life is to guard the dead. That's why you find them hanging around cemeteries so much."

"You think Mortem is a hellhound?"

"I'm certain of it, in part at least," he said.

"Did you find him in a cemetery?"

"Found him in the alley behind the beer joint. He was laying up across Old Man Freeze's neck, who had passed out behind the dumpster. I figure he mistook him for dead."

"So that's when you knew him to be a hellhound?"

"Half-breed, as I've said, half rat terrier and half hellhound."

"Seems a stretch to me," I said.

"Ain't the only sign of it, though," he said. "Any number of things suggest it."

"Like what?"

"Well, hellhounds are almost always black. You can see there that Mortem is black as black, even after a bath. Sometimes I have to whistle him in 'cause I can't see him in the dark. And his eyes glow red, just like all hellhounds, and his breath is fierce from all that infectivity in his teeth. It's well known that if a hellhound bites you, you're likely dead by sunrise."

"You ever see a full-blood hellhound, Duny?"

"One or two," he said.

"I've never," I said.

"It's best that way, 'cause it's damn dangerous. If you look straight in their eyes three times in the same day, you'll fall over dead as a carp. They say it ain't no way to go either. And here's the thing, hellhounds hate baptized people more than anything else in the world. You've no doubt seen how Mortem avoids your Uncle Ward."

Duny wiped off the neck of the bottle with his elbow and handed it to me. I took a swig, and water gathered in my eyes. I looked at Mortem, who was lying under the bus polishing his balls. Clearly Duny was right about one thing—Mortem's eyes were glowing red in the firelight.

"You must've looked into Mortem's eyes lots of times," I said. "Why ain't you dead?"

"I'm cautious about it, just a glance now and then. Even so, I fell sick a time or two. I 'spect being a half-breed cuts down on his powers. Mostly he's just somewhere between mean and stupid."

I took another swig and shuddered. "Uncle Ward says God will walk you through the valley of death so you won't fear evil," I said.

"I've walked that valley a time or two myself. I can tell you up front, no one offered to walk it with me."

"Maybe it was because you ain't baptized, Duny? Uncle Ward says God looks out even for sparrows."

"He didn't look out for that one went through the bus grill over on Highway 14 the other day."

"Don't you believe in God, Duny?"

He leaned into the firelight, and I could see the sweat on his forehead. "Say a tornado comes sweeping into Dunyville, killing all your neighbors off, even that little crippled boy what was swinging down at the park on his birthday. Say there ain't a house left standing, save for one, yours."

"Just my house?"

"That's right. Now, suppose the local reporter comes along and says, 'How is it your house is the only one left standing, while all those other folks are dead or dying, including that little boy was down there on the swing?' Say you take a long look back over your shoulder and sure enough, no one's left but you. How do you explain that?"

I sat there trying to think. Pretty soon, I said, "It was God's will."

"You being so special and all?" he said. "All those other poor bastards got what they deserved, while God reached down among all the wind and hail and blood and plucked you out, you being such a pure and fine fellow, better even than that innocent little boy what died?"

"Don't hardly seem right," I said.

"That's why your Uncle Ward isn't baptizing me. My neighbors go up in a storm, I'm going up with them."

Until that moment, I hadn't realized the courage my Uncle Duny had stored inside him. It made me proud. I stood up to say so, but then couldn't remember what it was I intended to say.

"I'm going to bed, Duny," I said. "I'm wore out bucking bales."

I rolled all the windows down on my Mercury and stretched out in the back. Even though the night was clear, and the stars circled overhead, I had trouble settling in. I thought about Rachael and what she might be thinking that very minute. I thought about the way she smelled, like powder and lipstick, and the way her mouth turned up and how her eyes looked like puddles of melted green glass. Maybe she'd be coming to visit her grandparents soon. Maybe we'd go for a spin in the Mercury and park under a big tree. Maybe we'd make love and stir about in each other's souls.

I figured to write her more letters soon as I got out from under bucking bales, 'cause bucking bales turned my thinking to misery. For now, I'd just write the ideas as they came to me and put them in the wooden box at the end of the shelterbelt. And when the hay season ended, I would write it all out, say it the way it was meant to be said, say it so the truth of the words showed through.

I slept in a shallow and fretful way, dreaming and stirring and climbing the same hill. I awakened once to something in the night. I could see the fire and Duny curled like a fox up next to it. I could see the whiskey bottle still clutched in his hand. I wondered if I'd stay with Duny to face the storm or fly off to safety with angel wings. While I liked Duny, maybe it *was* God's will to kill all those other people, even if Duny didn't like it. Duny didn't know no more than anyone else. I dozed again to dream of Rachael lying naked on her stomach, with my head cradled in the warm curve of her back.

I slept hard after that, moving deeper into the blackness. When something woke me, I turned to listen. My heart beat in my ears, and clouds, edged by moonlight, raced through the night sky. Lifting onto my elbows, I could just see someone under the bus. He was bent over Duny, someone big with shoulders hunched. Maybe it was one of those killers, a murderer come for his due.

But the moon broke through the clouds, lighting the camp in silver, and I could see the outline of Uncle Ward's rolling cross leaning against the bus. Uncle Ward was down on one knee with a bucket in his hand. He looked skyward and said in a bold voice, "Whoever believes and is baptized will be saved, but whoever does not believe will be condemned." Before I could call out to stop him, he poured that bucket of water straight onto Uncle Duny's head.

Uncle Duny rose up like a dead man from the grave, water dripping from the end of his nose and off his chin. "You son of a bitch,

Ward," he yelled. "I'll get you for this, you hear? I'll get you sure as I live."

Uncle Ward threw his bucket down and raced off into the night. Uncle Duny paced and cussed and threw his wet shirt on the ground. He took his pint and tipped it high. Once, I considered to go to him, to console him for the thoughtless baptism, to assure him that being baptized might not be as bad as all that. But Duny could be unpredictable, and in his current state, I decided against it.

Had it not been for the exhaustion that comes with bucking bales, I'd have never gone back to sleep. But I did, and I didn't awaken until the sun blasted through the Mercury's windshield and into my eyes. Uncle Ward had not come back, and Uncle Duny was sleeping under the bus like a hibernating bear. His wet shirt hung on the bus mirror, and the empty bottle of whiskey was lying on the ground. The campfire still smoked, and in it, half covered with ashes, were the wheels and the smoldering stump of Uncle Ward's rolling cross.

CHAPTER 23

Bucking bales finally stopped, and not an hour too soon. Old Man Hinkle paid me off in cash. I had enough to make a payment on my lots, and with some left over for a day in town. I found Danny at the hotel. He looked older to me, or not so much older as more grown up. He wore a tie and had a fresh haircut.

"Hey, goofball," he said. "Where have you been?"

"Working," I said. "What's with the tie?"

He picked up the tail end of his tie and looked at it. "The customers expect it; otherwise, they think they're getting ripped off."

"I never knew you to care much about customers, Danny."

"Yeah, well, I'm turning this dump into a money maker."

"What about your grandma?"

"She died."

"Oh," I said.

"I own it now. I guess you hadn't heard the latest?"

"What's that?"

"I'm getting married too."

"You?"

"We'll be moving into the hotel."

"Damn," I said.

"She's from out of town. What about you?"

"Me? No."

"What about that Rachael girl?"

"We're just friends. I think she's coming for a visit, though."

"Maybe we'll have you guys over or something."

"Yeah," I said. "Maybe so."

Danny laughed. "Maybe we'll drive around with you in the trunk. Scare the shit out of everyone."

"Yeah," I said. "Well, I better be going."

"What's up with you, Jacob?"

"What do you mean?"

"I mean, where does it go with you from here?"

"I'm making some land investments, stuff like that, and I'm thinking to go to college."

Danny leaned back in his chair and slid his pencil behind his ear.

"You're a good guy, Jacob, but maybe college isn't for you."

"What do you mean?"

"I like you, but you're a little weird, that's all. Maybe you should talk to someone."

My ears went hot. "And maybe you should go to hell, Danny."

"Come on, Jacob. Just saying."

I turned for the door and paused. "I don't want you to talk to me anymore, Danny."

I walked out of the hotel before he could answer. Danny was a liar and a braggart. He did creepy things, always pressing in, making me do things I didn't want to do. I don't know why I hung around him in the first place. I was glad to be rid of him.

I filled the Mercury with gas, filled it as full as it would go, and drove home. Mom was in the kitchen making fudge for the kids. She dried her hands on the dish towel and looked me over.

"You're getting awful skinny," she said.

"It's bucking bales," I said. "And the heat."

"You come home to stay this time, Jacob?"

"A visit," I said. "How's Dad?"

She hung the dish towel over her shoulder. "He's not been the same since Gea. He goes to work when he can find it, but we don't talk anymore. It's like something died in him too."

"He was always crazy about her," I said. "How are the kids?"

"Kids are kids, aren't they? But they need more than an old lady to raise them. But that's how it is." She pushed her hair from her face with the back of her hand. "I'm sorry if you feel like you were pushed out."

"Naw," I said. "It was time to make my own way. Look, I think I'll take a little walk before dark. Check the ol' place out."

"Sure, you go ahead. Your dad should be along pretty soon."

I walked the length of the shelterbelt to where my wooden box was hidden. I went through its contents, reading the notes and meanderings that had grown into quite a stack over the years. Gea's blouse was still in it, the blood stain darkened and dried with time. I touched it with my finger to know that it was her blood, Gea's, to feel the injustice of it all. There was so much loneliness with it. Uncle Duny was right. We lived by chance and nothing more.

I stayed long enough to eat supper. Dad listened as I related my summer before he retreated to the front porch for a smoke. Mom wrapped up some fudge and slipped it into my hand. We stood at the door.

"Where now?" she asked.

"There's plowing jobs now that the wheat's in," I said.

She laid her hand on my shoulder. "You still think about college, Jacob? You still want that?"

"It's a good job I'm looking for, a solid job, like the railroad or something."

"You come visit us soon," she said.

I nodded, closing the door behind me.

Somewhere between the farm and Dunyville, I made the decision to drive up to Casket Hill. It was a starless night, and a southwest wind swept through the valley as I pulled the last curve to the top of the mesa. Shutting off the lights, I searched out her grave, now sunken with time and rain and marked with a small stone. I listened for her voice, for some sign.

"Where are you?" I asked. "Where have you gone?"

There was no answer, save for the wind moaning through the valley in perfect alto.

I woke to Uncle Duny unloading a hay wagon of used lumber onto his lot. Mortem was asleep in the shade of the wagon. I approached with care, what with Uncle Duny still brooding over his illicit baptism. Uncle Ward had caught the doodlebug to town and had been gone for several days now.

"What you doing with the lumber, Duny?" I asked.

He tossed a 2x4 onto the pile before answering. "What do you normally do with lumber?" he said.

"Build something?" I said.

"That's right. That's good, Jacob."

I poured a cup of coffee and set the pot back on the fire. "What is it you're building exactly?" I asked.

"Well, now," he said, "I'm building my business building out of the lumber what was left behind when Bob Wilson's barn fell over. You be sure and mark that coffee down in Ward's record book, hear, or the ol' tight ass will be after you."

I nodded. "What kind of business, Uncle Duny?"

"A saloon," he said.

"A saloon? You talked to Uncle Ward about this?"

"What the hell I need to talk to that Bible thumper for? It's my lot and my lumber. There's nothing in the charter says Ward has approval over what kind of business can be run in Dunyville. I'm calling it 'Duny's Drinks.'"

Duny's face was red, red as blood, which sometimes happened when he was agitated or had had a little too much the night before.

"Who's going to come clear out to Dunyville for a drink when they can get one in town?"

"Anyone wants to see dancing girls while having that drink, that's who," he said.

"Dancing girls?"

"That's right. Girls that dance."

"How many girls?" I asked.

"One," he said.

"One?"

"Goddang it, are you dim-witted? One is one, isn't it? It only takes one to dance, you know, and I already got her contracted."

I tossed my coffee dregs into the fire and listened to them sizzle. The charred wheels of Uncle Ward's rolling cross were still in the ashes. "Which one would that be, Duny?"

"Hazel Morford."

I turned and looked at him. "What lives in that shack down by the stockyards?"

"That's right, Hazel Morford."

"She's got a mustache, Duny, and one eye that shoots off into the yonder. You can't tell if she's looking at you or the moon."

"It don't make a damn if she's looking at the moon or somewhere else. Hazel Morford's got moves to drive men insane."

Just then the doodlebug sounded off at the crossing. In short order, Uncle Ward came walking down the road. He had a box in his arms and his hat pushed to the back of his head.

Setting the box down, he looked over the stack of lumber. Uncle Duny said nothing while he continued to unload the wood from the wagon.

As Uncle Ward approached, he said, "What's all this?"

"Uncle Duny's building his business building," I said.

Uncle Duny paused, then said, "I'm building my building right here on these two lots, which I own outright, free and clear."

Uncle Ward said, "And what kind of business would that be?"

"A saloon," Uncle Duny said.

"With a dancing girl," I said.

"And who gave you permission to build a saloon in my town, and with a dancing girl at that?"

"I don't need permission from no one, especially you," Duny said. "There's no restrictions in the charter, and that's the business I'm building."

"It's Hazel Morford," I said.

"That cockeyed woman from the stockyards?" Uncle Ward said.

"She's got insane moves," I said.

Uncle Ward crossed his arms over his chest. "You see that box there, Duny?"

"I see it."

"There's over two hundred flyers in that box inviting the Christian community to a revival meeting I'll be conducting in this very town. I got men coming out to build a brush arbor and to unload an upright piano for singing. I'm telling you now, Duny, there will be no saloon and no dancing girl long as I'm alive."

CHAPTER 24

The structures went up, separated by a dirt road—Uncle Ward's brush arbor on the west, Uncle Duny's saloon on the east. Whenever Ward and Duny crossed paths, which was inevitable, given the closeness of their buildings, they would look at the ground or pretend they didn't see each other.

As soon as the piano was brought into the brush arbor, Uncle Ward's flyers went out, stating the date, time, and place and noting that the word of God would revive souls and set them on the path of righteousness.

That same week, Uncle Duny advertised in the local paper the grand opening of Duny's Drinks, touting free rounds the first hour of the opening and exotic entertainment by the ever-seductive Hazel Morford.

In the meantime, Old Man Hinkle asked me back to plow his fields, which I accepted, mostly to escape the pressure from both Ward and Duny, each seeing it as my moral obligation as a nephew to be supportive of his new endeavor.

It was on a Friday evening that I checked my mail and found a letter from Rachael. She would be coming on the bus for a short visit with her grandparents and would like to see me.

When the day came, I showered under the water barrel and shaved in the Mercury mirror. I didn't have all that much to shave, but I wanted to look my best. Living in a car didn't make for nicely pressed clothes, but I still had the clean Levi's in the trunk that Mom had washed for me.

As I waited for time to go, I listened to the radio and watched Duny hang a door on the front of Duny's Drinks. My stomach was in knots at the thought of seeing Rachael again. Sometimes I couldn't remember exactly what she looked like, except for her mouth. She had this mouth that turned up at just the right spot. Across the road, Uncle Ward was nearly finished putting the brush on the roof of his brush arbor, but the whole thing was a bit shaky, like some kind of African thatched hut.

I hoped I'd have something to say to Rachael, something smart and funny, but it had been a long time since I'd talked to anyone in a personal way. Old Man Hinkle barely spoke, 'cept to bark out orders of one kind or the other, and neither Ward nor Duny could get over his mad long enough to talk in any real way. Rachael, on the other hand, was always rich with news about the latest book or movie or what her friends were doing. At times the anxiety in me was so intense that I almost wished I didn't have to go.

When I pulled up in front of her grandparents' house and shut off my lights, I could see her grandmother and her granddad sitting at the table. My hands went wet.

Her grandmother answered the door, dressed in a black dress with lace around the neck, and with black heels. A single strand of pearls hung about her neck that matched her ear rings, with each showcasing a single pearl.

I cleared my throat. "Is Rachael here?"

"Please come in. She's not quite ready." Turning, she said, "John, you remember Jacob from church, Rachael's friend."

John looked over his paper. "The boy from down the road."

"Hello," I said.

"And how are your parents?" he asked. "We don't see much of them anymore. The drive to the country was simply too much, though we loved your little church."

Rachael's grandmother placed her hands on the back of one of the chairs. "You remember Jacob's sister, Gea. The girl who sang alto."

"Oh, yes," he said. "Lovely voice."

"Such a tragic situation," she said.

"And so what are you doing now, Jacob?" John asked.

"Me? Oh, I've been doing field work this summer, though I plan to go to college in the fall."

"How wonderful," her grandmother said. "The local college?"

"Yes," I said. "It's handy, you know."

"Rachael has been accepted to the University of Colorado," she said. "She's quite excited."

"Yeah," I said.

"Most of her friends are going there, sororities and all that. I have such fond memories of those days myself."

"Yes," I said. "A great university."

"And about the children?" she asked.

"Children?"

"I understand your mother is raising the children."

"Oh, yes," I said. "They're fine. Growing up."

"So difficult to have children at her age and then with Gea's death."

"She manages just fine," I said.

"Oh, here's Rachael. Oh my, you do look nice, Rachael."

Rachael stood in the doorway. She'd grown taller, graceful and lean, and her hair was the exact color of wheat. Her bosom was full and lush, and unlike the other girls I knew, her skin was untouched by the sun.

"Hi, Jacob," she said, smiling. "I'm ready."

"Where will you kids be going?" her grandfather asked.

"We haven't decided yet," Rachael said. "There are some excellent movies just released."

"Be back at a decent hour," he said.

I nodded and followed Rachael to the door. "Good night," I said to her grandmother. "Nice to see you again."

"Give your mother my regards," she said. "I do admire her so."

Rachael hooked her arm through mine as we made our way to the car. I opened the door, and she slid in, smelling of gardenias or something like that. I could see her profile against the streetlight, the perfect curve of her nose and mouth.

We drove around for a while, trying to decide which movie we might want to see. Finally, she said, "Isn't there somewhere we could go to talk? I'm leaving in a couple of days, and I've seen nearly all the movies."

"Sure," I said, my mouth going dry. "There's this old abandoned farmhouse. No one ever goes there. We could park for a bit."

She turned and smiled. "Yes," she said, "let's."

We parked under the big cottonwood that had grown up in the yard. I rolled the windows down. The mourning doves were settling in with their throaty coos back and forth in the high branches of the trees.

"It's so quiet out here," she said.

"Yes," I said. "Sometimes I go to my place just to listen to the mourning doves. Their sadness, you know."

She slid over close to me, and I could feel the heat of her arm on mine. My head reeled. "Your place?" she asked. "You have a place?"

"Oh, it's nothing like that," I said. "It's a place I go to at the end of our shelterbelt, a place to be alone, mostly."

"What do you do there?"

"I think. Sometimes I write things. I write you letters there lots of times."

"You write other things too?"

"Not really write, not like a real writer or anything. Just things that come into my head, things I can't really talk about with people."

"What do you do with them?"

"Do with what?"

"The things that you write."

"Nothing. I mean, just write my thoughts. It puts things in order for me, and I like to see the words. It lets me know what I'm thinking."

"Do you keep them?"

"Not really. I have this wooden box, and I throw them in there. I don't know why. They aren't of value to anyone but me."

"I love words too," she said. "That's why I'm majoring in literature. I love books and poetry and all that."

"What do you do with a degree in literature?" I asked.

"Oh, I don't know. Have you read Heller's *Catch-22*?"

"No," I said. "I've been working the field all summer."

"Or *One Flew over the Cuckoo's Nest*? It's crazy and wild. It reminds me of you."

"I'm not crazy *or* wild, either one," I said.

"Not crazy crazy," she said, taking my hand. "But sensitive crazy, you know. You have a way of going off to places where other people aren't allowed."

"Maybe," I said. "Danny thought that if I lived anywhere else in the world, they'd have me in the loony."

She reached over and kissed me on the cheek. It burned a place there on my cheek like a permanent brand.

"There's nothing wrong with being different, Jacob, but you really should broaden your horizons. I know you are bright, and there's so much to learn. When you get to college, you need to be able to relate, to interact with other people."

"We never had much time for reading and stuff like that," I said.

"There were place payments, and the railroad was forever laying people off. Seemed like all we ever did was chores and field work and then more chores."

"There's a whole world out there, Jacob. You really should prepare yourself. How do you plan a future otherwise? Now," she said, turning my face toward her, "are you going to kiss me or not?"

We kissed, and she leaned into me. And when I thought the kissing had stopped, she leaned in some more. A sensation twisted inside me, and my breathing faded. She laid her hand on my thigh, and I pulled her in close. I touched her neck, and her heart beat under my fingers. I put my lips into the hollow behind her ear. I traced her mouth and her eyelids and the curve of her brow with my finger. I let my hand wander to her breast to feel the heat and density of her body, and when she relaxed beneath me, I stopped. She was not to be mauled and mistreated, no more than I would abuse anything that I prized. She was to be valued and adored like a sacred object.

Accepting my reluctance, she fell quiet, and then we talked. We talked until late, kissing now and then to seal our secrets. And when I walked her to her door that night, I was more in love than I thought possible.

"I'll write," she said, closing the door behind her.

Uncle Ward opened his revival meeting the same night Uncle Duny opened his saloon. A dozen people showed up for the revival and twenty or so for the free drinks at Duny's. "Amazing Grace" drifted out of the brush arbor, while "Devil Woman" was turned up high on Duny's new juke, vibrating the windows. Unwilling to participate in either function, I sat in my Mercury, knowing there was no way things could end peacefully.

I could hear and see it all, like watching a horror movie at the drive-in. There was Uncle Ward, his hands lifted above his head, delivering his best lines on damnation and hellfire, while Hazel Morford humped and gyrated around the pole in Duny's Drinks. The pole, having been constructed from an old water pipe Duny dug out of the ground, swayed precariously under Hazel's enthusiasm.

Though tensions were high, all remained peaceful, until the pole gave way, dumping Hazel onto her back in the middle of the dance floor. One accusation led to another, and a fistfight spilled into the street. Duny's patrons, now lubricated, followed the fight out to join in with shouts of *Kill him! Stick him in the ribs!*

Mesmerized by the scrap, I failed to notice that Uncle Ward and his Christian soldiers had gathered on the opposite side of the street. Ward's piano player, a stout woman who played regularly at our church, was particularly agitated by Hazel's bare breasts swinging hypnotically in the light cast through the saloon window.

I can't be certain who threw the first punch, whether Christian or sinner, but soon enough, the whole town of Dunyville was embroiled in a street brawl. Taking sides struck me as a no-winner, so I cranked up the Mercury and drove to the top of the hill. From there, I watched the battle unfold, a battle similar to the ant wars I'd instigated as a child.

I couldn't tell the origin of the fire or who might have started it, but soon flames licked at the thatched roof of Uncle Ward's brush arbor. A short time later, another fire lit up the windows of Duny's Drinks. It was as if the Rapture had come at last.

The sirens of fire trucks and police cars soon filled the valley. I cranked up the Mercury and pulled away with the lights off. There was little anyone could do now. Maybe Duny and Ward could settle it over a domino game in county jail; meanwhile, I had made my decision to leave Dunyville and to make something of my life, just as Rachael had said.

CHAPTER 25

Before Mom had a chance to speak, I said, "I've decided to go college."

She stepped back and gave me a long look. "That cost money, Jacob, and there is the place payment, you know."

"A part-time job is all I need," I said. "Enough to get by."

"And the children," she said. "And your dad being out of work."

"I'm not asking for anything."

She dried her hands on her apron. "You're a grown man. I guess you got a right to your decisions."

"I came to pick up my things."

"Your clothes are washed up," she said.

I packed my clothes in an old suitcase that had been under the bed for as long as I could remember. The kids watched from the doorway. When I came out, Mom was dabbing at her eyes with her sleeve.

"You kids get on out of here," she said. "It's too pretty a day."

I stood at the door with my suitcase and watched the kids dash across the yard.

"Are you going to see your dad before you leave?" she asked.

"I'll catch him next time, Mom," I said, opening the door. "Don't you be worrying about things; I'll be just fine."

The campus set atop a hill overlooking the town. The administration building, known as the Citadel, looked just like its name, with octagonal towers, bastions, and fortifications, missing only the moat and drawbridge. Students, absorbed in conversation, passed by me on their way to class.

I stood at the front door of the Citadel, never more uncertain about what I was about to do. With a deep breath, I went in. A woman, who was sitting behind a metal desk, looked up. She was thin, with a sharp nose, and her glasses hung about her neck on a ribbon.

"Yes?" she said.

"I came to enroll," I said.

"Enrollment is not in this building," she said.

"I mean, I came to start."

"You are a new student?" she asked.

"Yes," I said. "That's it, I'm a new student."

"Have you taken your entrance exams?"

I shook my head. "No," I said. "They've sent my records, though."

"You'll have to take your entrance exams," she said. "We have to know where you are, you see."

"I graduated from high school," I said.

"I'm afraid that doesn't tell us much, does it? Come back after lunch, one o'clock. The battery of tests will take about three hours to complete."

The entrance exams took three hours, like she'd said, three hours of regretting ever having come. The monitor took my answer sheets and slipped them into a drawer.

"Come back tomorrow morning," she said. "A counselor will go over your results."

"I understand that sometimes there are jobs on campus?"

"Our funds are reserved for the better students, the ones more likely to succeed academically. Come back tomorrow, and you can ask your counselor about financial aid then."

Not wanting to return home, I parked on a country road just outside of town and slept in the Mercury, though it was hardly sleeping. Even though I'd spent many nights in that back seat, this was different, because tomorrow I faced a reality of a different sort. I knew that the sprinters were already far ahead, already at the turn. Would I turn back, or would I finish the race?

The counselor pushed her chair back from her desk and crossed her legs as she read over my test results.

"You are Jacob Roland?"

"Yes," I said.

She laid the papers on her desk and threaded her fingers together. "What made you decide to come?" she asked. "College, I mean."

I looked out the window. A sparrow was sitting on the ledge with an enormous grasshopper in its beak.

"I want to finish the race," I said.

"Excuse me?"

"I want to know things," I said.

She picked up her pencil and doodled something on her desk pad. "This isn't high school, Jacob. No one here will do things for you. It will be up to you to make it or not."

"It's my scores, isn't it?" I said.

"I'd like to be more encouraging, but your test results indicate a number of weaknesses in your academic abilities."

I swallowed. "They do?"

"Particularly in verbal development, a skill demonstrated to be essential for succeeding at the college level."

"I could work on them," I said.

"Verbal ability comes from living in a nurturing environment, from discussion, reading, and thinking in words. It's not something that can be picked up overnight. I'm afraid you will have difficulty succeeding with college-level work."

My heart pounded in my chest. "I can't go?"

"I didn't say you couldn't. I said it's unlikely that you could succeed. It would be disingenuous of me to tell you otherwise."

"Disingenuous?"

"Dishonest."

"I'm a hard worker," I said.

"Sometimes work isn't enough, Jacob. The others will be ahead, will be moving on while you are trying to catch up."

"I want to do this," I said. "Isn't there a way?"

She opened her desk drawer and pulled out a large book with a picture of the Citadel on the front. She thumbed through the pages. Pausing, she said, "There is a remedial track. Most of the course credit will not apply toward a degree; however, if you're willing to do that, and if you're successful, we will reconsider your application."

"Remedial?"

"A basic course of study. Frankly, it's what most students should have learned in high school."

"I could catch up that way, if I didn't quit the race, I mean?"

"Hypothetically, but you must understand that catching up is the hardest job of all. No one will wait for you to catch up."

"I'll do it," I said. "And if I could find a job—"

She tapped her pencil on her desk. "You have no financial means?"

"No, but—"

"How does one work and catch up academically at the same time? You do see the problem?"

"I can do it," I said.

She leaned back and folded her arms over her chest. "Well, I did see a part-time job advertised in the newspaper. Something at the courthouse. Custodial, I believe. You could check that out. It takes the university a while to get the tuition bills out. Perhaps you could get a payment together in the meanwhile. You'll have to come in for follow-up consultations here. The university can arrange a payment schedule, if necessary."

"Like place payments," I said.

"Excuse me?"

"Nothing," I said. "I'll see you soon."

CHAPTER 26

By the end of the week, I'd enrolled at the university, landed the job at the courthouse, and bought used textbooks from a kid who had quit the remedial track to join the army. In the meantime, I went to the public library and checked out Heller's *Catch-22*.

The county jail was housed upstairs in the courthouse, while the showers for the inmates were in the basement. After I'd finished cleaning the courthouse at night, I'd go into the inmate shower room with my pass key and clean up. From there, I'd seek out an inner office, one with no exterior windows, and do my reading.

I wrote Rachael long and detailed letters about *Catch-22* and then *One Flew over the Cuckoo's Nest.* I read the literature textbook that I had purchased for remedial English class, even though much of it made no sense to me. I ate sparingly, bologna sandwiches, which I kept in a paper bag in the jailer's little refrigerator. I purchased nothing else, save for gas for the Mercury and stamps to write Rachael. I had made it halfway through the literature textbook when classes began.

Nearly all my daylight hours were devoted to attending class, my evenings to my job, and late nights to completing class assignments. The one thing I had little time for was sleeping, but I found the energy. I found it from my professors and from the other students in class. I discovered a passion for the exchange of ideas, for understanding my world in this new way.

As the weeks passed, I became more organized, extending my reading time. I checked out more books from the library, which the librarians, who had come to know me by name, often reserved for me. I worked harder than I'd ever worked before and made certain that I was not losing the race.

I wrote letters to Rachael, detailing my passion for learning and how someday I would prove my worthiness to her. Rachael wrote back, but less often as the semester wore on. When she did write, she talked about her sorority and about the dances that were held on Saturday nights, about dorm life and football games and about how she was thinking of changing her major.

I made the first place payment on my tuition, and by midterm, I had passed all my tests, not with high grades but with passing grades.

I went back to see the counselor, who looked over my midterms and made small humming noises.

"I must say you've managed to do pretty well, Jacob. Now if you can finish with grades like these, perhaps we can move you into a regular-track program. Have you thought about a major?"

"English," I said. "I like the writing."

She laughed. "Majoring in your weakest area? Yes, that makes sense."

But I had discovered writing to be a way of tying things together, of making sense out of the absurd, even the problems that I struggled with personally. I started organizing my journal, too, and discovered I had a need for it, as a way of imposing discipline on my undisciplined mind.

"And what about your employment?" the counselor asked.

"I clean the courthouse at night. It fits into my schedule and still leaves time to study."

"And when do you sleep?"

"I'm a little short on that," I said.

"If you don't mind me saying so, it's beginning to show. You look a bit weary. Perhaps you should reconsider your credit load."

"I'm coming up from behind, gaining on the competition," I said. "I'm not stopping now."

By semester's end, I had brought my grades to a B average and was given permission to enroll in a regular summer term. Determined to get my major under way, I took as much literature as I could, not realizing that I'd have half the time and twice the work in each class. Research papers abounded in the major I'd selected, and finding time to get the reading done was increasingly difficult.

I had managed to save enough money for a deposit on a single room above the Bradey Flower Shop on Main. The room was a bit spare and a lot hot but better than sleeping in the Mercury. There was a private shower, a kitchenette, even a table where I could study.

Rachael wrote, saying that she and her family were going to Europe during the break. Though she didn't want to go, had planned for a visit with me instead, her father had insisted, and she hoped I understood. She said that her father had discouraged her from liberal arts, thought it of little value in the real world, and while she still liked literature, she'd decided to change her major to economics.

My summer classes were fast and difficult and cut ever more into my sleep. I studied every minute I could manage, sometimes falling asleep at the table. I cooked less and ate less, not so much from lack of money as from lack of time.

My professors, who at first had been skeptical of my abilities, were now encouraging. My weight continued to drop. My pants hung on my hip bones. Dark rings appeared under my eyes, and my physical endurance waned. Sometimes at work I'd stop on the stairs or on the couch in the lobby to rest, but I was making progress, overtaking the other sprinters, passing them by one by one.

That semester, I made a 3.7 GPA, and my determination to forge ahead strengthened. But I had paid a price. My hands shook, and the twitch returned to my nose. Still, I was in the pack and headed to the finish line.

With the few days I had before the next semester started, I decided on a brief visit to my family. After returning a stack of books to the library, I loaded up my journal notes in the Mercury and headed home.

Mom and the kids met me at the door. Mom drew me in, while the kids grinned back at me from the doorway.

"I've been worried about you," she said. "Just look at you, skin and bones."

"I'm fine," I said. "How's Dad?"

"He's building fence up on the Reynolds place. It's awfully hard work. He's not a kid anymore, you know, and the pay is not so good. But, we're getting by as you can see. Can you stay?"

"For a bit," I said. "I have to get back to my job."

"Well, come on in," she said. "We just picked the corn, and your dad has a clothes basket full of homegrown tomatoes."

After we had eaten, the kids took me out to show me the fort they were building and the labyrinth of tunnels they'd dug to connect the rooms. They danced ahead of me all the way out and all the way back to the house. Mom was sitting in her chair when we got back. She looked tired, and streaks of gray that I'd not seen before ran through her hair.

"Mom," I said, "I'm going to run in and see Danny. I'll be leaving early in the morning."

"I'll have your bed made on the porch when you get home," she said, waving me off. "It's a lovely breeze out there this time of the year."

The last time I'd seen Danny, I'd told him to go to hell. I hoped he didn't remember, because I didn't feel that way anymore. Danny knew me better than most anyone in the world. That made him special and, at the same time, dangerous in a way. He'd spent far too much time in my head and had seen things in there that no one else had.

I found him sitting at the reception desk of the hotel reading a newspaper. He looked up and didn't recognize me at first.

"Oh, hey, it's goofball," he said, with sudden recognition.

"Hello, Danny," I said.

He stood up and reached for my hand. "You still pissed at me?"

I shook my head. "I can't even remember why I was mad. You probably deserved it, though."

Danny looked different, kind of down, like the light had gone out of him.

"I hear you're a college man now," he said.

"Yeah, hard to believe, isn't it?"

"Well, it beats living out at crazyville with those whacky uncles of yours."

"Yeah," I said.

"I heard they put your Uncle Ward and your Uncle Duny in the same cell together. They said it was like throwing tomcats into a pillowcase and shaking it up."

"They had some issues between them," I said.

"It's no wonder you turned out a goofball," he said.

"I'm beginning to remember why I told you to go to hell, Danny."

"Just kidding," he said, grinning. "Sit down. The wife's not back from her shopping spree."

I moved some magazines off a chair and sat down. "How goes it, Danny? How goes the business and the marriage?"

He shook his head. "The train crews come in, and the train crews go out. I check 'em in, and I check 'em out. We talk about the weather, the ball games, and who is screwing who. I sometimes think I'll wither up and blow away to tell you the truth."

"What about all those inventions, Danny, all those thing you were going to do?"

He shrugged. "Kid stuff," he said. "Just that. We all have to grow up, I guess. By the time I get the rooms cleaned and the paperwork done, I'm lucky to make it to bed."

"Any kids yet, Danny?"

He opened the desk drawer and tossed in his pencil and pad. "No kids. Here's the thing, goofball. There's no faking it in marriage, see. When you live together, eat together, use the same bathroom, day in and day out, there is no faking anything. They know you, and you know them. No matter whatever shit it is you've been hiding, what crummy little secrets you have, they will all have been uncovered by the end of the first month of marriage."

"And I had you down for some big invention by now," I said.

A man cleared his throat as he came down the stairs. He wore overalls, and his jaw was loaded with tobacco. At the door, he cocked his engineer's hat on his head and spit in the ash tray.

Danny looked away. "No inventions," he said, "just weather talk, ball games, and cleaning dirty rooms. What about you?"

"No wife," I said.

"What happened to the girl with the big knockers?"

"Come on, Danny."

"Hey, you remember that time we drove around with your arm hanging out of the trunk?"

"I remember."

"What a hoot," he said.

"Yeah," I said.

"Old Chester Finley is dead, you know."

"I didn't know."

"He went to work for the electric co-op as a lineman and got caught up in a high-voltage wire. They said he hung midair for two hours before they could get him down."

"Damn," I said. "Finley was a good guy."

"He was dumb as a lug nut," Danny said.

"You still window peeking, Danny?"

"I see more than I want by accident," he said.

The front door opened, and a woman came in with her arms full of packages. She wore sweats, and her hair was stacked on top of her head.

"It's Florence," he said, standing. "My wife." She set her packages down. "This is Jacob Roland," Danny said. "We went to high school together."

She looked at me, and I nodded. "Nice to meet you," I said.

"We used to do some crazy shit," Danny said.

"Are those rooms finished, Danny?" she asked.

"I was just getting to it," he said.

"Those crews are due in at three," she said.

"Yeah," he said, "I'm on it."

I stood. "Well, I better get on my way. Nice seeing you again, Danny."

"Yeah," he said. "Hey," he said as I reached the door, "you remember what we called that arm-out-the-trunk thing?"

"The friend test," I said.

"Yeah, the friend test. I always figured you'd pass it," he said.

CHAPTER 27

I walked into the next semester still hungry for the world. Seeing Danny caught up in a dull marriage and a life of mediocrity motivated me to forge ahead. There were things I wanted to learn, books I wanted to read, people I wanted to know. I was determined to make it happen.

That semester, I enrolled in a class taught by one Dr. Foss, allegedly the most inspiring professor on campus. Normally, she taught only graduate-level classes, but a scheduling conflict forced her into teaching the undergraduate Introduction to American Literature class.

She showed up first day with her arms full of books, no makeup, wearing a plain cotton dress and black loafers. Had it been anywhere else, she would have passed for the cleaning woman or the old lady on the park bench feeding pigeons. But the moment her lecture started, I was swept into a world I didn't even know existed. It was a feast laid out in front of me.

I read the books she brought—Hemingway, Steinbeck, and Fitzgerald. I read late into the night, ignoring my need for rest, neglecting my job at the courthouse, forgetting family and friends. I filled my notes with thoughts, and I composed long and idealistic letters to Rachael, who had grown increasingly tardy with her responses. During this process, I discovered how powerful narrative could be, how it could make abstraction and confusion comprehensible. This was my new secret weapon. This made me formidable, perhaps immortal. I had to have it, perfect it, and live forever within it. So, I read everything she suggested and more. I took my scattered letters and words and made them whole.

What I failed to do was rest. At times I'd fall asleep unexpectedly, waking on the stairwell or behind the Mercury steering wheel or on the bunk in the basement of the courthouse. I developed tremors and a stammer that would start and stop unexpectedly, leaving me exasperated. My concentration failed, and my stamina weakened to the point that I could no longer sustain my reading or complete my assignments. Finally, my grades began to suffer.

It was during the last week of that semester that I awoke in the middle of the night to a noise. I lay in the darkness listening, trying to identify what it might be. There were occasions that the owner of the flower shop returned for something he'd forgotten, but this was different. There was something alarming about it. I dozed once again but was startled awake once more and left staring into the darkness. A figure materialized in front of me, murky but at the same time familiar.

"Who is it?" I asked, my voice breaking. There was no answer. "Who the hell are you?" I asked again with bravado.

"It's me, Danny," he said.

"Danny?"

"Danny, goofball. How many Dannys do you know?"

"What are you doing here?"

"I want to talk," he said.

"About what?"

"About the girl with the big knockers."

"Cut it out, Danny."

"Girls like her got no interest in guys like you. I tried to warn you, but you wouldn't listen. She's looking for smarts and money. You don't have much of either."

I sat up. "Don't talk that way, Danny. I'll punch you in the nose."

"Yeah, you and who else? Have some pride, goofball."

I heard the door close, and he was gone. I lay down, uncertain whether I had been dreaming. Maybe Danny was right about Rachael, that I'd been fooling myself all this time. But why would he come all this way, and in the middle of the night, to say it?

Unless—unless he wanted Rachael for himself. He'd always been obsessed with her, talking about her that way, and he was married too. So, what business was it of his, unless he was trying to convince me to get out of his way so he could have her? Maybe that was it, the son of a bitch. Maybe he was looking to steal Rachael away from me.

When I arrived the next evening at the courthouse, I had been fired. My check was waiting, along with a brown bag of sandwiches that I had left in the jailer's refrigerator. They said I had failed to do my job and that they would have to find someone else who could work unsupervised.

The following morning, I received a letter in an envelope that had a picture of the Citadel on the front of it. It was from the dean of students, informing me that I had been placed on academic probation and would not be allowed to enroll the following semester. I could reapply in one year to have my status reconsidered. There would be no refunds this late in the semester, and a letter had already been sent to my parents explaining the reasons for my suspension.

No sooner had I finished reading the letter than the telephone rang. It was Uncle Duny.

"Where do you live?" he asked. "I'm coming over."

"Above the Bradey Flower Shop on Main. What's wrong?"

"Did I say anything was wrong?"

"No, but—I thought you were in county?"

"I'm out, legit, if that's what you're thinking."

"I'm just surprised, that's all."

"I'll be there shortly," he said, hanging up.

I'd barely gotten dressed when the downstairs doorbell rang. Uncle Duny stood there, looking like he'd just hopped off a freight train.

"Jesus," he said. "You really do live on Main Street?"

"Just a room," I said.

"Beats sleeping under a bus," he said.

"What you doing here, Uncle Duny?"

"You know that crazy bastard Ward burned my building to the ground," he said. "I got nothing left. You going to let me in or what?"

We climbed the stairs, and I could hear Uncle Duny wheezing behind me. I pointed him to the chair, and he slumped down into it. He dabbed the sweat from his forehead with his handkerchief.

"You OK?" I asked.

He pulled out his cigarette makings. "Hell no," he said, sprinkling tobacco the length of the paper. "I got water gathering up in my ankles and feet. Look like a goddang hippo. The county croaker tells me I got the liver of a ninety-year-old. I tell you, boy, I got no money, no job, and I'm too sick to give a damn. I'm too old and crippled for farmwork, and I can't run fast enough to steal. I'm used up and no one to care."

"You got family, Uncle Duny. And you got Mortem."

He lit his cigarette and studied the end of it. "Damn dog took off," he said. "Hellhounds got little use for baptized humans. Anyway, your mom tells me you're going to the university and landed a job at the courthouse."

I walked to the window and looked down on Main. "I lost my job," I said. "Been kicked out of the university too."

"Well, damn," he said. "We got more in common than I thought. Is your rent paid up?"

"Until the end of the month," I said.

"Well, that's something," he said.

"It all went off the rail," I said.

"Been there," he said. "Once, I was selling encyclopedias over in Albuquerque. Made thirty dollars in two days. I was hauling it in. Franklin charm, you know. Anyway, I was fixing to close a deal with this gal, a twelve-volume leather-bound deluxe set, when this cop showed up with his nightstick and threatened to soften up my head."

"Why?" I asked.

"Don't know. All I did was show her a full-page illustration of an erect penis."

"You want something to eat, Uncle Duny?"

"Maybe a whiskey?"

"I don't have whiskey," I said.

"What the hell is all those notebooks for?" he asked.

"Just some journal notes I been keeping. My professor said I had a knack for it."

"Get it from the Franklin side," he said. "Your grandad could lie his way out of a cattle stampede. Say," he said, "you still writing love letters to that girl?"

"We're still writing," I said. "Trouble is—"

He squashed out his cigarette on the bottom of his shoe and palmed it. "Trouble is what?"

"I think Danny is trying to steal her away."

"Danny?"

"He was here last night, telling me how I wasn't good enough for her, and how sooner or later she was going to find someone else."

"Danny Armstrong? That little son of a bitch who runs the Railway Hotel?"

"That's right."

"You saw him last night?"

"That's right."

"Peculiar," he said. "Danny Armstrong shot himself in the head a week ago. Train crew found him bleeding out on the hotel register. Dead as a carp, he was."

CHAPTER 28

Uncle Duny, being more sensitive than one might surmise, didn't pursue the matter further. I found some relief in that, because I didn't understand it all myself. In any case, a man owning a hellhound and scared of being baptized didn't have much truck worrying about my life.

Having acquired fair cooking skills over his many years of bachelorhood, Uncle Duny fixed pinto beans and fatback as good as I ever had. That night he slept on the floor, and I slept in the bed. I offered the bed, but he declined, saying as how sleeping under the bus had taught him how to sleep anywhere at any time.

Neither of us had a clear notion as to where we went from here, but I could see that Uncle Duny's health was not what it should be. He'd slowed down some to be sure, no doubt due to his heavy drinking and his uncontrollable appetite, and he didn't have life direction far as I could tell. If he did, he wasn't saying. He had a way of just disappearing, showing up again at odd times and without explanation.

I missed going to my classes, which had served to keep my mind occupied. Now, with nothing specific to think about, I thought about everything in the most random and illogical ways. I stopped going out any more than was necessary. I had no interest in seeing anyone, most especially Mom and Dad, now that they would have received the suspension letter.

Sometimes the world would fall about me like a dark cloud, like a weight on my chest that kept me from breathing. I feared closed rooms and large crowds more than anything, any place where there was no clear escape route. It was as if a great hand were pushing me underwater, holding me there as my lungs filled.

On better days I worked on my notes or listened to the radio. But then sometimes Danny would come at night, telling me how Rachael was his now and how I was a bad friend who had deserted him. Asking why I wasn't there the day he put a bullet in his head. Where was I when it came down to it?

One morning, Duny showed up with a sack of groceries in his arms and a grin on his face.

"Guess what?" he asked.

"What?"

"I got a job."

"You mean like a real job?"

He pushed the sack of groceries over to me. "With a paycheck and everything," he said.

"Where? Doing what?"

"Cleaning the courthouse at night," he said.

I looked at him over the sack of groceries. "You took *my* job?"

He shrugged. "I knew it was open. Now we can eat, buy gas, pay the rent. Come on, boy, I just as well have the job as someone else."

And so he paid the rent, bought eggs and milk, and made cornbread smeared with real butter. Duny said it would all work out. Said he found college generally a waste of time, but if that's what I wanted, he'd let me stay in the apartment until I could come up with a job for myself.

But I didn't know if college was what I wanted anymore. I had this big hole in my life. I didn't want much of anything anymore, 'cept to be left alone. I'd been thinking that others were right about me. I'd always be running behind, never catching up.

A week later, when I came home, I found Uncle Duny passed out on the stairwell. He didn't smell of liquor, but his face was red and bloated, and his shirt was wet with sweat. I put a wet rag on his forehead and waited for him to come around. He sat up and leaned against the wall. His breathing was labored and shallow.

"What is it, Duny?" I asked. "What's wrong?"

He pushed me aside. "Get the hell out of the way, kid," he said. "It ain't your business."

After that, I looked for work in earnest, knowing now that I could not depend on Duny much longer. Three days later, I spotted a help wanted sign down at the gas station. The owner had oatmeal on the front of his uniform when he came out. He said the job was pumping gas and doing oil changes. He said it was cleaning the public toilet every night before going home, that it wasn't so bad, save for when some bastard missed the stool or clogged it with toilet paper. He said the other guy was filling out notice time and I could come back later if I wanted.

Danny's visits commenced in earnest again, usually in the wee hours of morning. Sometimes he'd talk, while other times, he'd just watch from the doorway without saying a word. I came to realize at some point that he wasn't just watching but was making me do stuff with his presence, making me think things I didn't want to think.

Uncle Duny said Danny had killed himself, and that if I believed otherwise, I was crazier than Danny had been. In some ways I knew he was right, but then there Danny would be standing in the doorway, real as real. I couldn't stop him.

While Uncle Duny was cleaning the courthouse, I'd write my notes. I'd write things that were happening to me and things that I'd been thinking. It didn't stop me from thinking them, but sometimes I'd change them up, make them the way I wanted them to be. I had the power to do that.

One night Uncle Duny came home early from work, and I could tell something was different. I'd seen him drunk plenty of times, knew how he walked, and how he talked with his words all jammed up together. But this was different. He sat down on the chair and held his head in his hands.

"What's the matter, Uncle Duny?"

He looked up at me. "Who said anything was the matter?"

"You want me to fix you some food?"

He coughed and held his stomach. "What did your cooking ever cure?"

"Just an offer," I said.

"You ever think about dying, boy?" he asked.

"Everyone thinks about it some, I guess."

"You know, I ain't never been to a single funeral in my whole life. Even my own mother's."

"Why not?"

He lowered his head. "I didn't want to be drawn into it, I guess. I didn't want to look at it straight on."

"Everyone dies," I said.

He pushed himself back in his chair. "Now ain't that a goddang insight to behold? It doesn't make a damn that everyone dies when it comes to your own dying, does it?"

He jumped then like he had a pain, and he took a deep breath. "Damn beans lay up in a man like beer wort," he said.

"Maybe we ought get hold of someone, Duny. See a doctor or something."

"You thinking I might die, leaving you to pay the rent?"

"I wasn't thinking that," I said.

"Anyway, I'm baptized, ain't I?"

He groaned and slid his legs out in front of him. The hair on his leg was dark against the whiteness of his skin. I could see the scar on his shin and remembered when that bumper jack gave way and came down on his leg. Duny didn't even holler.

I sat down on the step next to him, my nose twitching.

Duny took a couple deep breaths, and his eyes focused in on me. "Will you stop," he said.

"Stop what?"

"Twitching like a goddang rabbit."

I held my nose still with my finger. "It just goes off like that," I said.

"Maybe you need a carrot," he said.

"I don't even like carrots."

He rubbed at his neck and looked at the ceiling. "It's the Roland blood what makes you crazy, you know. Next thing you'll be looking for a cross with wheels on it."

"Dad says it's the Franklins who are drunks and ne'er-do-wells."

"Something is wrong with my insides," he said. "I can't go to work like this."

"I can do it," I said. "Who knows that job better than me?"

"Suppose no one would know the difference," he said.

"We need the money, Duny."

"If you get caught, it was none of my doings," he said.

I worked the shift without a hitch, staying clear of the night jailer by ducking out the side door at the end of the shift, and I was nearly back to the room when I saw red lights flashing up ahead. As I got closer, I could see the ambulance pulled into the alley behind the flower shop and a cop car parked behind it. The stairwell door to the apartment was wide open, and all the lights were on.

Just as I reached the door, two men came out carrying a stretcher with Uncle Duny on it. He was naked, save for his jockey shorts. His eyes were shut, and his jaw was clenched.

"What's going on?" I asked.

"Would you mind moving out of the way, sir?" one of the attendants said.

"Where you taking him?"

"To the hospital," he said.

"Is he going to be OK?"

"Not if you don't get out of the way."

I stepped aside. The cop came out of the door and said, "Who are you?"

"Jacob Roland. I live here. Is he going to be OK?"

"How should I know?" he said.

"That's my uncle, Duny Franklin."

The cop hooked his hand over his sidearm. "There isn't a law officer in the country doesn't know Duny. He's the one called for an ambulance. These rides don't come free, you know."

I looked down at Uncle Duny, whose face had the pallor of milk, and he was wet with sweat. He was groaning and mumbling something, but I couldn't make it out.

The attendant said, "He looks like shit, boys. We better get him in."

"I'll follow," I said.

The cop moved past me. He turned and pointed his finger at me. "Don't mean you can break the law so stay back clear, you understand."

My foot jumped on the clutch as I pulled in behind the ambulance. The siren went off, shriveling my stomach. I followed as best I could. Pulling into the hospital parking lot, I headed for the emergency room, and I could hear Duny screaming, screaming something dreadful as they unloaded him from the ambulance.

The emergency room doors swung open, and they wheeled him in, his screams filling the hospital and the hearts of everyone who heard them. Only I knew that in those screams was all the rejection and fear that Duny had suffered throughout his life.

My eyes brimmed, and my throat closed. I covered my mouth and leaned into the wall. And when the screaming stopped, so did my hope.

I sat alone in the waiting room. People came and went. A baseball game played out on the television that sat in the corner. Finally, a doctor came, a big man with a farmer's hands. He sat across from me and told me that Uncle Duny had suffered an abdominal aortic aneurysm, that, in short, his aorta had blown out like a retread tire. I searched for my handkerchief to blow my nose, and when I looked up, the doctor was watching the ball game over my shoulder.

I didn't go back to the room that night but drove home instead. I'd have to tell Mom and the others what had happened. Uncle Duny had had his faults and was always full of complaints, but whatever they were, they were silent now.

CHAPTER 29

My mother grew quiet and turned her head away when I told her that Uncle Duny had died. The kids stood at her side, twisting back and forth. While they knew Duny, they knew him in a different way than me and Mom. Dad listened from the kitchen and then went out to finish his chores. In the end, Duny's death didn't come as much of a surprise to anyone, I suppose. Things had been going downhill for a long time, and we all knew it.

Arrangements were made with the local funeral home for his burial on Casket Hill, a simple casket and a single spray of flowers. He'd left nothing behind, save for a grocery bag full of paperback westerns and his old military uniform. I didn't tell anyone how he died, the details, the way his aorta had blown out and how he'd screamed that awful way. Some things were just best left to eternity.

Turned out that there wasn't a preacher in the county willing to preach Duny's funeral. He'd lived his life pretty rough and had left little doubt about his skepticism of religion in general. For a while, it looked like he'd have to be buried without the assistance of clergy, that is, until Uncle Ward knocked on our door. He had dark circles under his eyes, and he stood there with his hands in his pockets.

He said to Mom, "I'd like to preach Duny's funeral, Vega."

Mom looked at Dad and then at me. "I don't know, Ward," she said.

"It was a misunderstanding between us," he said. "I'd like to make it up. I've been called as a proper servant of God, and I could send him off right."

"What do you think, Abbott?" Mom asked.

Dad shrugged. "He's your brother, Vega."

She looked at Uncle Ward. "I'd expect scripture read and maybe a song."

"Therefore we were buried with Him through baptism into death," he said.

"Well, I guess we'll figure on it," Mom said. "There's not much in the way of pay what with the place payment."

"This being family, we'll make do," he said. "Casket Hill?"

She nodded. "You got a suit, Ward?"

"Burned up in Duny's fire."

"Jacob, go get your dad's suit."

"That's my only suit," Dad said.

"You can stand in the back, Abbott, but the preacher's got to be up front. Bring it back here when you're done with it, Ward. Abbott's figuring on being buried in it himself."

That night after supper, Mom and I went out on the front porch. Dad went on to bed, being tired as he was from building fence. She fixed a pallet for me, and then we sat in the swing. The night was clear as glass, and the stars were sprinkled out in the blackness.

"We got that letter from the college," she said.

"I know," I said.

"What happened?"

"I was never much for coming up from behind," I said.

"We could fix up the separator house," she said. "You could get a job fence building with your dad."

"I shouldn't be moving back home at this age," I said. "I'll look for a job in town."

"No one figured on a second family, Jacob, and your dad losing his railroad job. No one figured on Gea dying like that and then me coming up pregnant at my age. It's not all your fault, you see."

"I just got to thinking I was something I'm not," I said. "But it was like riding a mule in a horse race. This new job's going to get me through, so you aren't to worry. I'm relieved to be out from under all that college nonsense anyway."

"Well," she said, "I better get on to bed. Duny's viewing is tomorrow."

"Looking on the dead is a hard thing to ask of folks," I said. "I wish there was another way."

She walked to the door and paused. "Just look at his hands, Jacob. Everything you want to remember is there."

We buried Uncle Duny on a clear and fine day. The Cimarron sprawled out beneath the mesa like a silk braid, and the air smelled of sunflowers and sage. Locusts sounded out from the grass like a string orchestra.

The undertaker arranged Duny's casket over the open grave, having no pallbearers as such. Uncle Ward stood next to it, Bible in hand, looking a bit saggy in Dad's suit. Dad stood in the back, wearing a white shirt and tie and managing the kids.

Uncle Ward took a moment to survey the surroundings and gather up his thoughts. Adjusting the knot on his tie, he said, "We have come here this day to bury Duny Franklin on Casket Hill. Let it be duly noted that he's on the Franklins' side, though there is an empty Roland slot not that far away.

"Most of us know that Duny lived his life as he saw fit. While I can't tell you he was a godly man, I can tell you that he was baptized by my own hand, which should reassure any doubters of his intentions. But of course judgment ain't ours altogether. It could be a hard case to be made for Duny, given his building of that saloon and hiring up a pole dancer, not to mention the destruction of my own rolling cross. Whether he gets in or sent elsewhere is a matter settled between him and God, who might be more forgiving than some of us humans.

"Now, Duny's dear sister Vega has asked me to read some scripture. While we all know that Duny had his faults, who among us does not? Some called him stubborn. I prefer to think of him as a strong and determined man whose natural tendency for goodness was destroyed by drink.

"With that in mind, I have chosen Isaiah 5, verses 11–12." He cleared his throat. "Woe to those who rise early in the morning, that they may run after strong drink, who tarry late into the evening as wine inflames them! They have lyre and harp, tambourine and flute and wine at their feasts, but they do not regard the deeds of the LORD, or see the work of his hands."

Uncle Ward closed his Bible. "Now shall we sing 'Blessed Assurance'?"

Ward's voice rose high and confident above everyone else's, a haunting rendition of the hymn, and a cloud drifted over, casting its shadow on the mesa. I could see Duny's Mortem up on the cap rock, watching over the dead as was his duty. And then I spotted Danny, too, standing next to him. He had his hat in his hand, just like that day we buried Gea.

Uncle Ward finished his song and stepped back from the grave to wait for the casket to be lowered into the ground. He said a quick prayer, and we all turned to go to the car. Mom took me by the arm. "I'll be along shortly," she said. I waited a bit to make sure she was all right. She approached Ward, and I overheard her say, "Get that suit back liked you promised, Ward. And never darken my doorway again."

CHAPTER 30

I drove back to my room that night, mostly to pick up my things and try to make some important decisions. I found Uncle Duny's last check in the mailbox and signed his name to it. He wouldn't have minded, and it was enough to pay up the rent and give me some thinking time.

I laid my latest notes out across the bed in the order they'd been written. I cut sections out with scissors and arranged them in such a way they might be understood more or less as a whole. Those pages represented a lot of hours, wasted hours, I suppose, scribblings that in the end no one cared about but me.

I barely slept that night or for several nights thereafter. I let the words consume me, take me back to places that I could just remember. I can't be certain why I did it. I just needed to, I suppose. Sometimes I fell asleep on the floor, papers stacked all around me, only to awaken in the night and begin again. Now and then Danny would show up, looking on from the doorway with his hands in his pockets, saying nothing the whole time. I think he was mad at me, because if I asked him anything, he would just shrug and walk away.

Maybe things got away from me a little during that time, I mean what with Duny's death and me getting kicked out of college. That twitch came back into my nose with a vengeance, and I developed this sort of shuffling walk, like I had one leg shorter than the other, like an old peg-leg pirate, and I couldn't make it right.

The days passed, but it wasn't long before I ran out of food and money. I was on my way to the store to spend the last of it when I decided to stop in at the station again. The owner was sitting on an old school bus seat that had been bolted to the floor.

"Yeah," he said. "It's open still. I'll be needing a part-time lube man. You got experience?"

"I grew up around machinery," I said.

He took the ring of keys that was fastened to a retractable chain fastened to his belt and opened the pop machine, pulling out an Orange Crush. He took a swig, set the bottle down on the seat, and crossed his legs. The hair on his leg had been worn away by the top of his boot.

"My name's Clyde," he said.

"Jacob," I said. "Jacob Roland."

"You a college boy?"

"Farm kid, mostly," I said.

"Last boy I had in here left the oil plug loose on a Chevy pickup. Cost me a month's income. The little son of a bitch is lucky to still be alive."

"You'd have to be pretty damn stupid to do that," I said.

He looked me over. "I need a man here from three to closing time, Mondays through Fridays. Sometimes you'll have lube jobs. Other times it's filling up gas and washing windshields. When you ain't doing neither one of those, you can sit on your ass and listen to the radio."

"Sounds like my kind of work," I said.

"The one thing I won't truck is stealing. I catch you stealing, it's all over. Understood?"

"I ain't a thief."

"You look a tad frail for the work, but I'm willing to give you a try."

"When do I start?"

"Tomorrow, and see if you can't stop that goddang twitching. I don't want you scaring off no customers."

"Yes, sir," I said. "Tomorrow at three."

I was down to tomato soup and soda crackers before I got my first check. But I figured out right away how to jimmy the vending machine at the filling station for candy bars and peanuts. Cleaning the bathroom was ever as bad as the courthouse bathroom, but late in the evening things usually quieted down, giving me a little time on my own.

So, one Monday morning, I went to the college bookstore, picked up the required reading list for English majors, and headed for the library. Having gotten considerably faster at doing lube jobs and cleaning restrooms, I managed to squeeze in several hours of reading time right there on the job.

Two months later, I'd read every book for every introductory class for English majors. Not only did I manage a substantial reading schedule but I was able to maintain my notes with some regularity.

What I hadn't managed was my physical downhill slide. My sleep was sporadic at best, and my weight dropped almost weekly. My left leg went numb to the point that I sometimes had to drag it along behind me. People watched me, especially children, who would stop and stare and stick their fingers up their noses. Sometimes I would lunge at them or make loud noises just to watch them jump. One mother turned me in to the store manager, who threatened to call the police.

I started taking long walks late at night, going nowhere really. I'd walk until exhausted but would still struggle to sleep. I wrote long letters to Rachael, who had nearly stopped responding. But with each letter I received, hope returned, and I'd flood her with more letters.

I found bathing to be time consuming and tedious. My boss threatened me, saying as how his customers were complaining that I smelled. So I started bathing again but quit shaving to compensate for the loss of time I spent bathing. My boss just shook his head, saying as how I looked like a goddang serial killer.

Sometimes my words didn't come out right, or I couldn't find the right one without thinking for a long time. People would look at me funny and walk away. On those days, I would hit bottom, convinced that my life was not worth living, and I would return to my notes. There was something about the process that I needed.

The welcome back sign was set up on the campus lawn and a new year began. With increasing anxiety, I watched the students return. They came by the station with their backpacks and their books and their excited chatter. At some point, my courage returned, I suppose, or my fear receded enough that it no longer blinded me.

I needed to talk. I needed to talk to someone who understood. I thought about Rachael first, of course, but she was busy with her own classes. If only Danny were around. He could call me goofball, and everything would suddenly fall into place.

And so on a Friday morning, I took a bath, shaved the beard, and went to the bursar to see if I could enroll. The answer was no, not until I talked to an advisor. I was sent to another building and assigned a number that would be called at the first available opening. I waited for an hour. The twitch in my nose returned, and my palms sweat. I stood to leave, and they called my name.

"Cubicle three," the secretary said. "Ms. Kate Hilton will see you, and take this folder with you."

Ms. Kate Hilton was tall and slender and stood to shake my hand. She had long auburn hair that she'd pulled back over her shoulder. She smiled, and her eyes lit, affirming the smile as authentic.

"Mr. Roland?" she said.

"Yes," I said. "Jacob Roland."

"Please sit. May I have your file?"

I handed her my file and waited as she glanced through it. I could smell her perfume, a light citrus smell, and she wore a small cross on a gold chain around her neck.

"You're an English major?" she asked.

"Yes."

"And you've been on academic suspension?"

My ears heated, and I nodded. "Yes," I said.

"And now you are wanting to re-enroll?"

"Yes."

She finished reading my folder and closed it, placing her hands on top. "I'm only a graduate assistant to Dr. Foss, the department chairperson, Mr. Roland, and do not have the authority to grant your request one way or the other. However, Dr. Foss does take my recommendations seriously. Now, would you care to tell me why you think this semester will be different?"

I sat there for some time looking at my hands. "I don't know that it will be. I mean, I can't know for sure."

"You understand that there are limits to the number of suspensions you can have before you're permanently restricted from enrollment?"

"Yes," I said. "I have read all the books this time."

"Pardon me?"

"I've read all the required intro books that were listed for the major."

"All of them?"

"As far as I know."

"That's quite remarkable."

"My background is pretty limited," I said. "I thought it might give me a head start."

"Your previous grades will have to be averaged in. It takes a long time to raise them. You do understand?"

"Yes," I said.

"And you hold a job as well?"

"Part time," I said.

"And no other financial assistance?"

I shook my head. "I live pretty close to the bone," I said.

She stood, opened the filing cabinet behind her, and placed my file inside. She sat down and pushed her hair back with her fingers.

"I'm going to recommend to Dr. Foss to give you another chance, Mr. Roland. I'd suggest you limit your credit hours to half time."

I started to object, but she held up her hand. "It's only a suggestion, but it's for your own good. Classes begin in two weeks. Come back in a week, and I'll tell you what Dr. Foss has decided."

"Half time?" I said.

She nodded. "If she approves your application, you will have to maintain at least a 2.5 grade point average with no failing grade. Are we clear?"

"Yes," I said.

"Do you have a phone number where you can be reached?"

"At work," I said, and gave her the number. "Miss Hilton—"

She looked up at me. "I'll call when I know," she said.

CHAPTER 31

She didn't call until Friday, leaving a message that I should come in the following Monday. That meant an entire weekend without me knowing the decision. Early Monday morning, I was waiting on her when she arrived.

I opened the door and took the books out of her arms. "Mr. Roland," she said. "You're early."

"You've a lot of books," I said.

"Graduate school," she said. "There's never enough time. Come on in."

I waited as she set her books down. She turned and said, "Have a chair, Mr. Roland. Now, I talked to Dr. Foss, and she has agreed to let you continue with your studies, but with one caveat: you will be on probation until such time as you get your grades in order."

"I will," I said, smiling. "I promise I will."

"I do have a question."

"Yes?"

"An English major strikes me as an odd choice for a farm boy."

"I'm not sure," I said. "But it is basically about stories, isn't it?"

"I suppose it is in a way."

"That's what I like. If things get out of order, they can be set right. It can all make sense then. That's how it is. That's what I want."

She looked at me. "Well, you're right about one thing. Telling stories has been a human pastime for millennia, since they painted hieroglyphics on cave walls, I suppose. OK, so make it work this time, Mr. Roland, and I'll see you in here after midterms."

I started immediately and with a determination just short of maniacal. I reread the books I'd just read. I made comprehensive and detailed notes. I sat on the front row and listened to the lectures with total concentration. On one occasion, I looked up to see my professor standing at my desk.

"Mr. Roland?" she said.

"Yes, ma'am?"

"Class is over. You can go now."

I looked around at the empty seats. "Oh," I said.

"While I admire your dedication, Mr. Roland, you need to remember that this is not the only thing to life."

"Yes," I said. "I'll remember."

By midterm, I'd taken a dozen pop quizzes and written my first essay. I handed them to Ms. Kate Hilton and waited as she examined them.

"Great," she said, looking up. "These are commendable."

I smiled, hearing her say it that way. "I could have done better," I said.

"Mr. Roland—"

"Do you think you could call me Jacob?"

"If you prefer, and my name is Kate."

"Yes, Kate," I said.

"Your professors tell me that, well, that your obsession with perfection may be getting out of hand."

"I don't understand."

"That you might be trying too hard. You don't have to be perfect, you know."

"I'm far from that," I said.

"And you are still working a job as well?"

"Yes," I said.

"And how is your financial situation?"

I lowered my head. "It's the books mostly," I said. "They are costly. I have trouble coming up with the money for all of them, and the library copies are always checked out."

Kate got up and walked to the window. "I'm impressed with your progress, of course. And I don't want to see you fail because of financial difficulties."

"I'll make it one way or the other," I said.

"I've a suggestion, a way that might help. You see, it so happens I have many of these books in my possession, many of which are the ones you'll be using in your classes."

"Your own personal library?"

"Not exactly a library, but I've kept most of the books I've used over the years for reference. I have a small building back of my house. I'm offering it to you as a place to study. You can use the books as well." She turned. "It's an offer, that's all. You're welcome as long as you leave things as you found them."

"It would be OK, you think?"

"You might find a few of them outdated, but most are solid intro books that haven't changed for some time."

"It would get me through," I said.

"I'll leave the key under the mat. You may go there any time you wish. Here's my address. Be sure to turn out the lights and lock the door when you've finished with your work."

I flew home, my papers stuffed in my back pocket. To have made such grades and won the confidence of Kate was more than I could ever have anticipated. I was taking the steps two at a time when I noticed an envelope in the mailbox. Maybe it was a letter from Rachael? Could my winning streak really end with yet one more prize? I held the envelope to the stairwell light and recognized my mother's hand. Mom never wrote. I opened the letter.

> *Dear Jacob:*
>
> *I'm writing this to let you know your dad has been sick. He's been to the doctor, but they aren't sure what is wrong. They are going to make some more tests to find out. Sometime when you are off work, you should come see him. p.s. The sheriff picked up your Uncle Ward when he tried to preach a sermon at the high school prom dance.*
>
> *Mom*

Dad sick? He was never sick, and I'd never known him to go to the doctor for anything. Soon as I got ahead a little to buy gas for the Mercury, I'd go. In the meantime, I'd drop her a note and tell her all about my grades.

I waited until the next day after work to look up Kate's address. Her old study was a small one-room building near the alley behind her house, a converted storage shed by the looks of it. There was a small air conditioner in the window and an old desk against the back wall. Some of Kate's personal things were still on the desk: a photograph of her high school graduation, a certificate for academic achievement, and a small porcelain doll with the nose chipped off. From the desk, I could see the back of Kate's house and a gray cat sleeping in the window.

I went there every day that week, and every day that cat was sleeping in that same window, but not once did I see Kate. With its privacy and books, the study allowed me to move more deeply into my work than ever before.

It was on a Saturday morning when I noticed the cat was gone from the window. And that's when I spotted Kate in the backyard. She was in her pajamas picking flowers from her garden.

I opened the door. "Good morning," I said.

"Oh, my God," she said, putting her hands on her chest. "You scared the life out of me."

"Oh, I'm sorry," I said. "I didn't think about it being your day off. Maybe I should go now?"

She pushed her hair back from her face. "Don't be ridiculous. You startled me is all."

It was the first time I'd seen Kate without makeup, like a pencil sketch with all the colors yet to be added.

"But you might need it yourself," I said.

"I have an office at the university, so the place is yours to use."

"It's been a big help," I said.

"And the books?" she asked.

"They're almost all still in use, and I don't have to worry about getting them back to the library."

"I have coffee on," she said. "Would you care for a cup?"

"I wouldn't want to bother."

"I wouldn't have asked," she said.

"Sure, I'd love a coffee."

She finished gathering her flowers, and I followed her into the house. Books and papers were scattered about on her kitchen table.

"Grading research papers," she said. "It's endless."

"I bet you're good at it," I said, taking up a seat.

She put the flowers in a vase and poured our coffees. Taking a chair, she said, "I hear you're doing well in your classes."

"The study has been a big help," I said.

She sipped her coffee and looked at me through the steam. "Dr. Foss tells me your essays are quite good, that you have a natural ability."

"I write a lot that way," I said. "I just record things, for no reason really."

"You keep a journal? That's commendable, Jacob, and a bit old-fashioned."

"Like a girl and her diary?" I said.

"Or like someone who thinks deeply about things."

"I've this box full buried at the end of our shelterbelt. It's under a tree that looks exactly like a woman holding a broom. She's the witch, I'd guess you'd say."

"Perhaps I could read some of your entries sometime, something you would share?"

"You wouldn't care about any of that old stuff," I said.

"What do you intend to do with them?"

"Do with them?"

"You have a purpose, I assume?"

"They help me think," I said. "That's all."

"More coffee?"

"I better get going," I said, rising.

"Jacob," she said, "I don't give out much personal advice, because it's rarely listened to anyway, but I'd like you to remember that the world will always underestimate you, so you don't need to do it to yourself."

"Yes," I said, "I'll remember, and thanks for the coffee."

CHAPTER 32

With work, and the increasing pressures of school, the days passed like minutes. To date, my grades were in the top percentiles, though the Chaucer class remained difficult and remote for me. I anticipated the final to be a nightmare in the waiting, and to make matters worse, I'd not heard from Rachael in weeks.

Nor had I forgotten Kate's invitation to read some of my journal entries, though I'd failed to follow through. Her request, frightening in its way, was also encouraging. Finally, I made the selection. Though the entries were personal, I trusted her and so placed a dozen pages in an envelope and left them on her back porch. An hour hadn't passed before I regretted the decision with everything in me.

That evening, I closed up the station as usual, drove within a block of Kate's house, and parked. Perhaps she hadn't spotted the envelope. Perhaps it was still there on the back porch. I got out and walked to where I could see her bedroom window. Her light was on, but the curtains were drawn. Slipping through the darkness, I made my way to the back porch to find the envelope gone.

I barely slept that night, or the rest of the week for that matter, thinking about those entries, about her reading my thoughts and what she might think. I'd just finished the Chaucer test and was putting my things in order when someone called my name from the doorway. I looked up to see the department secretary signaling with her finger.

"Are you Jacob Roland?" she asked.

"Yes," I said.

She handed me a piece of paper. "Ms. Kate Hilton asked me to deliver this."

"Oh, thanks," I said, my heart pounding.

As soon as she was gone, I opened the note. It said, "Could you stop by to see me tonight after work? Kate."

That afternoon I left the gas cap off one of the customer's cars by mistake, and he had to come back to get it. When closing time finally came, I couldn't find the key to the door, searching in vain for ten minutes, only to find it where I'd left it on the counter next to the cash register.

By the time I reached Kate's back door, I was in a breathless state. I knocked and waited. When the porch light came on, I jumped and nearly stepped backward off the porch.

Kate, dressed in jeans and a white T, smiled at me through the screen door. "Hi," she said. "I'm glad you've come."

"I got your note."

"Come in, Jacob."

I followed her into the kitchen, and we sat at the table where we had sat before. "I wanted to visit," she said. "Could you wait a minute?" She returned shortly with my journal notes in hand. "I've had a chance to read these," she said.

"I should have picked those up," I said. "It's just stuff. I mean—"

"Jacob," she said.

"Yes?"

"Could you shut up now?"

I nodded and buried my hands between my legs.

"I was busy the first part of the week and just got around to reading these yesterday. What I want to say is that I'm impressed with your writing. You still have plenty to learn, so don't get overconfident. But you've an innate ability. You see yourself and the world through a curved glass, which makes the common uncommon. Do you understand what I'm saying?"

I sat there for several moments, my head humming. "I think so."

"I would like to show these to the department chair. I would like for her to see your work because . . . because I think you have potential, and Dr. Foss can go a long way in getting you headed in the right direction. Sometimes classroom assignments don't get at the real person, you see. Sometimes you have to know the person up close, and that's what these do."

"Maybe I can find something better for her to read," I said.

"What you gave me will do fine, but I need your permission."

"What if she doesn't like them?"

"I wouldn't do this if I didn't think it worthwhile."

"I don't know," I said.

"Jacob, it's time for you to step up and let the world know who you are."

"I'll do what you think," I said.

She came to where I was and put her hand on my shoulder. It burned, and I could smell her perfume. "You remember what I said about believing in yourself?"

I nodded. "Yes."

"Well, this is one of those times. I'll let you know."

It was nearly a week before I could get loose from the filling station to go home. With only a few days of break left, I locked up my room, filled the Mercury with gas, and headed out. As I drove from town, I could see the campus in the rearview mirror. It was an exciting place to be now, a dream in the making.

When I turned into the yard, Dad's pickup was parked under the old elm tree, and the kids were playing on the rope swing down on the creek. The rope had been tied high in the branches of an old cotton-wood tree. I knocked on the door and waited.

When no one answered, I opened the door and stuck my head in. "Hello," I said. "Anyone here?"

"Jacob?" Mom said from the back of the house.

"Can I come in?"

"I'm doing the washing," she said.

I set my things inside the door and made my way down the hall. The house was a shambles, something Mom never permitted. She hugged me.

"I'm glad you could make it," she said. "Your dad isn't doing well."

"What is it?"

She shrugged. "He's lost weight and won't eat more 'n a sparrow. Most of all, he's given up hope, I think. He just sits around pining about how he can't work and how the world has left him behind. His breathing is all rough, too, like he can't take a breath deep enough to do him some good. I don't know what's going to happen if he don't come out of it soon."

"How is it for money, him not working and all?"

She held her elbows in her palms and looked out the bedroom window. "Gea's Social Security money came through, and we get some government surplus coming in, flour, sugar, peanut butter, and such. The kids been helping out with picking the garden. Cash money is short, but when was it ever otherwise? Miss having milk and cream, but your dad just ain't up to fighting cows morning and night."

"Where's he now?" I asked.

"Back there listening to the ball game on the radio. That's about all he does anymore."

I found him sitting in his chair. He had a pillow behind his head, and a dirty dish was sitting on a nail keg next to his chair. The game was turned up loud.

"Dad?" I said.

He looked up at me as if at first he didn't recognize me. His skin was pale, the color of wheat straw, and his hands lay in his lap like broken twigs. There was a staleness about the room.

"Those idiots couldn't hit a ball if it was tied on a string," he said.

"How you feeling?" I asked.

"When you finishing up with that school? Your mom could use some help around here."

"I'm done for the summer," I said. "You feeling out of sorts, are you?"

"Can't breathe," he said. "Can't tie my shoes or take a piss without hanging on to something."

"What you think it is?" I asked.

He looked up at me, his eyes faded and milky. "Who the hell knows? Maybe I'm as crazy as that goddamn Ward. Maybe they ought to take me to the lunatic asylum too."

"What do the doctors say?"

"Say I smoked too many roll-your-owns and ate too much dust on the back of a John Deere. But what the hell do they know? Nothing, that's what."

Heat crawled up my neck and settled in my ears at his words. "You'll get better, you'll see."

"I want to finish my game now," he said.

"You can't just give up," I said.

"I can't breathe. I can't eat. I can't sleep."

"Why is this happening to you?" I said.

"It ain't," he said. "It's happening to all of us."

CHAPTER 33

I didn't wait for Mom to finish the wash or the kids to come in. I drove instead to Casket Hill, pulled over, and shut off the engine. I walked through the little cemetery, Duny's grave, Gea's, and, just beyond, the Rolands', all so much a part of my life, now silent with their gods and their sins.

I smoked a cigarette under the soft hooting of an owl far up in the rocks. I thought about where Dad might lie, and where I might some day lie as well. I thought of all the hard work he did to protect us and how it might now fade away forever in the silence of this lonely place. I had failed to save any of them. My penance was to lose them forever.

I drove down the mesa with its narrow curves and looming rocks. My intent was to go home and say good-bye, but as I approached, I cut westward instead to Dunyville. To go home now would be to watch him die and to listen to Mom rise alone in the cold dawns.

At Dunyville, I could see the railroad tracks racing off in the moonlight, could smell the ashes still hanging in the wind. I could see the stone foundation of Duny's saloon scattered about the prairie.

From there, I drove straight back to my room and put home and sickness out of my mind. I moved into my work with as much concentration and force as I could muster. I tried not to think of other people reading my personal thoughts or what they might think of them. But it was there in the back of my mind the whole time, like a stone in my shoe.

I saw little of Kate during this time, what with her being so busy with her own work. Sometimes we'd see each other in passing during the day, but neither of us had a moment to spare. I'd been back several weeks when she came to the door of her study on a Saturday morning.

"Jacob?" she said, opening the door. "Are you here?"

"Yes," I said. "Do you need to use your books?"

The open door framed her against the morning sun, and the smell of her flower garden came in with her. She pushed her hair back from her face.

"No," she said. "I just wanted to tell you that Dr. Foss got around to reading your journal entries."

My heart raced. "Oh," I said.

"She is sorry in taking so long. She's quite busy, you know."

"It's all right," I said.

"Well, while she finds your writing is good, it lacks a certain maturity, a polish, but she thinks you have a natural ability, that you might well flourish given the right circumstances."

My ears burned at the words. No one had ever said anything like that to me before. "Gosh," I said. "She really said that?"

Kate sat down in the chair across from me. She was wearing shorts and was barefoot. Her legs were brown, and there was a delicate gold chain drooping about her ankle.

"And so do I," she said. "But here's the thing, Jacob, ability isn't always enough. What I'm saying is that it's necessary to make the most of one's opportunities."

"I'm working hard," I said.

"I know that, but you're trying to hold down a difficult job, pay tuition, buy books, meet your rent. In the end, there's simply not enough time or energy to take full advantage of your education."

I closed my book. "It's the only way I have."

"It isn't the only way."

"What do you mean?"

"The department has a budget available to hire work-study help."

"Work-study?"

"Students who show promise in the discipline are employed by the department. They work for the professors. They do whatever needs to be done."

"They do?"

"While it doesn't pay a lot, it gives students an opportunity to see how things work, to meet the right people. It's an education within an education. It's how I started myself, and it led to a graduate assistantship. I've learned so much from just being around the office."

"Yeah," I said. "I can see how that would help."

"The thing is, Dr. Foss thinks you might be a good candidate, and, frankly, so do I."

"You mean for the work-study?"

"Exactly."

"And I wouldn't have to work at the station?"

"You'd be working for Dr. Foss and the other professors. What do you think?"

"You think I could do it?"

"I want you to have a chance, and this is an excellent opportunity. There is another item I'd like to discuss. I rarely use this little building for anything other than storage for my books. It has all the amenities needed to make a livable room out of it. I'm offering it to you as a place to live while you complete your degree."

"To stay here?"

"We could store the books elsewhere if they are in the way."

"I don't mind the books," I said. "But I don't know if I can afford it."

"You can afford it," she said. "I want you to stay here for free, with the understanding that you will fully apply yourself to your studies."

A lump came to my throat. "I don't know what to say," I said.

"You don't have to say anything. People helped me out along the way. This is part of my payback. Now, you give notice at your job, make application for the program, and I'll tell Dr. Foss of your decision." She reached into her pocket. "Here's the key to the room."

"I could mow your lawn," I said.

"Yes," she said, "you can mow my lawn."

I hummed all the way to work, canceled a late oil change appointment, and ate three candy bars out of the vending machine. At the end of the shift, I wrote out a note saying that I wouldn't be back to work and put it on top of the cash register.

I spent the next three days moving my things into my new room, and bright and early on Monday morning, I applied for the work-study program. Three days later, I received a letter of acceptance and reported to work at the English Department.

The department was located in the basement of the oldest building on campus. The floors were marble, the ceilings were high, and the windows looked out at ground level. The professors' offices surrounded a main suite where the secretary sat. The work-study students each had a small cubicle and a locker for their belongings. I was given a key to the main office and told that I could use my cubicle day or night but that I was never to enter the professors' offices uninvited or to breach their private files. I was then taken to see Dr. Foss, who looked up at me from behind her desk. She was frail, with piercing eyes, and had the slightest hint of a mustache.

"I've looked over your journal," she said. "I've read your writings, and you have been recommended by Kate Hilton, for whom I have a high regard. That's why you are here." She took off her glasses and laid them on the desk. "Your job here is to do whatever the professors ask, on time, with full commitment, and with absolute integrity. Do you understand?"

"Yes," I said.

"This is an opportunity for you to see the inner workings of academia, to meet people who might matter in your career. I expect you to fulfill your obligations to the department and to maintain your grades while doing so."

I nodded. "I will."

"Because you will be working closely with the faculty, you will be privy to information and conversations that other students will not. It's incumbent on you to exercise discretion about what you see and hear. To do otherwise will lead to your dismissal."

My mouth had turned to dust. "I understand," I said.

"Good. Congratulations on your new job. My door is open, and you're welcome to talk to me about anything at any time."

"Thank you, Dr. Foss."

She handed me a note. "Here is your first task."

I was to go to the library and find research articles for a speech that she would be giving at an upcoming conference. And it was with some trepidation that I presented my first task to the university librarian, who then personally guided me through several options. At the end of three hours, I handed the articles to Dr. Foss, who looked them over, nodding her approval.

And I was to be paid for this, without the heat and sweat of manual labor, without the humiliation of sweeping floors and cleaning toilets. By some miracle, I had been lifted from the dirt and set on a high shelf. Yes, it was the lowest job in academia, but the highest for me in what had before been a world of grind and blisters.

Driven by new possibilities, I doubled my efforts. My grades soared to new heights, and my reputation as an excellent student was secured. The demands of the department were onerous, the deadlines demanding. But they always came first, my own work to be completed in the wee hours of the night. To sit still was to fall dead asleep. Time was of the essence, and it sped away without limits. Focus and concentration waned. Dreams morphed into vivid and terrifying nightmares.

More often than not, I would climb from bed with my heart still pounding for what was surely near death. By the time spring break arrived, I'd dropped ten pounds, now slack, exhausted, and in need of peace. Personal duties lay dormant, lay waiting for some imaginary point in the future. I'd heard nothing from home or from Rachael, but in that lack of contact, I'd scrubbed out one more minute for myself.

Kate had taken on an undergraduate class in addition to her normal assignments and was seldom accessible for conversation. She'd stopped coming to her garden, though on occasion I would see her bedroom light on late at night.

Spring break came at last, like the sliding back of a cell door. It came with a blinding light after months of near darkness. It came with freedom and escape and the first letter I'd had in weeks from Rachael. Her folks had left for a two-week vacation to Florida. She was coming to visit her grandparents, and would I care to pick her up Wednesday at seven?

I sat back and reread the letter. She was coming, and it was like a voice from an alien world, from out of the distant past. I'd awakened suddenly from a dream and was now at last ready to step into the daylight.

CHAPTER 34

I stood on her grandmother's porch, the same as I had so many months earlier, and with the same proportionate terror. The fact that I had carved out a place in academia, unfathomable to me then as now, still failed to calm me. I had thought so long and hard about being with Rachael that the reality of it was now terrifying.

I rang the doorbell and ran my fingers through my hair. I could see her grandmother through the diamond-shaped window in the door. She was slower to rise and more bent in stature than I'd remembered, but she approached with the same poise.

She turned on the porch light and opened the door. "Jacob," she said. "Won't you come in? Rachael is not quite ready."

I tried to clear my throat but emitted a peculiar hooting sound instead. "Yes," I finally managed to say.

I followed her into the living room, where she pointed to a chair across from where Rachael's grandfather sat. He had a newspaper in his hands, which he folded across his lap to look at me. He had that dried apple look that old men in particular get.

"Rachael tells me you're in college now?" he said.

I threaded my fingers together. "I'm on a work-study program," I said.

Her grandmother sat down on the couch next to me. I could smell her perfume, like vanilla, like cookies baking in the oven.

"Is that like a scholarship?" she asked.

"I work for the university, for the English Department."

"They pay you for working while you attend college?"

"Yes," I said.

"Doesn't that take away from your studies?"

"It's a real opportunity to learn about how things function."

"I should think one would be better off as a full-time student," she said. "But then I suppose things have changed a good deal since I was a student. And we were so sorry to hear about your sister."

"Yes," I said.

"So terrible, and then with the babies so close together."

"They're the size of bucket calves now," I said.

"Bucket calves?"

"You know, healthy, a little ornery."

Her grandfather set the newspaper on the coffee table. "And what about your father?" he asked.

"Oh, he's fine."

"I understood him to be out of work?"

"You know the railroad," I said. "But he's been working here and there until it opens up again."

"I should think that kind of labor would be hard for a man his age."

"He's pretty tough," I said.

Her grandmother crossed her legs and bobbed her foot. "Oh, here's Rachael now."

Rachael stood in the doorway with her shoulders back, the way she sometimes stood, erect and proud. She smiled, and my heart leapt. She'd changed, too, though I couldn't tell exactly how. She was more adult somehow, with her hair back and with small earrings that glittered under the lights.

"Hi," she said.

"Hi," I said, standing. "You look really nice."

"So do you. You've grown so tall."

"Oh," I said, looking at my feet. "You ready?"

She nodded and took my hand, leading me to the door. "Don't wait up, Grandmother," she said. "We'll probably get a bite to eat after the show."

We didn't speak until we were out of town. She sat at a distance, looking out the window. "I'm glad to see you," she finally said. "It's been forever, hasn't it?" She turned and looked at me, her eyes green in the dash lights. "Let's skip the show," she said. "We could have dinner somewhere and then talk. I've only a couple days before I have to leave. Do you know a place, just a burger or something?"

"Sure," I said, turning, "not far from here."

She slid over next to me and put her hand on my leg. "I've missed you," she said. "Life has been whizzing by, and you aren't anywhere to be seen."

"There it is," I said. "You can have burgers or burgers, your choice."

"To go," she said.

So we ate burgers in the car and listened to the radio. Afterward, she laid her head on my shoulder, and I could feel her warm breath on my neck. Then I drove up to Dunyville and parked on my lot. The sun set, and the stars winked on in the blackness. She took my hand, and we kissed.

"Do you come here often?" she said.

"I'm a landowner here," I said.

She looked at me through the darkness. "Oh, stop. Do you come up here with other girls, I mean?"

"I come here sometimes," I said. "But not so much with other girls."

She snuggled in. "That's what I wanted to hear."

I pulled her in close and kissed her again. She put her hand on my chest and nudged me away. Her eyes were jade buttons, and my head whirled a little at her being so close.

"You haven't written to me much lately," she said.

"I know," I said. "Going to college, working, and then with Gea's accident."

"Are you are still majoring in literature?"

"Same as you," I said. "So now we can talk about things."

She tuned in a radio station. "Don't you remember? I changed to economics. Literature is nice, I suppose, but one must prepare for the real world."

"I forgot, I guess. But you loved it so."

"Everyone talks about art and literature and all that, but what does it really matter when it comes down to it?"

"You mean it's not about money?"

"Money is important, Jacob. It's hard to deny it doesn't matter."

"This is your father's decision?" I said.

"My father is a successful businessman. What's wrong with that? It shouldn't just be dismissed."

"But you were so keen on the other," I said. "It seemed like it was everything to you."

She turned. "We all have to grow up, Jacob, especially if there's family involved. I mean, in the end, one's family must be taken into account. This is especially so for the man, the one who must provide. Don't you think?"

"The thing is, I rather like what I'm doing now, Rachael, and I'm pretty good at it. It feels right for me, like dropping an anchor in a storm. And my professors have been really supportive. They even like my writing, they said. They think I might have a knack for it."

"I'm sure they are supportive, but, well, it is *their* program, isn't it?"

"What do you mean?"

"I'm sure they want students in their program."

"I suppose, but—"

"I don't doubt what you're saying, Jacob, but a person should consider the consequences of his decisions on others as well. Oh, this is not something we have to resolve tonight, is it? We've plenty of time to work these things out." She took my face in her hands and kissed me again. "When people love each other, they make sacrifices. That's all I'm saying. They adjust. I want to be with you, but I also want my future to be secure and safe. You do see that, don't you?"

"Well, sure, I guess I do."

"You're just a bit impulsive, that's all, and it's fine to enjoy what you are doing while you're young. Of course, in the end, we all have to face the reality of making a living."

She leaned in and kissed me again, passionately this time, and I melted into her. Her breasts were warm and considerable against my chest, and I touched them briefly. She let me, and I touched them again, fervently, and then with abandon. She pushed me gently away.

"I hate to bring this up," she said, "but Grandmother will be worried."

"You mean now?"

"We should, really. She's old-fashioned that way."

"But I'll see you again before you leave?"

"The truth is that Grandmother has me scheduled to the last second. I was hoping we could have more time, but we'll write, won't we? And next summer, I plan on coming for the whole summer." She paused. "Jacob?" she said, turning my head with her hand.

"Yes?"

"You do love me, don't you?"

"I do," I said.

"Then nothing else matters, does it? We belong together, and we will do what we must to be together."

CHAPTER 35

I drove back that night thinking about Rachael and the things she had said. I drove with an ache inside me, like something had gone wrong that I was powerless to stop. I couldn't deny the influence she had over me. I would be what she wanted me to be. I would do what she wanted, because who was I to set the course of our lives?

As I came into town, I could see the Citadel on the hill and a few remaining lights still on in the dorms. Rachael had seen something in me that I had not. She'd seen my lack of focus, purpose, how my heart drove me into places I shouldn't go. Perhaps it was not too late to change, to become what she wanted. Perhaps when the semester ended, I would check out alternative majors, those more practical. I would find something every bit as fulfilling, and I would write her. She would be waiting, though she'd not said as much.

The semester ended with the same crushing weight as the others had. I scarcely had time to sleep. And with the praise of my writings still glowing in my memory, I worked at my journal whenever time permitted. In between, I'd get a letter off to Rachael, but mostly I studied.

Kate, too, labored under the demands of the semester's conclusion. I would sometimes see her bedroom light on in the night or hear her leave at sunrise. Her dedication was no less than mine, and the demands on her were burdensome.

On a Monday, I received a letter from Rachael. She had enjoyed seeing me very much and hoped that our talk had been useful. She had changed sororities and found the girls there much more interesting. They'd held two dances, complete with live music, and were having a garage sale the coming weekend in support of a local charity. She'd planned a weekend visit with her parents, and so perhaps I would not hear from her for a while. Her closing was simply "Rachael."

It was on a Saturday morning that I spotted Kate standing at her back door. She was still in her robe and unaware of my presence. I hesitated before opening my door to greet her. This was, after all, her home, and she had a right to expect privacy. But I stepped out and acknowledged her anyway.

"Good morning," I said.

"Good morning, Jacob," she said. "Excuse the robe. Just got up."

"Me too," I said. "I haven't seen you around."

She came out, shading her eyes with her hand against the morning sun. "Oh," she said. "You know, everything ends as it started, in a rush."

"Yeah," I said.

"Would you like some coffee?" she asked.

"Well, sure," I said. "But I wouldn't want to bother."

"I have a fresh pot on," she said.

I stepped into her kitchen and into the aroma of fresh coffee. There were books stacked about, and her briefcase lay open on the table. She poured our coffees and asked if I'd like a sweet roll as well.

"I'm fine," I said. "Are your classes over then?"

"Yes, over," she said, sipping at her coffee. "You?"

"Nearly," I said.

"And how has your work-study program gone?"

"I've learned so much from just being there, like you said."

"Are you still writing?"

"My journal mostly," I said.

"I've been meaning to talk to you," she said, lifting the pot. "More?"

I nodded. "Talk about what?"

"You see, I've made application for the doctoral program at State. I've been accepted actually."

"Oh," I said. "Congratulations."

"I'll start in the fall, you see, full time. The thing is, I'll be putting the house up for sale."

"Oh?"

"I won't be able to maintain two households."

"No, I suppose not."

"I'm afraid you'll have to move, Jacob. I'm very sorry. I hadn't antic-ipated this, but I'm sure you'll be able to find another place."

"Yes," I said. "There are lots of places."

"I don't want you to get discouraged."

"No, I'll be fine," I said.

"You are a capable person, and you mustn't let anything stop you."

"Thanks," I said. "I'm not sure this is the thing for a man to be doing in any case."

"What do you mean?"

"For a family man and so forth. I mean, there are more practical ways to make money."

"I see."

"A man's obligation is to first provide for his family."

She reached for the cream and stirred it into her coffee. I'd not seen her like this, fresh from her bed, the tangle of hair about her face still soft and warm from sleep.

She said, "We should do what we're meant to do, I think. Money follows success. It doesn't lead."

"There are things about me," I said.

"What do you mean?"

I told her then more than I had intended, about my family, about how the Franklins drank to excess and how the Rolands' behavior was sometimes erratic. I told her how that left me as an unpredictable brew of the two. I told her how Rachael, my friend, had probably learned all this from her grandparents and was now having her doubts that I could be a responsible person.

I shrugged and added, "She was trying to tell me all this I guess, that I must take control and make sound decisions or risk our relationship."

Kate didn't say anything as she stirred her coffee. Finally, she said, "Young girls can be insecure, Jacob. Maybe she senses your passion for something other than her. Maybe it's that, or maybe she just views the world from a different place. But you're right about one thing."

"What's that?"

"You are an unpredictable brew. I've seen it in your journal writing, the way you whirl away into the unknown sometimes, the way you blaze a path, and the world be damned. It is a particular madness that can be frightening to others. In any case, you cannot change what you are. Go back to what you do, and do it with all your might."

As the sun set that evening, I stood at my door and could see Kate's light on in her bedroom. The blinds were half pulled, and she was combing her hair in front of her mirror. At first I thought to turn away, to not see what I was seeing. But I didn't. The dishonor of spying failed to sway my conscience, so I watched her as she arched her back like a beautiful and rare violin. She turned once and looked out, and for a moment, I thought our eyes met through the darkness.

That night, I lay in bed and considered the conversation Kate and I had shared that day. She was leaving to a world far removed from my own, and we might never meet again. I would soon have no place to live and an uncertain future. Perhaps it was Kate, instead of Rachael, who had abandoned me.

CHAPTER 36

I stopped first at the gas station. "No notice given, no job now," he said, turning his back. Just as I reached the door, he added, "Been able to prove all them candy bars missing, I'd have your ass in jail too."

I found after a thorough canvassing of the town that any job that was available was not worth having. If I couldn't pay rent or buy groceries with the pay, what was the point? By the time I got back to my room at Kate's, a moving truck had pulled into the driveway. I looked for Kate, but she was not to be found.

I'd no sooner finished my lunch when there was a knock at the door. Kate stood there with her hair tied up in a red bandanna.

"Hi," she said.

"Hi."

"I just wanted you to know that I hope to be moved out very soon. They're wanting me settled in before the summer session starts."

"No time to waste," I said.

"Listen, I hate to press, but I need this place on the market soon as possible. I mean, when do you think you'll be moving?"

"Oh," I said. "I should be out in a couple days."

"I do hope you understand?"

"I've been thinking I might go home for the summer anyway. That will give me time to find the right situation."

"A good plan," she said.

"And I'll get your lawn mowed before I go."

She turned and paused. "I'm going to miss our talks," she said. "You'll keep in touch?"

"Oh, sure, I'll keep in touch."

"And you might want to do something with that journal. It's quite good, you know."

I nodded and watched her walk away. She hesitated at her garden gate but didn't turn.

A day later, the van was gone. I loaded the Mercury with my few belongings, and by the time I turned onto the highway, I had a knot in my stomach the size of a coffee can. Going home, even for the summer, had the feel of defeat. I rolled down the window and turned up the radio to drown it away.

But then I still had my work-study money coming in for the fall. I had an impressive transcript and was tight with the departmental faculty. Not bad, really, for an old farm kid who'd barely known his way around a book when he'd started.

The mesas cropped up on the horizon in front of me, their cap rocks lost in the blue haze of the morning. I could see the red dirt road that led to Casket Hill, where my sister and ancestors lay, while the rest of us who remained struggled on.

When I pulled into the yard, Dad's old pickup was still sitting under the elm tree. It looked as if it hadn't been moved since the last time I was home. I turned down the radio and shut off the Mercury. The garden was overgrown with spring weeds, and the chickens were scratching under the shade of the lilacs. There was a flat tire on the water truck and a battery sitting on the running board.

I knocked and opened the back door. "Mom?" I called

The house smelled of cold wood ashes, and the sink was full of dishes. "Mom?" I called again. "It's me."

"Lord," she said from the front room. "You home?"

"Semester's done," I said.

She came from the hallway and patted my shoulder. Pulling a chair out from the table, she said, "Sit down. You hungry?"

"I'm fine," I said. "Where are the kids?"

"They aren't kids anymore, growing up, and they find all kinds of reasons for staying in town now. You remember how that is, I guess. Won't be long until they jump track."

"And Dad?"

"He's not up just yet," she said.

"This time of day?"

She drummed her fingers on the table. I guess you've a right to know. He's not doing so well, Jacob."

"What is it?"

"They're saying it's cancer." My heart tripped. "They're saying it's in his lungs, and there's not much they can do. He's quit eating mostly, a little soup or such, and he stays angry all the time."

"Angry at you?"

"Angry at dying, I suppose, or not dying. Who's to know? He doesn't talk much except to ask for this or that, or complain about the chores. It's been a struggle for me to keep them up."

"You should have let me know," I said.

"I figured you had your hands full. How long can you stay?"

"I was thinking through the summer."

"And then back to that college?"

"I thought I might get a job around here this summer."

"I wish there was more we could do to help out with your schoolin', but with the place payment and now Dad's sickness—"

"There's no need for you to fret over all that."

"I'm sure he heard you drive in. Maybe you should go in and see him."

I found him sitting on the edge of the bed. He hadn't shaved, his face gray with whiskers. Gone were those once powerful arms, now thin and atrophied, and his skin was pale as milk from lack of sun.

"Dad?" I said.

He turned and looked at me, his eyes large and empty. "Help me back in bed," he said.

Lying down, he struggled to breathe, his lungs rattling something awful, and there were specks of dried blood on his pillow.

"Your mom needs a load of water," he said.

"All right, Dad."

"And the weeds takin' over the garden."

"I'll get on it." I said. "How you feeling?"

He turned his face into the pillow. "Just great, ain't I?"

I closed the door behind me and searched out Mom.

"I'm going for a load of water," I said.

"The battery's dead," she said. "I didn't know how."

I changed the tire and charged the battery, jumping the posts with a screwdriver to check for spark before I installed it. The old truck fired off, and blue smoke rose into the sky. I nursed her up the hill in second gear and could see the county well up ahead. It leaned a little northward now, and one of the blade fins had fallen off. I pulled in and shut down. There was a water puddle where the tank had sprung a leak. Not many were using the well anymore, and maintenance had been neglected. I put the hose in the tank and opened the valve before taking up residence in the truck to wait. The old windmill squawked and squeaked in a slow breeze. I thought about the day I hand-pumped Duny's chaser for his whiskey and how we'd roared down that hill with no brakes and no hope of living. It was probably the only time Duny ever gave serious thought to the hereafter.

Once I got back to the house, I filled the cistern and then went to the garden to hoe weeds. By day's end, I was as tired as I'd been for some time. Study was one kind of weariness, a kind that can't be slept off. Manual labor was a different kind altogether, one that would sink you into your pillow at night like melted butter.

As the days passed, I found that being underfoot in the house had made things complicated, what with the kids needing their own space now and Dad demanding more of Mom's time.

One morning over breakfast, I said, "I'm thinking to move my bed to the separator house."

Mom set a plate of pancakes in front of me and turned for the coffee pot. "You're welcome enough in here, Jacob. You know that."

"It would be easier for everyone," I said. "Me and the kids wouldn't have to share so much."

"It's his coughing keeps you up?" she said.

"I'm just used to being on my own," I said.

"If that's what you want," she said. "I'll get your bedding together. You come in for meals or when you need a visit."

"I'm not missing any meals," I said.

By week's end, I'd planted tomatoes, repaired the gate, and moved the cattle to the north field. I'd written Rachael about my move home for the summer and where to send her letters in the future. I'd contacted Old Man Tuttle about building fence in my spare time, and he'd agreed. The pay wasn't much, but my living expenses were minimal.

Mom was right about the kids. They were far more interested in their friends than anything else and were gone whenever they could arrange it. The inevitability of Dad's illness escaped them altogether, I guess.

On occasion Dad would put on his robe and come out on the front porch, but he never stayed long, his strength waning more every day. Now and then I'd stop in and give him an update. He'd grunt his approval or tell me not to forget this or that. Beyond that, he demonstrated little interest in anything more than the world he now occupied.

There were times I struggled against a great emptiness inside me, the realization that this farm was not mine, nor my dream. It was his dream, and I was trying to live it for him. In those moments, I knew I had lost my way.

I had heard from Rachael only once during this time. She was taking a weekend trip to New York with some friends, where they planned to explore the city. She hoped to see me when she came to visit her grandparents again. Though increasingly discontented, I took solace in the possibility of seeing her soon.

Come July, the temperature soared to 103 degrees, an unrelenting assault on the senses. I moved my bunk to the front porch in an effort to catch any available breeze, but even the night air failed to cool me. Locusts gathered in the darkness, a mob chanting through the night. My sleep was sporadic and shallow. I would awaken to my bedsheets soaked with perspiration and with the certain knowledge that by noon, the heat would once again soar to painful heights.

Dad's condition deteriorated. He had to be assisted to the bathroom, a task most often coming in the wee hours of morning. With the slightest exertion, he would struggle for breath or lapse into a coughing spasm that left everyone shattered. His skin would tear like paper. At times he would demand his medication, other times refusing it with his hand over his mouth. His anger and pain permeated the house, a place now reeling under the throes of his pending death.

Mom, too, weary with stress, faltered. She cried alone in her room at night and took long, solitary walks. Her world was crumbling, and there was no way to stop it, while I, trapped in a web of a different sort, turned once again to my journal.

He died in the night with his back to the door. Mom found him first and came out to the separator house where I was again sleeping.

"He's gone," she said.

I sat up, uncertain as to what she was saying. But then I could see her standing in the door, her fists clenched at her sides, and I knew.

I rolled onto the side of the bed and reached for my shoes. "I'll be in," I said.

"There's no need," she said. "I've covered him with a blanket and called for the undertaker. You get the kids off somewhere. Come back at daylight, and we'll make arrangements."

"All right," I said.

Three days later, we buried him on the Franklin side of Casket Hill, though Uncle Ward had protested such, saying as how it was unsanctified ground and no place for a Roland to be awaiting the Rapture. Mom insisted, however, pointing out that it was the Rolands who had failed to accept her when she'd married Dad, and she had no intentions of lying up for an eternity on the Roland side of the graveyard.

There was generally little crying among the family the day of the funeral, not that the sorrow wasn't deep, but the crying had been going on within us for many weeks. Now that it had happened, there were few tears left to shed. Abbey and Silas felt it the most, I suppose, youth being where it is. Though Dad could be aloof and silent, he was still their stability and their security. When things went awry with any of us, there was always Dad to shore up the dam.

Not many of the Rolands came to the funeral that day. Like most families, each new generation had slipped further away from the old until few close connections remained. I did see Uncle Ward standing off at a distance, his arms crossed and his hat squared. And there was Danny, too, sitting on a rock up on the hill, his legs pulled up in his arms. And next to him was Mortem, keeping the death watch as was his way.

I took over the family duties, as was expected of me, rising early to milk, to pick the garden, and to do whatever other arduous tasks remained. I worked alone and with a brooding resentment at the loss of my own life. I went through Dad's clothes, taking what fit and what bolstered my authority, before moving everything permanently to the separator house.

Rachael's letters continued to come, but sporadically. They were most often detailed accounts of her classes and the plans she and her friends had made for the weekends. I resisted telling her of Dad's passing. Having not experienced such things in her own life, she probably wouldn't understand them in mine.

Mom fell quiet, fixing meals as always, washing clothes and cleaning the house. Our conversations circled around our duties, all of which failed to fill the emotional vacuum left in Dad's absence. Abbey and Silas moved into their adult lives without us.

Even as the weather cooled, I continued to sleep in the separator house. Rats scurried under the floor at night, and the timbers creaked as they settled under the cold. Frost gathered on the windows and scattered the morning sun into rainbow colors. Mom, still trapped in her own sorrow, had little to spare for anyone else. In the end, there was nowhere for any of us to turn, except inward.

Sleepless nights followed with me rising at two and three in the morning and the tic returning to my nose. I bought whiskey, but it failed to console me. I couldn't eat, and my weight dropped. My temper erupted with the slightest provocation, and I would sometimes fall suddenly asleep. Night terrors followed, a place where breath failed me, where water filled my throat, and my arms flailed about as they searched for a single hand to take my own. There was none.

CHAPTER 37

The letter arrived on a Monday in the afternoon mail. At first I thought it was from Rachael, until I spotted the Citadel logo. The return was from Dr. Janet Foss, Chairperson of the English Department. Perhaps it was a tax form required for the fall term employment, or perhaps I was to arrive early to prepare for the fall semester. I opened the letter in the privacy of the separator house. The message was short and to the point:

Dear Mr. Jacob Roland:

We regret to advise you that due to a budget shortfall, the work-study program has been discontinued for the upcoming academic year. If needed, other financial arrangements may be pursued through the business office. We will notify you if there is any change in our situation. We are looking forward to seeing you this fall.

With warm regards,
Dr. Janet Foss
Chairperson, English Department

I sat on the bunk and reread the letter. Without financial backing, I would not be able to return. I had already exhausted my search for other sources. Wadding up the letter, I threw it on the floor. I was stuck here for the rest of my life. Everything I wanted had vanished in a single paragraph. I struggled to think of alternatives, of other ways to come up with the money, but it was too late. I was a fool ever to have believed things could be different. My world crashed down about me. There had been only a thin chance for me to make it, and that chance had just vanished.

Weeks passed, dark weeks, void of all but the drudgery and hopelessness of the farm. Sometimes, while building fence alone at the back side, or cutting wood for the fire, or shocking feed in the field, I could hear Rachael's voice saying how much she missed me, how much she wished we could be together at last. But then it would go as it had come, as a whisper of wind on a summer day.

So I filled my notebooks with scribbles and carried them to my place in the shelterbelt, where I buried them ceremoniously in the wooden box under the tree. There were times Danny would appear to me, stepping out as was his way, grinning the way he could do.

On this day, he startled me with a tap on my shoulder. "Hey, goofball," he said. "What you doing?"

"Jesus, Danny, you scared the life out of me."

"Still scrawling in those notebooks, are you?"

"What's it to you?"

"You should keep that shit to yourself," he said.

"You still at the hotel, living off your kin?" I asked.

"Don't ask so many questions, or I won't come around anymore."

"Like I care?"

"You ain't jack without me, goofball, and you know it." He leaned against the tree and kicked his foot back. "I thought you were going to be a big-shot university man."

"I ran out of money," I said.

Danny laughed. "You just ran out, goofball. You never could finish a race."

"I gotta go now, Danny."

"Ain't you got any naked pictures or anything?"

"No," I said.

"Kools?"

"No."

"What's the matter with your nose?" he asked.

"Nothing's wrong with my nose."

"It's ticking," he said.

I put my finger on it. "No, it isn't."

"It's ticking like a clock."

"Maybe a little when I'm nervous," I said.

"You still writing letters to that big-titted girl?"

"Knock it off, Danny."

"Maybe she don't like tickity noses," he said.

"You can go to hell, Danny. You didn't even come down to my dad's funeral, you and that dog just sitting up there staring like you're something special."

"You can't go around ticking your nose," he said. "It ain't natural. You don't see me ticking my nose."

"Maybe you don't feel the things I do or think the same way."

"I'm sure glad of that," he said.

"I gotta go," I said.

"Yeah," he said. "You go, 'cause time is ticking away."

I couldn't sleep that night for thinking about Danny and what he'd said. I guess down deep I figured what he said might have some truth in it. I didn't sleep well that night, or several nights after that, to be honest. And there were some days I could barely lift my arms, like they had lead weights tied to them. But each morning I got up, put on my clothes, and stepped out the door.

Mom never came back full power after Dad died either. Abbey and Silas sensed the weakness in her, I think. Silas took to staying in town instead of catching the bus home, and I found his whiskey bottle hidden in the barn. Abbey stole down the road late one night to meet someone. I saw her go. I thought to call her out, but who was I to do so? Who was I to tell someone else how to live?

Sometimes Mom would come to the separator house at the end of the day. She'd say from the door that such and such needs doing and that your dad always had it done by now. Or she'd say how it wasn't good for a boy my age to be moping around all the time, and how I needed to come out of it.

Every day, I'd walk to the mailbox and check for Rachael's letters. Sometimes they'd be there; more often the mailbox would be empty. Those few letters that did come were disappointing. She said how her dad had started an investment fund for her and how by the time she graduated with an economics degree, she'd have enough to start her own business. She said how I ought to start thinking about the future myself.

I wrote her how my Uncle Duny had been in business and how successful it had been for him. I didn't tell her about Hazel Morford, the pole dancer, or about the riot that burned down the entire town of

Dunyville. She wrote back and told me that she hadn't been aware of
the entrepreneurial side of my family and how together we could be
financially secure and how comforting she found this to be.

Unable to sleep one night, I rose in the early hours and looked out
the window of the separator house. I could see Casket Hill off in the
distance, just sitting there all silent under the stars. I'm not sure why I
wanted to go. Perhaps it was no more than facing the unresolved issues
with Dad, the way we'd left things undone, or perhaps it was just the
night calling as it sometimes did. Whatever it was, I drove with my
lights off as I climbed up the winding mesa road to the cemetery.

Once there, I pulled over and rolled the window down. The tomb-
stones dotted the little cemetery and cast minute shadows in the moonlight. A coyote wailed somewhere upriver, and crickets chirped with
singular measure. The old Mercury creaked in the night as she cooled
down, and a faint smell of salt rose from the Cimarron below.

I wondered if Dad knew I was there, if he understood how hard
things had been since he'd left. I wondered if he knew how Mom
grieved and how the kids were beginning to scatter. Did he know these
things, or was there only the cold and silence of the grave?

I got out of the car and made my way down the path, the same path
that I had helped Dad clear so many times in my youth. In such a
private and small cemetery, the grounds overgrew quickly and had to
be cleared before each new burial.

I walked on until I could see the headstones clearly through the
mesquite. I stopped there to reconnoiter, to listen to the hum of the
universe and the beat of my own heart. The gypsum cap rock, being
soluble, had washed away to ravines and caverns and housed several
degrees of dangerous creatures. Large boulders sometimes dislodged
and plunged headlong into the Cimarron below.

I'd nearly reached the graveyard when I heard a peculiar sound. I
crouched in the shadows, and it came again, a determined clanking
and huffing. My pulse ticked up, and my hands proceeded to sweat.
Peering through the darkness, I could see a man with a shovel and

with shoulders squared. Only then did I realize that he was opening a grave—not just any grave but my dad's.

CHAPTER 38

I stepped from my hiding place, my fists clenched. "What the hell you doing?" I asked.

The man looked slowly toward me. "What the hell is it to you?" he said.

I moved closer, prepared to defend the sanctity of my father's grave. But there was something familiar in the voice. "Who *are* you?" I asked.

"Ward Roland," he said. "Who do you think?"

He'd no sooner said it than I spotted his bus parked back in the trees. "Uncle Ward?"

"You go on," he said. "I got the Lord's work to be doing."

"That's my dad's grave," I said, my voice trembling.

"Now ain't that clever. It says so right there on that tombstone."

"You can't be doing that," I said.

"Says who?"

"Me *and* the law."

"It's God's law I follow," he said. "This here is a Roland, and he's got no business being buried on unholy ground."

I circled around for a better look under the moonlight, and I could see it in his eyes. What he was hearing was most in his own head.

"Mom placed him next to her where she wanted him," I said.

He spun around on his heel. "Did you hear that?" he said.

"I didn't hear anything," I said.

"Germans," he said. "Goddamn Germans everywhere."

"The war's over," I said. "It's been over a good long while."

"Duny burned up my rolling cross," he said. "And he opened that saloon in my town, bringing in that woman to dance and tempt men with her body. Duny turned my town into Sodom and Gomorrah. Then him and those other heathen bastards burned it all to the ground. Abbott ain't going to rest in Franklin ground long as I'm alive. Come the Rapture, he'll be rising up in sacred ground."

"I can't let you do that," I said.

"Germans," he said. "You can't kill 'em fast enough."

I held out my hand. "Give me that shovel," I said.

Uncle Ward swung, catching me upside the head. Stars swept across the sky, and a church bell rang in my head. I pitched forward, never feeling the ground as it rushed up to meet me.

When I came to, dirt clogged my mouth and nose and blood was caked down my front. My head pounded, and a knot the size of a hen's egg protruded from my forehead. I sat up and waited for the world to stop spinning. Uncle Ward's bus was gone, and his shovel was leaning against Dad's headstone.

I can't be certain how long it took to shovel that dirt back into the grave, but it was something I couldn't leave undone. By the time I was finished, I could barely stand. I drove home, coasting into the yard so as not to awaken anyone.

It wasn't until late that morning that Mom knocked on my door.

"You still laying up in bed?" she said. "Your dad would have had chores done three hours ago."

I pulled myself out of bed and opened the door.

"I'm up," I said, shading my eyes.

"Good Lord," she said. "What happened to your head?"

"I ran my car off the road last night," I said.

"You been drinking? You know that runs in the Franklins' blood."

"Went to sleep, I guess. Anyway, I'm up."

"Did it wreck your car?"

I shook my head. "Not so you can tell."

"Well, those cows can't wait all day to be milked."

"OK," I said.

She closed the door and then opened it again. "You're going to hear it soon enough," she said. "I just as well tell you."

"Hear what?"

"Your Uncle Ward."

"What about him?"

"June Elliot called and said they got him in the city jail again."

"For what?"

"He parked his bus on the lawn of the Baptist church, and he was behind the podium preaching to empty pews. It took the county sheriff and two city cops to bring him in."

"He's always been headstrong," I said.

"I'm just glad Abbott wasn't around to see it," she said.

The weeks and months passed as one. Mom had taken to her bed, just laying up and waiting for time to pass. It wasn't that she was sick so much as her spirit was broken. The kids were now in their last year of school. Abbey had taken up with a boy who worked the oil patch, and Silas fussed with his old car day and night. Uncle Ward got out of city jail with the understanding he'd clear out of town and pay for the damage to the church lawn.

As for me, I worked at what needed to be done, though as absent in my own way as everyone else. I failed to tell Rachael about not going back to the university, even as she wrote about her own plans. What I had sought for my life had slipped away, and it was no longer in me to care about others.

The cumulative result was a breaking of my resolve. I slept poorly, often waking from vivid dreams, dreams that set me upright in the darkness with my heart pounding. My concentration waned, and my memory faltered. I sometimes would come up lost or confused and have to reconstruct the events around me. Mom said I mumbled to myself like some danged fool, and the neighbors were beginning to talk.

It was in such a condition that I walked to the mailbox on a crisp fall morning and found a letter from Rachael. Mom was still in bed, and the kids were gone to school. Leaves swirled in eddies about my feet as I made my way back to the separator house to open it.

Dear Jacob:

I wanted to write and let you know that I'm planning on being married over the Christmas holidays. He is someone I've known since high school. I never set out to deceive you. Things just turned out this way, and I've got to be true to my feelings. While I will always cherish our time together, I know this is the right thing for me. He and I have much in common and want the same things in life. I ask that you not contact me or try to dissuade me from my decision. I will always remember you as the boy who stole my heart one summer.

Rachael

CHAPTER 39

Rachael was gone, and there was nothing left, my life crushed by her words. I locked my door and lay down on my bunk, failing even to get up for evening chores. When I didn't go in for dinner, Mom came out to check on me.

She knocked on the door. "Jacob, you OK in there?"

"Not now, Mom," I said.

"Open the door."

"I'm not dressed," I said. "I'll be out later."

When she didn't answer, I peeked out my window and could see her making her way back to the house. No sooner did I lie back when there was another knock at the door.

"Go away," I said.

"Open the door, goofball."

"I don't want to talk, Danny."

"Open the door, or I'll burn you out."

I opened the door. Danny stood there, his hands tucked in his back pockets like James Dean.

"What do you want?" I said.

"She dumped you, didn't she?"

I started to push the door closed, but he held it open. "Like you care," I said.

"Winning races isn't something you do, is it?" he said. "Don't you know who you are? You were never getting that one, not in a million years. I told you, didn't I? And you trying to fit into that snooty university with manure on your shoes."

"Like you know so much," I said.

"I'm no phony."

I sat down on my bunk. "I've got something in me, Danny, something important that needs to be said."

"You got nothing," he said. "The sooner you understand that, the better off you'll be."

"You better go now, Danny, because I'm thinking to knock you down."

He stepped out, laughing, and I locked the door behind him. Who was he to say anything about me? I reread her letter in my head. So she didn't want me to dissuade her. *Dissuade*—what the hell kind of word was that? I hated her.

I awakened in the dark, except for the dim glow of the moon framing the window. I'd been gutted and thrown on the bank to die. My nose ticked, and I tried to stop it with my finger. And then I heard her.

"Jacob," she said.

I sat up and swung my feet onto the floor. "Is that you?" I asked.

"This is not where I wanted to be. You can understand that. I could never be happy here."

"I was going to be more," I said.

"You were all dreams and clouds," she said.

"I taught Rudy how to read," I said.

"But you didn't finish the race."

"They didn't tell me," I said. "I didn't know."

There was no answer. Rats gnawed at the floorboards, gnawing and stirring under my feet. My heart pounded in my ears, and blood rushed through my veins. I got up and looked out the window. The yard was empty, except for my Mercury. The house was dark. They were all gone—Dad, Mom, Rachael, even Danny.

So that's how it was. They wished me away, the lot of them. There was no one I could trust, so it was up to me now. I put my ear against the door to listen. It smelled of sweat and soured milk. I eased it open and looked out the crack. The night air was thick and dank. Crickets chirped from the creek bottom, and droplets of moisture clung to the trees like diamonds. I made my way to the house, knowing that my life had changed forever.

The house door was unlocked, as it always was, and the smell of baked chicken still lingered in the kitchen. He kept his rifle in the closet, always the same, and the shells in a box on the shelf above. It was the rifle he always hunted with, the one he wanted me to learn to use, and it was the only thing standing between me and the others.

The rifle was heavy and cold in my hands, and the shells clicked into the magazine with machined precision. Armed and ready, I made my way back to the separator house and locked the door behind me. I sat down to wait. Though I didn't know who would be coming,

I knew they would be here. Satan rats stirred and gnawed beneath the floor.

When the knock came, it came like the crashing of cymbals. My insides turned to ice, and my scalp crawled.

"This is Sheriff Brunsetter," a man said. "Unlock the door."

"Go away," I said.

"Your mother is worried about you. She wants you to see a doctor."

"We have place payments," I said.

"She asked us to check on you. Come on out, and we'll see that you get help."

My arms stiffened, like rigor mortis. "There are rats under the floor," I said. "Satan rats."

He pushed against the door, making it creak. "No one is going to harm you," he said.

"You cannot dissuade me," I said.

The door hinges groaned and then gave way with a crash. I pointed the rifle, but the sheriff knocked it away.

He kicked out the shells and set the rifle in the corner. "It's over now," he said, cuffing my hands behind my back. He took me to his patrol car and pushed me into the back seat. It smelled of sweat and whiskey. "You do things the hard way, don't you, boy?" he said, closing the door.

As we drove away, I could see Mom standing on the front porch under the yard light. She had her arms folded over her chest. Danny was sitting on the bottom step with his chin in his hands. Neither of them waved good-bye.

The sheriff lit a cigarette and looked at me in the rearview mirror. His eyelids drooped down on the sides, and his eyes were slits. "Keep your feet off the back of the seat," he said. "I just cleaned this thing up."

The cuffs cut into my wrists, so I turned sideways. I could see the farmhouse disappearing behind me, and all the lights were on now, like a celebration.

CHAPTER 40

I sat on a wooden chair while the sheriff filled out a form. My heart beat in my ears, shallow and fast, and the room spun a bit, like I'd had too much to drink.

"What is it?" I asked.

"A Blue Paper, a petition to have you committed," he said.

"Committed?"

He looked up from his desk. "That's right. You're a danger to the community, pointing that rifle around like that."

"I can't even finish a race," I said.

"Just like that crazy uncle of yours," he said. "What the hell do you Rolands eat?"

"I'm not dangerous," I said.

He signed with a flourish and said, "A man with a rifle is always dangerous."

"I've shot at an ant once, and I missed it," I said.

He stood. "Come on, we're off to see the judge."

Western State Hospital, an old territorial fort that had once housed the infamous General Custer, had gone through a number of transformations, including its present status as a state insane asylum. It sat on the open plain, surrounded by little more than sagebrush and an ancient cemetery filled with ancient bodies.

"How long will they keep me?" I asked, looking out the window of the patrol car.

"Not long enough," the sheriff said.

He handed me over to an orderly, who was dressed in a white coat and smelled of bacon. The sheriff looked at me, adjusted his holster belt, and headed for the door.

"My name is Vern," the orderly said.

"Sperm?"

"Vern," he said. "Short for Vernon."

"My name is Jacob," I said. "Short for the ladder that goes up to heaven."

"I know your name," he said. "We're going to take you up to the staff psychiatrist now."

"What's his name?"

"What difference does that make?"

"I have to call him something," I said.

He rolled his eyes. "Call him doctor, Jesus."

"What if I don't want to go?"

"I hadn't considered that. Do you know what a straitjacket is?"

"No."

"Believe me, you'll go," he said.

He took me by the arm and directed me to the stairwell. At the top, we turned down the hallway. Light seeped through the window at the end of the hall, and I could hear the *bump, bump* of a wasp against a windowpane.

Sperm's hand dug deep into my arm. "In here," he said, opening the door.

The secretary's typewriter clacked, the exact same clack as Old Man Hinkle's alfalfa baler. "You're late," she said, pulling the paper out of the typewriter.

Sperm shrugged. "That sheriff is a three-toed sloth," he said.

"The doctor's on the phone," she said.

I looked around. Danny was sitting on the couch looking at a magazine with naked girls in it. He put his finger to his lips to shush me from saying anything.

The buzzer rang, and the secretary picked it up. "He's ready now," she said to Sperm.

The doctor's office smelled of pipe tobacco and coffee. The doctor, in his late forties by the looks of him, peered at me over his glasses. He pointed to the chair, and I sat down, wedging my hands between my knees. Sperm handed him my file.

He looked it over and said, "Was he in restraints when he came in?"

Sperm nodded. "Cuffs."

"It says here that there was a firearm involved in his arrest."

"He couldn't work the safety," he said.

"I'll ring you when he's ready," the doctor said.

Sperm paused at the door. "I caught Bailey jerking off under the stairwell again."

The doctor made grunting noises. Looking up, he said, "Isolate him. It freaks the nurses." The doctor looked at me. "Roland," he said.

"That sounds familiar."

"It's my name," I said.

"Roland," he said. "I'm Dr. Jesus."

"I'm Jacob's ladder," I said.

"It says here that you've never finished a race?"

"I wasn't told," I said.

"One must always finish the race," he said. "I should think you would know that."

"People should have told me," I said.

"So, Roland, have you had problems in the past?"

"I couldn't teach Rudy Joe words," I said.

"Not even one?"

I shook my head.

"Do you have headaches?"

"When Duny gives me liquor."

"Who is Duny?"

"My uncle. He's dead."

"We don't talk about the dead here, Roland. Do you hear voices?"

"I hear yours," I said.

He clicked his pencil against his teeth and studied me. "Being a smartass will get you nowhere in here, Roland."

"OK."

"Have you had that tic long?"

"The doctor took it out."

"The jerking in your nose? You look like a rabbit."

"I can make it stop with my finger," I said.

Doctor Jesus made circles on his notepad and shaded one in. "Will you describe what you think your sickness is?"

"I'm not sick."

"You haven't noticed that your behavior is different from others'?"

"I threw up on the teacher's desk once."

"How about friends?" he asked.

"No, just the teacher's desk," I said.

"I mean, do you have many friends?"

"Rachael was my friend, but I couldn't dissuade her. And there's Danny, of course."

"Who is Danny?"

"He's sort of a friend, but you never can tell when he will show up."

"What do you mean?"

"I'm not supposed to say."

"It's all right to say."

"He's out in the reception area right now."

"What's he doing out there?"

"Reading a naked girl magazine."

"And does Danny tell you what to do sometimes?"

I looked around to see if he was in the room, sitting on the couch or something. "Maybe," I said.

The doctor got up from his chair and walked to the window. He had a bald spot on the back of his head.

"Tell me about Rachael," he said.

"She has to be true to her feelings," I said.

"I see. Are you close friends with Rachael?"

"She's getting married," I said.

"And how do you feel about that?"

"Just great," I said.

"So, are Rachael and Danny your only friends?"

"There was Kate. She gave me a place to live, but she's gone now."

Dr. Jesus sat back down, looked at his watch, and said, "How would you feel about me talking to some of your friends? Sometimes it's beneficial to see what someone else thinks about things."

"They're gone, except for Danny," I said. "He doesn't talk to other people much."

"What about your mother and father?"

"My father is buried on Casket Hill."

"And your mother?"

I shrugged. "She's alive."

"I would like to talk to your mother."

"Does it cost money? She has place payments."

"No, it's free."

"I guess it would be OK," I said.

Flipping through his calendar, Dr. Jesus made a note. "Have you ever thought about taking your own life?"

"I've thought about taking Danny's," I said.

"But have you thought about killing yourself?"

"They ought to feed people around here," I said. "I'm starving."

"Your life, Jacob?"

"Who hasn't?" I said.

"Do you think about it often?"

"I'm thinking it right now."

"I need a serious response," he said.

"Some, when I was a kid," I said.

He wove his fingers on his chest and rocked back and forth in his chair. "And why has that changed for you?"

"I know how to live forever now," I said.

He looked up at me. "You do?"

"Yes."

"That's quite a development. Would you care to share it?"

"As long as my thoughts are alive, I'm alive."

"Your thoughts?"

"As long as someone knows my thoughts, I'm not dead because they are the same thing."

"But how does someone know your thoughts?"

"I write them down," I said.

"So you write your thoughts down and that keeps you alive?"

"Yes," I said.

"I would like to read them sometime," he said.

"They aren't finished," I said.

"When will they be finished?"

"When I'm dead," I said.

CHAPTER 41

They X-rayed my lungs, listened to my heart, tapped my knees with a rubber hammer. Sperm went with me everywhere. He didn't like to talk much, so when he wasn't around, I talked to Danny instead. Danny said that Sperm didn't say much because he didn't know much. He said that I talked *too* much for the same reason. I didn't understand that altogether, but Danny was that way. He'd throw something out like that and just let it lie there.

A man with a mustache gave me a test in a little room without windows. I listened to numbers and repeated them back. I answered questions about history and literature. I put puzzles together, and he kept starting and stopping his watch. After the test he told me that I was smarter than I looked. I don't think he thought that for sure, so I didn't say it to anyone, not to Sperm, and especially not to Danny.

Sperm was taking me back to my room when he stopped between the buildings to smoke a cigarette. It was cold, and he pulled his collar up against the wind. I didn't have a coat.

"Hey, Spook," he said. That's what he called me sometimes, Spook.

"What?" I said.

"You have a girl?"

"Not anymore," I said.

"Wouldn't she let you do it?"

"Don't talk that way about her," I said.

He spit between his legs and blew smoke in my direction. "You didn't even try, did you?" he said.

"She couldn't be dissuaded."

"You didn't give her what she wanted, so someone else did. What a spook."

I could see Danny standing in the shadows at the end of the building. He had his fists clenched, and I knew what he meant by that. So I doubled up my fist and hit Sperm in the nose. I was strong from bucking bales. His nose slid sideways, and blood spewed all over my shirt. He tried to scream, but with all that blood in his throat, he just gurgled.

I ran across the compound fast as I could, but I didn't know where I was going for sure. I only knew that I had to get away. I'd nearly reached the front gate when two men caught me from behind. They dragged me across the compound and into a room that had bars on the door. Sperm was waiting in there. Blood was encrusted in his nose, and his eyes were nearly swollen shut.

They put a white coat on me with long sleeves that they tied behind my back. I couldn't breathe. They set me down in the corner of the room. I tried to get up, but without my arms, I couldn't move. Sperm sniffed his nose.

"That's a straitjacket, you little son of a bitch," he said. "We use it with spooks like you." When the other two men left, he walked over and looked down at me. He pulled at his crotch and then kicked me in the face.

He shut off the lights and closed the door. It was dark, and I couldn't breathe. The jacket tightened around my body like a giant snake. I couldn't breathe. I needed to die, but I didn't know how.

No one came, not then, not for hours. I wet myself like a baby. The room was hot, and I smelled of urine. I made a mistake smashing Sperm in the nose. I should have killed him. And where was Danny, somewhere reading a naked girl magazine?

Later, Sperm showed up with the same two guys who'd tackled me in the compound. He turned the light on and kicked the bottom of my foot.

"Get up, you bastard," he said. "Your stay has been extended. Me and you is friends now for a long while, and you've been scheduled for a little insulin treatment."

I tried to stand but couldn't. The two men caught me under my arms and lifted me to my feet. "I can't feel my feet, and I don't have diabetes either."

"Not yet," Sperm said.

They untied the jacket, and my arms hung at my sides like pieces of meat. Pockets of blood had gathered in my elbows, and my fingernails were blue. They put a wool robe around my shoulders and walked me to a building across the compound. It was red brick with high windows and white double doors. The hallway was dimly lit and smelled of wax. We went into a large open room off the hallway. It was filled with iron beds, all occupied by old men with sunken cheeks and drool down their fronts.

"Who are these people?" I asked.

"Resident idiots," Sperm said.

We passed through another room full of women in rocking chairs, some swaying back and forth, some still and with their hands in their laps. Others giggled as we passed and held out their arms.

Sperm directed me into a room no bigger than a kitchen. It was full of nurses and doctors wearing white and with masks over their faces. They laid me on the table, stood over me, and made humming noises behind their masks.

"What are you going to do to me?" I asked.

The doctor with the horn-rimmed glasses patted my arm. "We are just going to administer some medicine," he said. "It's nothing to worry about."

"What for?"

"To induce a coma."

"Induce a what?"

"A coma."

"Like a coma before you die?"

"You just go unconscious for a little while. You won't even know it."

"I know it now," I said. "I don't want to go unconscious."

They put a belt over me and tightened it. "Not to worry," the doctor said. "Hypoglycemia is easily reversed."

"But what's this for?"

"To change the structure of the brain cells. Makes you better," he said.

"You are changing my brain?"

"I guess you could say that, but the procedure is well controlled. You might experience mild convulsions, sweating, perhaps temporary memory loss. Occasionally patients can get a little weepy, but then, who doesn't, right?"

"My God," I said.

"So just relax," he said, sliding the needle into my arm.

"Does it really work?" I asked, my head spinning.

"Oh, certainly," he said. "One way or the other."

When I came to, I was back in my room. My lip was bleeding, and my shirt was wet with perspiration. Sperm handed me a glass of juice.

"Drink this," he said.

"What for?"

"Because they said to. You have to question everything?"

So I drank it. "I'm hungry, Sperm," I said.

"They always are," he said. "And don't call me Sperm. It's *Vernon.* My name is *Vernon.*"

"Why did they do that to me, Spernon?"

"It's supposed to realign your brain, and believe me, yours needs it. They do it to all the schizos. Never helps." He took my empty glass and walked to the door. "I think they just like to wear white coats and use big words," he said.

After he was gone, I rolled onto my side and closed my eyes. My hands shook, like an old man's hands, and my brain was shattered glass. I slept then, I guess, and didn't wake up until someone called my name.

"Jacob?" he said from the doorway. "Your food is here."

I sat up, and there was Uncle Ward with a plate, with a sandwich on it.

"Uncle Ward?" I said.

He stepped in. "Who else?"

"What you doing here?"

"I like it here," he said. "No Germans. What you doing here?"

"They're realigning my brain," I said.

"Insulin shock," he said. "Electroshock is better. Makes your wee-wee stiff."

"Where did you get the sandwich?"

"I work in the kitchen for free," he said. "It's called occupational therapy."

"You nearly killed me with that shovel," I said.

"Did you move Abbott?"

"Mom wants him where he is."

"She'll be sorry, come the Rapture. Here, eat this," he said, handing me the sandwich.

I ate the sandwich. It was good, corned beef on rye. Uncle Ward sat in the chair and crossed his ankles while I ate. He looked older. His beard was gray; so was the hair above his ears. His eyes were squinted up, with wrinkles in the corners, but there was nothing behind them, like a bullet had passed through his brain.

"How is your mom doing?" he asked.

"She's got place payments," I said.

"She should have bought a lot in Dunyville," he said.

I picked the crumbs off my plate and ate them. "If you see Danny, have him come visit me."

"Danny what ran the Railway Hotel?"

"Yes," I said.

"He shot himself in the head months ago. They found him bleeding into the register."

"That must have been a different Danny," I said.

"You wouldn't think there'd be so many," he said.

"Tell him I want out of here."

"You want another sandwich?"

"I could use some paper and a pen."

"They won't let us have a pen. They think we might stab ourselves to death with it."

He took the plate and paused. "I couldn't leave Abbott on the Franklin side," he said.

"I know it," I said.

"And I'll tell Danny what you said, even though he's dead."

"Thanks, Uncle Ward."

"And don't let them do that fever therapy. It's the worst."

"Fever therapy?"

"They put you in a Hypertherm cabinet, a big toaster. By the time you pop up, you're as brown as shoe leather. And it shrinks your wee-wee into an earthworm," he said.

CHAPTER 42

The next day, Uncle Ward brought me the paper and a stub pencil, but it was butcher paper from the kitchen. I had to tear it into the right sizes to write on. I hid the sheets under my mattress. But the longer I was there, the less I had to say. Without thoughts to write down, how was I to continue to live?

Uncle Ward didn't come anymore after that. Spernon said Uncle Ward put cayenne pepper in the oatmeal at the cafeteria, and they'd banned him from occupational therapy. Said he wasn't surprised that Ward was in isolation, that that's where all Rolands would be had he his way.

My insulin therapy lasted for months before they called it off. Dr. Jesus said that keeping so many doctors and nurses on duty all the time was not cost-effective, and they had drugs now that did more for less. He said the drugs could turn a Mexican fighting bull into a Chihuahua.

So Spernon showed up one day with a pill and a glass of water and said, "Take it."

"Take what?" I asked.

"The pill," he said.

"What kind of pill is it?" I asked.

"It's a pill pill, what the hell do I know?"

"I need an answer, Spernon."

"The doc said it's chlor-pro-mazine or some damn thing. Just take it."

So I took the pill and didn't feel a thing. It was only later that I realized that not feeling a thing was what the pill did best. It pulled out all my wires and threw them onto the floor in a tangle. It turned my legs to posts, and I shuffled about like a two-year-old. My breasts grew large and leaked through my shirt.

I stopped writing in my journal or even getting up. Spernon stopped talking to me and slid my meals under the door.

And then one day, an orderly showed up with my mother in tow. She was dressed in an old cotton dress, and her glasses were smudged with grease. She hugged me and said that the kids were gone out on their own now. She smelled of stale bread.

She told me how hard it was on the farm trying to get things done on her own and that the doctors had found a lump in her throat. They said it was big as a hen's egg. She said that sometimes she spit up blood and that it made her feel all weak and wobbly.

She hugged me again before she left, and I could feel her ribs. She said she wished things could have been different for our family but that it was God's will, she guessed. She said that when the time came, I was to see that she was put to rest next to Abbott.

I told her at the door that she ought to see Uncle Ward before she left. She said she didn't have the time, what with chores waiting at home. When she was gone, I thought I should cry, but I couldn't. It's hard to cry with your wires on the floor.

After that, I stopped thinking about anything. I'd get up and wait for breakfast. After breakfast, I'd take my pill and sleep until lunchtime. Sometimes they'd ask me if I wanted to go eat with the other inmates. I tried it a few times but couldn't make my answers fit their questions. So then I didn't want to talk to anyone. For a while, I sat at the far end of the table, thinking I'd adjust or something, but I couldn't. Pretty soon they quit taking me to the cafeteria altogether.

Sometimes they'd take me to see Dr. Jesus, but he ran out of questions, except a few. He'd ask how I was doing and was I taking my medication. Sometimes he'd increase my pills. Other times he'd decrease them, and then they quit taking me to see him too.

Some days I'd awaken early and watch the sun come up through my window. On warm days, Spernon would take me out to the garden and leave me to sit on a bench while he smoked. I no longer wrote in my journal or thought about anything. Nothing mattered anymore.

I can't know how many days passed, or months, or even years. I can't know because I didn't count them. I'd grown old and weak. Once, I dreamed that Dr. Jesus gave me a whole bottle of pills.

"Take them," he said.

"How many?" I asked.

"All of them," he said.

"But they might kill me," I said.

"Wouldn't it be better?" he said.

One spring morning, Dr. Jesus and Spernon came to my door. I knew it was spring because I could hear the thunder and smell the rain. Dr. Jesus looked odd with his hair all wet.

"We have bad news," he said.

I looked at my bare feet. My toenails were long and curled under.

"What bad news?" I asked.

Dr. Jesus looked over at Spernon. "Your mother is dead," he said.

"When?"

"Last month," he said.

Spernon checked his pocket to see if he had brought his cigarettes.

"I didn't go to the funeral," I said.

"They found her dead at the kitchen table," he said. "You were psychotic at the time. There was no point."

"Did they bury her next to Abbott?"

"Your brother and niece took care of all that," he said.

"She wanted to be there next to him," I said.

The sun lit Dr. Jesus's face and cast his shadow on the wall.

"There was an auction, and the proceeds were divided among the heirs. The house was left to you."

"It was?"

"You have a house to live in now. This changes your situation. If you continue with your medications, there is no reason you can't live independently."

"By myself?"

"We have an acute shortage of beds here at the asylum. It would help us out as well. We'd expect you to come in for periodic checkups, of course."

"But there are place payments."

"That's something for you to settle with your kin," he said.

I looked over at Spernon, who was smelling his cigarettes. "Yes, I'll go," I said.

Dr. Jesus clipped his pen into his pocket. "Well, that's fine. Pack your things, and you can be released as early as this afternoon."

"I don't have a car here," I said.

"Spernon will take you, and the pharmacy will have your medications ready before you leave."

After they'd gone, I packed my things, which didn't take long—the clothes I'd been wearing when they brought me in, my shoes, which had dried and curled up on the ends, and my butcher paper notes stacked beneath my bunk.

Spernon showed up twenty minutes late. He said he had the scours from eating raw oysters and drinking beer. I think he just wanted to make me wait. We stopped at the pharmacy and got my pills. Then we walked out through the same rooms we'd walked in through when I had arrived. Not even the smell had changed. The women still rocked, and the men still drooled, and nothing was different.

At the front gate, I looked back at the towering buildings. It was a place where life had paused for me, where there was but silence and pain. It was too much to bear, and I knew I would never come back.

Spernon drove with both arms looped over the steering wheel and said nothing. We crossed the Cimarron River with its braided streams and climbed into the Gloss Mountains. When he missed the turn, we passed Casket Hill, and I could see the gravestones flickering by through the trees. Spernon cussed and said that finding the Roland place was like hunting for a goddang outlaw's den.

Soon the county well loomed up ahead, and I remembered Duny and the way he'd drank whiskey and wiped at his mouth with his sleeve. We passed the church, now empty and sad. I thought of Rachael and how she'd stood at the door looking back at me

When we pulled into the farmhouse yard, memories rushed back from somewhere deep inside me.

With the motor still running, Spernon looked over his arm. "Damn," he said, "this place is sad, man."

I gathered up and slid out. I'd walked only a short distance when he called to me.

"Which way out, Roland?" he asked.

I pointed him north. It *was,* after all, a way out, though a very *long* way out.

I stood at the door of the house, expecting it to open and be welcomed home. No one came because they were dead. My shoulders slumped with weariness. The place smelled of mice, and dust covered the furniture. Mom's coat still hung behind the door, and the floor creaked under my feet the way it always had. Each room greeted me with a cold and empty silence, and the damper on the wood stove squeaked against the downdraft of the chimney.

I pulled the shades up to let the sun in before walking the yard. The outbuildings were tired and weathered and leaned against the wind. I opened the door to the separator house where Uncle Duny had stayed before me, his old westerns still stacked under the bunk. I placed my hand in Gea's handprint on the storm cellar and remembered the stormy nights and how Dad willed them to pass around. I walked the yard, pausing at each building to remember its place in my life.

I sat in Dad's old chair and wondered, Where might he be? Where had they all gone? Why had I been left behind?

CHAPTER 43

I found my Mercury parked behind the barn. There was a rat's nest in the glovebox. It took a while to clean it up, but even so, the smell lingered. I gathered up my journal notes and put them in chronological order. Hungry, I looked for something to eat, settling for crackers and plum jam that had been left in the pantry. At sunset, I walked the shelterbelt, searching for the broom tree and nearly missing it, what with its new growth. It now looked more like an old man with a cane. I dug up the box, placed my papers inside, and watched the moon rise over the horizon.

That night, I tried to sleep in the house, but I woke to Mom's voice, clear as spring water. "I could use some help in this kitchen," she said. I sat up, drowning in the blackness, the hair crawling on my neck. I wanted to talk to someone, so where the hell was Danny when I needed him? I lit the lantern and watched the shadows dance up the wall. If he wouldn't come to me, I'd go to him.

The town was empty, save for the cop's car sitting in front of city hall, and Danny's Railway Hotel was dark and vacant. But it was late, and the crews had probably all been called. I knocked on the door, but no one answered. I pushed it with my shoulder. It creaked and dragged on the floor but opened. At first I couldn't see anything, but as my eyes adjusted, I spotted a figure hunched over the front desk.

"Danny?" I said. He lifted his head, and the streetlight flickered in his eyes. "It's me, Jacob," I said.

"So, what do you want?"

"Everyone is gone," I said. "I'm alone."

"Why did they let you out?" he asked.

"An acute bed shortage," I said.

"We aren't open anymore," he said.

I walked closer. A column of light shot through the window and onto the floor.

"You mean the hotel is closed for good?"

"What does it look like?" he said.

"But why?"

"Because I'm dead."

"No you're not," I said.

"You ever see me dead before?"

"No."

"Then how would you know?"

"I'm talking to you," I said.

"You'd talk to a fence post," he said.

"What happened, Danny?"

"I killed myself."

"But why?"

"I wanted to."

"What about your wife?"

"She wanted it too."

"Did it hurt?"

He turned his head and pointed to a hole just above his ear, where brain matter and blood leaked down his cheek.

"Any more questions?" he asked.

"We can still talk, can't we?"

"I don't think so," he said. "They are tearing down the hotel soon, and I'm pretty much through with this shithole anyway."

"I can't win," I said.

"You have to finish the race," he said.

The next night, I slept on the floor in the separator house. It turned cold in the night, and I could hear rats under the floorboards again. When I woke up, I thought I had died and the floorboards were my casket lid.

I looked out the door at all the old buildings, twisting and leaning every which way, like the ground had suddenly given way under them. This was my inheritance—an old house, outbuildings, and the few acres they sat on.

I'd just lain down on the bunk when a knock came at the door. I opened it to find Uncle Ward standing there. His face was worn and old, and his hair was gray. He was smoking a roll-your-own, and his fingers were yellow with nicotine. His shirt was wrinkled, and there was dirt in the cuffs of his pants.

"Where's your dad?" he asked.

"Dad's dead," I said.

"Oh, yeah," he said. "Where's your mom?"

"She's dead too," I said.

"That's right," he said. "I forgot. Are you dead too?"

"What are you doing here?" I asked.

"They kicked me out of the loony," he said.

"Did you put cayenne in the oatmeal again?"

"Acute bed shortage," he said.

"I'm living here now," I said. "I inherited the place."

He ground out his cigarette under his foot and looked around at the buildings. "Looks like shit," he said. "Get any land with it?"

"Some."

"Place payments?"

"Some."

"I'm living in Dunyville," he said. "You could live there, too, except we're expecting the Rapture soon. I don't think you'd fit in."

"It's OK," I said.

"If you see Abbott, tell him I came by."

"I will," I said. He started to walk away, and I called after him. "What if there isn't any?"

"Any what?"

"Rapture," I said.

He studied his feet for the longest time before answering. "Well, Hazel Morford is a hell of a pole dancer," he said.

I called Rachael from the pay phone in the courthouse, the one just inside the door.

"Hello," she said.

"Rachael?"

"This is she."

"How are you doing?"

"Who's calling, please?"

"This is Jacob," I said.

There was a long pause, and I could hear her breathing. "Jacob Roland?"

"Yes," I said.

"What do you want?"

"I just wanted to hear your voice."

"You can't be calling," she said. "I'm married."

"Mom and Dad are dead, and the kids are gone," I said.

"That has nothing to do with me."

"Did you graduate?"

"This won't do," she said.

"I didn't," I said. "I quit the race."

"My husband wouldn't like this, Jacob. Don't call again."

"So, did you graduate?"

"We're both in graduate school getting our MBAs," she said. "We'll be working in my father's company."

"I see."

"A person has to be prepared, you know."

"It's best that way," I said.

"I gotta go," she said. "I'll be late for class."

I drove that evening to the university and sat in the parking lot of the Citadel. Later, I slept in the Mercury outside of town. It wasn't so bad, except the wind blew all night, rocking the Mercury back and forth like someone trying to break in. The next day, I walked around town for a while, then checked out the old apartment where Duny and I had lived, which was now occupied by frat boys, who gathered on the back steps to smoke.

I took a nap in the library before driving over to Kate's old house to see it. There was a broken window in the study behind the house, and her flower bed was full of weeds. A couple of kids came out of the house, playing tag and laughing. They looked back at me as they ran down the street, trying to trip each other.

After that I drove to the campus and parked in the faculty parking lot, where I could watch the students going to class. My coat, the one I had used as a pillow the night before, had slipped off onto the floorboard. When I bent to pick it up, I spotted my old class notebooks under the seat. I took one out and thumbed through the pages. The notes were clear, organized, and pretty damn good. All in all, I'd been a pretty fair study. A group of students came by, laughing and talking on their way to class. I got out, put the notebook under my arm, and followed them into Burnham Hall.

The professor had not yet arrived, so I took up a seat at the back of the room and opened my notebook.

Shortly, an older woman came in. She wore horn-rimmed glasses, and her hair was wound in a tight bun on the back of her head. She carried a textbook with little pieces of paper sticking out of the pages, and she had a manila folder as well.

She looked around the room before opening the manila folder and proceeding to call roll. When the last person had responded, she laid down her roll sheet and looked at me.

"I don't believe I have you listed," she said. "What is your name, please?"

"Jacob Roland," I said.

"Were you here when the class started?"

My mouth went dry. "I just enrolled," I said.

"It's too late in the semester for drops and adds, Mr. . . . what did you say your name was?"

"Jacob," I said, my ears burning. "Jacob Roland."

"Mr. Roland, if you'll make an appointment to see me, perhaps we can get this straightened out."

"Yes," I said.

"Oh, dear," she said, "I've left my notes in my office. I'll be right back."

When she'd gone, all the students turned and looked at me. I stared at the floor. I had made a big mistake going there. I gathered up my notebook to leave when someone touched my shoulder. I looked up to see a campus policeman standing there. He wore a brown uniform, and his eyes were squinted.

"Sir," he said, "come with me."

I could hear the other students mumbling as I gathered up my things. He followed me into the hallway.

"I'll leave now," I said. "I'm sorry I interrupted the class."

"Put your hands behind your back, please," he said.

"I'll just go," I said. "I promise I won't do it again."

"This is the last time I ask you, sir. Put your hands behind your back."

I put my hands behind my back, and he cuffed me, lifting my arms until they hurt.

"What are you going to do to me?" I asked.

"It's up to the city police," he said.

"I just wanted to sit in this one time."

He pushed my arms higher, lifting me onto my toes. "Don't make this any harder than is necessary," he said. A white pain fired at the base of my skull. "You can't just walk into someone's class. Who do you think you are?"

CHAPTER 44

We walked across campus toward the security building. Some people turned and looked, while others pretended they didn't see us. We cut north at the fountain, and that's when I saw her walking toward us down the sidewalk. I was pretty sure it was Kate. She looked different, a little older, but as she passed by, she looked straight into my eyes.

They took me to the courthouse, the same where I had previously worked, except upstairs where the jail was. Two policemen questioned me. One was not much older than me, while the other was a lot older, fat, and smelled of liquor. They asked what I was doing there. Did I have nefarious intentions? When I said that I just wanted to be in class for a bit and didn't mean any harm, they looked at each other.

The fat one said, "You wanted to be in class?"

"That's right," I said. "Just for today. I didn't mean to make a disturbance or anything, I swear."

The young one said, "I think you have already; besides, what kind of loony wants to be in class? I figure you was going to wait around and rape someone or steal their purse. I mean, who knows what, but no one goes to class for the hell of it. You think we're idiots?"

After that, they took me to the courtroom, where I had to stand in front of the judge with my handcuffs on. He looked over my file, sucked at a tooth, and adjusted his glasses.

"It says here you broke into a college class with nefarious intentions."

"I didn't," I said.

"Keep quiet," he said. "If I want you to talk, I'll tell you. This kind of behavior cannot be tolerated in a college town. You can't just walk into someone's classroom and bring the whole education system to a halt. On top of that, you parked in the faculty parking spot? It's the kind of disregard for rules that leads to anarchy."

"I was just sitting in to see what was going on," I said.

"Thirty days in jail, or five hundred dollars fine, court costs, and impounding fees."

"But your honor—"

"Did I say talk?" I shook my head. "Do you intend to bond out?"

"I don't have any money," I said.

"Take him," he said to the policeman.

They put me in a cell with an old man who had been caught shoplifting raw hamburger from the grocery store. He had white hair, blue eyes, and no teeth. When he talked, he spit droplets of water into the air, and I could barely understand what he was saying.

"What you do?" he asked, wiping at his mouth with his sleeve.

"Went to a college class," I said.

"Goddamn smartass," he said. "Why they always bring the smartasses in here?"

"I hadn't paid any tuition," I said.

"You have smokes?"

"No," I said.

"Goddamn broke smartass," he said, flopping into his bunk. Within minutes he was snoring.

I was in that cell for three days, and that's all he said. They served fried bologna and toast for breakfast, a bologna sandwich for lunch, and a lettuce salad with chopped bologna in it for dinner, all three days.

It was on the fourth day that I heard a woman's voice downstairs. Pretty soon the jailer came up and unlocked the door.

"You've been bonded out," he said.

"What? Who?"

"It ain't my job to know. Get your stuff and get out."

I was gathering up my things when the old man turned on his side. "Where you going?" he asked.

"I don't know," I said.

"Goddamn smartass," he said, turning back over.

It was Kate Hilton waiting outside the door. She'd cut her hair, added glasses, and sported a stylish gray suit.

"Jacob," she said.

"Kate?"

"I saw you on campus," she said. "With the police, I mean. One of the students told me what happened."

"I didn't mean anything by it," I said.

"I know," she said. "But it was against the rules."

"Did you pay my fine?"

"Call it a loan," she said. "Hungry?"

I nodded. "But I'm broke."

"I'm buying," she said.

"As long as it isn't bologna."

She smiled. "Come on. We'll talk over a hamburger."

We drove to a small café on the edge of town and took a back booth. Kate slid in and handed over a menu.

"So," she said, "I take it you are no longer in college, enrolled, I mean?"

"No," I said. "It didn't work out."

"That's a shame," she said. "You have a lot of potential."

"People died," I said. "My life sort of fell apart."

The waitress came, and we ordered. When she'd gone, Kate said, "So, where are you living?"

"I inherited the farmhouse," I said. "It's pretty empty, you know."

"I'm sorry about what's happened to you, Jacob."

"So, what about you?" I asked. "I thought you were in graduate school."

"I finished," she said. "I was hired back here as an instructor in the English Department."

"You're on the faculty?"

"More or less," she said. "Bottom rung, you know. I need the experience and some time to figure out how far I want to take all this. Graduate school has a way of flatlining your brain."

The waitress set our hamburgers in front of us. "Anything else?" she asked.

"We're good," Kate said.

I struggled not to wolf down my burger. "You'll make a great professor," I said.

Kate smiled. "The policeman said he thought you had been sleeping in your car. They found your things."

"Just for a few nights."

"And what about tonight?"

"My car's impounded," I said.

"What about your girlfriend?"

"Rachael got married."

"I'm sorry."

"It's OK. We didn't have much in common anyway."

"And so you've been living alone on the farm?"

I finished my burger and pushed the empty plate aside. "That was great," I said. "Thank you."

"You're welcome."

"Truth is, I had kind of a breakdown, I guess you'd call it. I was in Fort Supply for a spell. I'm OK now, though."

"Look, I have a spare bedroom, a place for you to stay tonight. The impounding fee was part of the court costs. Tomorrow is soon enough to pick your car up."

"You think it would be OK?" I said. "You're on the faculty now."

"You must know I don't worry about things like that," she said.

"OK," I said.

"Good. Then that's settled."

"There is one thing," I said. "If you wouldn't mind, I mean."

"And what would that be?"

"Another burger. I'm famished."

Kate's house was small but finely decorated, with just the right furniture in just the right places and a bookcase that stretched the length of the living room. We sat up late talking about what plans she had for her future. It was Kate's way to know her goals and how she intended to achieve them. For her, life was a journey, she said, and one must always keep the goal in sight.

She poured another cup of tea for each of us and said, "What about you? Where do you go from here?"

"Well, I have the house," I said.

"Your future, I mean."

"I don't see things as clearly as you," I said. "I start down one road, only to find that I'm lost or several more roads appear in front of me, all looking the same. Sometimes I have to wait for a sign."

"What do you mean? I don't think I understand."

"Things come to me sometimes. It's like being asleep and awake at the same moment, like being in a dream where you can hear people talking, telling you things that no one else knows. There are times I can't make it stop, and I think I might die. Sometimes I wish I would."

Kate leaned onto her elbows, wove her fingers together, and studied me. "Is there no remedy for you?" she asked.

I watched the minute hand on the clock behind her head as it leapt from one second marker to the next. "This is going to sound strange," I said.

"It can't be as strange as what you just described."

"I have this way of fixing things," I said.

She checked my cup and poured the remainder of the pot into it. "Go on."

"I write it down," I said. "That's the secret. I turn it into words that *I* control."

"You are talking about your journal entries?" she said.

"Under the broom tree," I said.

That night I slept in the room next to Kate's. I say slept, but I hardly closed my eyes. Her door was open, and I could hear her breathing, the slow, steady breathing that comes with deep sleep. Being so near her kept me awake, being so near and so far at the same time. I thought about her lying there, about how she combed her hair in the mirror and the gentle bend of her back. I covered my head with my pillow and turned to the wall.

Sometime in the early-morning hours, I rose from my bed and put on my clothes. A flash of lightning lit the room. Wind swept rain against the window, and thunder rumbled in the distance. I gathered my things and stood in the darkness. When the lightning struck again, closer this time, it made a crackling sound that caused the hair to rise on my arms. I went into the hall. Her door was open, and I could see her lying there. She'd thrown off her blanket, her waxen body under the white sheet. I stepped into her room. I could smell her perfume in the dampness, and her clothes lay tossed over a chair.

"Jacob?" she said.

"Yes," I said.

"It isn't that way between us."

Stillness rushed into the room. "Yes," I said. "I know."

CHAPTER 45

I walked in the rain to the city shed where my car was impounded. It was Sunday, and the gate was to be opened at ten. I waited under the eve of the gate shack for nearly two hours before the attendant showed up in his pickup. He wore a raincoat and had a cigar stub sticking out the corner of his mouth.

"Who are you?" he asked.

"Jacob Roland. I came to pick up my car."

"I'll have to check the records," he said. "You wait out here."

I nodded. "It's a black Mercury," I said, "'49. The fine has been paid."

Fifteen minutes passed before he pulled up to the gate in my Mercury. "You better put some gas in this thing," he said, getting out. "And my advice is to watch your p's and q's around here before you wind up in state prison. They'll teach you how to be a real criminal in there."

The dust on the windows had turned to mud under the wipers, and my car smelled like cigar smoke. When I pulled onto the road, I checked the gas gauge. It was bouncing on empty. I checked my billfold, finding two dollars—enough to get me home if I could locate an open station.

The only open station in town was the one where I had previously worked. With mud on the windows and the rain coming down, I figured I might get by without anyone recognizing me. I pulled in, and the owner came out. I cracked my window.

"Two dollars, regular," I said through the crack.

I could see oatmeal on his coveralls, and he grumbled something about two dollars in a downpour. When he'd finished, I cracked the window a little more and pushed the two dollars out. He bent down and peered in.

"It's you," he said.

I started to roll up the window, when he opened my door. "I got a bone to pick with you, you little son of a bitch," he said.

"I gotta go," I said, reaching for the door.

He stuck his leg in. "That vending machine was damn near empty after you left. Cost me plenty too. I got a notion to call the cops."

I started up the Mercury and pulled away slowly. He hung on for a bit, finally falling back. In the rearview mirror, I could see his mouth working and his fist in the air. So I had taken a few candy bars. So what? It was little enough considering what the cheap bastard had paid me.

Determined to put my life back in order, I moved into the farmhouse. The wind rattled the windows at night, and the rats scurried inside the walls. I hung blankets over the doorways to reduce my space. Even so, the nights were long and filled with voices. I would awaken and lie there in the darkness, listening to the past and its loneliness.

Once, I was jolted awake by a noise, something outside. I got up and peeked out the window. The moon hung in the western sky, its silver light illuminating the distant mesas, and there standing in the road were Danny and Mortem, just standing there looking back at me. When I opened the door to call out to them, they were gone.

Without work, I soon came up short on groceries. I ate everything I could find from the pantry, mostly canned goods left behind when Mom died. I took long walks through the pasture and tried to figure out what I was supposed to do now. Sometimes I'd catch Danny following me, but I said nothing. If he wanted to talk to me, he was going to have to make the first move.

I grew skinny, living on green beans and canned beets. I hauled water from the county well in a five-gallon cream can. Sometimes I would kind of black out, a falling away that would suddenly overtake me. Other times, my heart beat out of control and I couldn't breathe. No one came to visit. No one wrote. No one gave a damn.

I thought once to go to Dunyville and see Uncle Ward, but he didn't want me either, what with the unpredictable arrival time of the Rapture. I tried to read Uncle Duny's westerns, but I couldn't concentrate. So lots of nights I just stayed up and waited for the morning to come.

And then summer set in hard, like only it could in this place. The temperature soared to a hundred and ten. It snuffed away my breath and my thoughts. Sleeping during the day was impossible and as bad at night. By morning, my sheets were wet with sweat. A rash broke out under my arms and in my crotch. The grass turned to straw, and the grasshoppers arrived, hoards of them, thousands of them, jumping on my clothes and in my face, eating holes in the feed sacks, copulating in the road, spitting tobacco juice on the windows of the house. They ate the leaves off the trees and then the bark. They ate the insulation off the Mercury plug wires and the bristle off the back door mat. The hotter the day, the more they ate. They left nothing living behind.

As the heat soared, the cicadas crawled up from the earth's bowels and clung to the window screens and the bare limbs left behind by the grasshoppers. Day and night, they beat out their cadence, a cacophony so intense as to cause blood to seep from my ears. There were times I could hear Mortem howling far away as Casket Hill, his voice lifting to the sadness of the circadian mantra.

At some point I decided to go see Uncle Ward, despite his reluctance to have me visit. Perhaps it was when I ran out of canned green beans, the last food I had in the house. I had enough gas to make it, so I took a spit bath, slicked my hair back with Dad's Brylcreem, and headed for Dunyville. I was excited, not so much to see Ward as just to be going somewhere.

When I pulled in, Uncle Ward's bus was parked in its usual spot, and smoke was rising out of an old barrel he'd brought in. Sacks of garbage were stacked by the door, and an empty whiskey bottle sat on the bus fender. Grass and sandburs grew up through a makeshift sidewalk he'd concocted from old barn boards.

I knocked on the door and waited. When there was no answer, I called out his name and knocked again. I was about to leave when the bus door opened, and Uncle Ward stood there in his underwear, his chicken legs white as snow. His T-shirt hung off him like a rag, and his hair covered his ears.

"What you doing here?" he said.

"Come for a visit," I said. "Didn't figure you for sleeping in the middle of the day."

Just then Hazel Morford stuck her head out from under his arm. "Who is it, Ward?" she asked.

"It's my nephew, Jacob Roland," he said.

She looked at me and twisted her mouth to the side. Her hair was mussed, and there were streaks of gray in it. I could see the plunge of her breasts.

"What does he want?" she asked.

"What do you want?" Ward asked.

"Nothing," I said.

"He wants nothing," he said.

Hazel looked at me. I could see lipstick gathered in the lines of her mouth. "You must want something," she said. "You're here, ain't you?"

"Yes," I said, "I'm here."

"Here for nothing?" she asked.

"I didn't figure Uncle Ward laying up in the middle of the day."

"He woke up at daylight looking for the Rapture," she said. "He didn't find it. He never does."

"He's been waiting a good long while," I said.

She pushed Ward's arm away. I could see the cut of her face, the way her nose turned up. She'd been a looker in her day. "Well, Ward, ain't you going to ask him in?" she said.

"I hadn't figured on it," he said.

"Ask him in, Ward."

"You wanna come in?"

I shrugged. "I guess," I said.

He stepped aside to let me in, and I could see that Hazel was wearing one of his old work shirts. It barely covered her nakedness. She sat in the seat across from me and slid back against the side of the bus. Her shirt edged up, and I could see she was wearing nothing underneath.

Uncle Ward took up a seat next to me and rolled himself a cigarette, sealing it off with his tongue.

"How's your dad?" he asked.

"Dad's dead," I said.

"Oh, yeah," he said. "Want a drink?"

"I didn't come for anything," I said.

He reached for a bottle under the seat and poured some in a coffee cup. "Here," he said.

I took the cup and sipped at the whiskey. My eyes watered. Uncle Ward poured himself some and then Hazel.

"You remember Hazel?" he said.

"Sure," I said.

"She was Duny's pole dancer," he said. "That was before he burned down Dunyville. Jacob here is a college boy," he said to Hazel.

"I gave it up," I said.

"I've been waiting on the Rapture myself," he said. "It hasn't come."

"I know," I said.

He took a drink and looked out the window. "Maybe it won't."

"Maybe," I said.

"So Hazel come out for a visit," he said. "Something to pick up my spirits while I wait."

"Yeah," I said.

"Hazel," he said, "do a little dance for Jacob."

"Oh, Ward," she said.

"Go on," he said. "He's never seen you dance."

She leaned toward me and dropped her chin in her hands. "Do you want me to dance?"

"I guess I would," I said.

She looked at Ward. "I don't have any music. How can I dance without no music?"

Ward took a drink and turned on the radio. "There," he said.

Hazel stood up. "It's poor enough music," she said.

She commenced swinging her hips from side to side, dipping low, and with each dip, Uncle Ward's old shirt lifted a little higher. Sometimes she'd looked up at the roof of the bus, as if the music were coming from somewhere up there, or she'd put her hands behind her neck and move her hips back and forth like riding at a trot. I looked at Uncle Ward, who was kind of smiling and patting his foot, and the heat rose in my neck and ears.

Gyrating to the music, Hazel pushed her fingers through her hair, all the while gyrating and unbuttoning Uncle Ward's old shirt. When her breasts spilled out, with nipples like ripe raspberries, I held my breath for fear of dying.

Her shirt dropped away like there was nothing to it. I'd never seen a woman naked before, not on purpose like that, and it struck me deep inside. Taking my hand, she lifted me up and brought me in until my nose touched her stomach, all the while her moving to the music. And when the music stopped, she reached down for her shirt and slipped it on. I looked over at Uncle Ward.

"When the music is over, Hazel's done," he said.

Hazel sat down, took a drink, and looked at me. "You remind me a lot of your Uncle Ward," she said. "Something in the eyes."

CHAPTER 46

I had gas enough to make it to Casket Hill, and by the time I got there, the sun was starting to set, a blaze of orange and yellow on the horizon. Shadows leapt out from the mesquite like cat claws, and the wind swept through the valley.

I parked on the side of the road and walked into the Franklin side of the cemetery. For a moment, I didn't comprehend what I was seeing. Dad's marker had been moved and his grave opened. A spider web bridged the gaping void left behind. A hundred feet away on the Roland side was a freshly mounded grave with Dad's marker planted at the head.

No one but Uncle Ward was capable of such desecration. My life clicked by like the shuddering frames of an old film as I stood at the edge of that black hole. I could see Dad clearly—how he worked in the field, how his physical presence filled the room when he entered, and how the distance between us was never traversed. I could see the things he'd missed in his life, things he never knew. I could see how, like all of us, he'd been trapped in the circumstance and flow of his time.

And now, a distance away, Mom lay alone in her grave as well. I thought of her in the kitchen, the sounds of her dishes, the aromas of her food, and how we'd pack up and go to the shelterbelt for picnics. She must have had dreams, too, things she'd wanted for her life. She'd never said, just working all those days in that hot and hopeless kitchen. Nothing was left for either of them now, nothing but the emptiness of a violated grave.

A howl lifted from the distant mesa, a cry of pain and disbelief that all had come to this place. Danny watched on from the mesa, his legs dangling over the side. Mortem sat next to him, his muzzle lifted skyward. I'd been abandoned by my own broken mind and by a heart as empty as the grave before me.

As I drove back to the farm, I thought to challenge Ward, to confront him with the awful reality of what he'd done. But even as I drove, I knew it was too late, because he would never understand. Though we existed together, we came from separate worlds. Uncle Ward had done the only thing possible for him, and my pain would never be his. I knew then what had to be done and who had to do it.

I found the shovel in the old oil house, the one Dad used for building fence. The end of the handle was worn sharp from tamping posts. Unable to fit it into the trunk, I laid it in the back seat instead. I found the cable he used for pulling the tractor. It was hanging from a rafter in the shed. Frazzled and worn from use, it refused to coil and so had to be shoved into the trunk with my foot and secured there by slamming down the lid.

I can't be sure what I was feeling as I drove back up that mesa. It could have been fear or dread or some combination of both. I didn't dare examine it. Some things were to be done, no matter the cost.

By the time I reached Casket Hill, the stars had clicked on in the blackness. I pulled in close to the grave so that the headlights lit the newly mounded dirt. He would have disapproved of his disinterment, of what his own brother had done, for he believed that a man should lie in peace until such time as God called him up from the grave. So for it to happen twice would have been incomprehensible. Uncle Ward was a good deal less than God, as was I, but I began the task, grim as it was, because there was no one else to do what had to be done.

The earth was soft under my shovel, so I worked fast and deliberate. I worked without rest, even as sweat dripped from the end of my nose and my cuffs filled with dirt. And when the thump of my shovel deepened at last, I stepped back, knowing what now lay beneath my feet. As I swept away the dirt, I found the casket as I remembered it, walnut, with hinges of brass.

I could never lift it alone, not from such depths, not with such weight, so I dug yet more, until the cable could encircle its circumference, and when it was secured, I fastened it to the bumper of my Mercury.

Not until the motor roared and labored against its weight did I fully appreciate the enormity of my act. And when its burden bore up out of the earth behind me, I cried out. I sat a while to gather my courage to finish what I had begun. Finally, with the casket resting at the grave's edge, I pushed it back once more into that terrible hole. And as the sun rose in the east, I filled the grave for a final time and set the marker in its rightful place.

Once home, I retrieved my notes from under the bed, where I kept them at hand, and scribbled in my confession as best I could. And with the words written, I surrendered my weariness and my guilt to them. I would take them soon, as I had done with him, to their final rest.

I rose early the next morning and within the hour pulled into the gas station where I had once worked. The owner came out, wiping the oil from his hands.

"You," he said. "What the hell you want?"

"I'd like to sell my car," I said.

"So? Why are you here?"

"I thought you might buy it."

"Why should I buy anything from you?"

"Because I'll sell it cheap, and you will make a tidy profit."

"How cheap?"

I told him, and he agreed. He left and returned with the money, counting it out through my window.

"Leave the keys in it," he said, going back inside.

I walked to Kate's house, but she was gone. So I walked to the campus, where I asked the departmental secretary to look up her schedule.

"She's in class," she said. "You can wait if you want."

"Where is her class?" I asked.

"Room 203, but it isn't over until two."

"I'll come back," I said.

I stood outside Kate's classroom door. I could hear her lecturing, confident and precise. I knocked, and there was silence as she came to the door.

"Jacob," she said. "What are you doing here?"

"Can we talk, Kate?"

"I'm in the middle of class," she said. "You'll have to wait."

Just then the door opened at the end of the hallway, and a man came in. He was looking at me.

"It's important," I said.

"You mustn't come to my class this way, Jacob."

The man came toward us, his shoulders squared, and I recognized him as campus security.

"Here's the money I owe you," I said, shoving it into her hand. "Good-bye, Kate."

I started down the hallway, my head lowered, and was nearly past him when he held up his hand. "Hey," he said. "Hey, you. What are you doing here?"

I broke for the door, and I could hear him running after me. Once outside, I cut to the left and dropped behind a thicket of bushes that had been planted under the window. Within seconds, he burst through the door with his baton in hand. Breathing heavily, he paused and looked around before heading for the parking lot. The second he was out of sight, I cut across campus in the opposite direction and a half hour later was walking the highway home.

CHAPTER 47

It was nearly midnight by the time I got home. I went into the house and sat on the couch, pulling off my shoes. Water blisters had formed on my heels, broken, and refilled with blood. I changed my socks and sat in the dark. I could see the moon rising through the window. I heard voices coming from the folks' bedroom. I checked, but it was empty, smelling of dust and mouse droppings. I looked for something to eat, but the pantry was bare, save for an old jar of dill pickles Mom had canned last summer.

I stood at the mirror that hung in the hallway and looked at the person who looked back at me. He had grown old and thin, and hope had vanished from his eyes. Mom and Dad were gone, the kids, Duny. They'd all left, Rachael and Kate too. What else could they do?

There was a flashlight in the kitchen, and Dad's hunting rifle in the closet. The shells I found in the box on the shelf. From there I stopped at the separator house to retrieve the journal pages from under my bunk and put them into a paper bag.

Even in the night, I found the tree without difficulty, where I cleared away the grass and dirt covering the box. I opened it to find the pages of my life recorded there, along with my writing tablets, now yellowed with age, a box of sharpened pencils, and Gea's blouse still folded at the bottom. The blood spot was barely distinguishable now, having given way to dampness and age. In the quiet and peace of that place, I made my final entry and reburied the box.

EPILOGUE

The last time I saw Jacob was the day he came to my classroom door, shoved money in my hand, and ran away. I first learned of his death over spring break when I came across his obituary in an old paper that had been left in the reference section of the university library. I can't say that it came as a total shock to me, though I did find it disturbing. I had grown quite fond of him during those days he occupied the study behind my house. Perhaps it was his hunger for learning, or perhaps it was just his intensity. There were times I thought him brilliant and other times quite troubled. I'm not sure that I know which prevailed in his life. But who's to say that insanity and brilliance cannot coexist in such a mind?

While the obituary was unclear as to the cause of his death, it implied that something untoward and sudden had transpired. It stated that he was interred at Casket Hill Cemetery, that he was preceded in death by his parents, Abbott and Vega Roland, and an older sister, Gea. He was survived by a niece and younger brother, both of whom now lived out of state.

Exhausted from graduate school and the demands of my new position, I decided to take the summer off from teaching. It wasn't until a few weeks into my idle time that I determined to track down the details of exactly what had happened to him. I had knowledge of where he was from and drove there with the intent of bringing closure to this haunting story.

I went to the local undertaker first, learning that what I had suspected was true—Jacob had been deeply troubled for years, committed at some point to an insane asylum, where he was unsuccessfully treated. The undertaker said that Jacob killed himself with his father's hunting rifle, a single shot into his head. He directed me to Casket Hill Cemetery, with a warning that the road up the mesa could be treacherous. So it was with some consternation that I found that lonely place.

It took only minutes to conclude that the Rolands and the Franklins were divided even in death. What puzzled me more was why Jacob was buried next to his mother, while Abbott Roland, his father, was buried yards away in the Roland section of the cemetery. Despite the considerable passage of time since his death, both graves appeared to have been freshly opened.

Though anxious to get home, I was unable to resist turning onto the road that led to the Roland place, which turned out to be a hardscrabble farm. A for-sale sign was in the yard. Standing there, I remembered what Jacob had said about his journal and how he had buried the pages under a tree that looked like a woman with a broom.

The walk was short and the tree easily discernible. Locating the buried box took a bit more effort. In it were letters, the remnants of a woman's blouse, and a large stack of journal entries. Sitting under that tree, I read them, deciding at some point that I must tell his story with all the truth he'd left behind. And as the sun lowered to the horizon, I came to his final entry.

"A particular madness has taken me," it said. "But I will reach back to you through these words that I have written, forever."

Acknowledgments

A special thanks to my editor and publisher, Holly Monteith, of Cynren Press. Her enthusiasm, encouragement, and finely tuned organizational skills made all the difference.

Lightning Source UK Ltd.
Milton Keynes UK
UKHW020634061121
393477UK00010B/527/J

9 781947 976269